life

unaware

life

unaware

Cole Gibsen

Entangled Publishing, LLC
2614 South Timberline Road
Suite 109
Fort Collins, CO 80525

Entangled Teen is an imprint of Entangled Publishing, LLC.

Visit our website at www.entangledpublishing.com.

Edited by Liz Pelletier
Cover design by Najla Qamber
Interior design by Jeremy Howland

Print ISBN 978-1-62266-396-5
Ebook ISBN 978-1-62266-397-2

Manufactured in the United States of America

First Edition April 2015

10 9 8 7 6 5 4 3 2 1

This book is dedicated to everyone and anyone who's ever been bullied and made to feel less than your amazing worth — whether by peers, family, or even yourself. You are never alone. If you need help, please call 1-800-SUICIDE.

PROLOGUE

"Regan?" Dr. Lee arched an eyebrow and rested the tip of his pen against his pad. The ink slowly seeped into the paper, a small pool of blue against a yellow backdrop. Fitting, because that was what reliving the last three months felt like—ripping open scars so the wounds bled onto the page. "Would you prefer we talk about something else?"

I shook my head. Bitterness burned up the back of my throat. Was that what shame tasted like? I swallowed and licked my dry lips. I was determined to get this out, the truth. "I wasn't a nice person," I said. "I mean, I guess I knew it then, too. I just didn't care."

Dr. Lee didn't move. "And you care now?"

I nodded, watching the pool of ink as it swelled around the tip of his pen. How many sheets would he have to flip through to get to one unmarred by the ink? Three? Six? Half the pad? It was funny how damage only appeared on the surface.

"What changed?"

I blinked, forcing myself to meet his gaze. "Everything."

He wrote something on his pad, but his sloppy handwriting made the words illegible. "How so?"

I shrugged. "I used to think the only thing that mattered was staying on top. I did whatever it took to make it happen. I was using people, but I didn't think it was a big deal because I wasn't technically hurting anyone. I had no idea..." My voice caught.

"You had no idea," Dr. Lee prompted.

I didn't want to say the words out loud, because giving them voice would only make them more real. "I had no idea that I was...*destroying* people. But when it happened to me, by someone I *thought* I loved—"

A sob choked off the words. I squeezed my eyes shut before the tears I felt welling up could fall. "I can't," I whispered. And it was the truth.

In the darkness behind my closed eyes, I saw *him*—the way he'd looked at me, how they'd *all* looked at me—and the pain crashed into me with enough force that I didn't understand how I wasn't dying. "I just...*can't.*"

"That's fine, Regan." I heard the soft *thump* of a legal pad falling on a desk. "We can end right there for today."

"No." Every breath, every beat of my heart brought a fresh wave of agony, but the only thing worse than talking about what I did was keeping it secret. Secrets were what

started the whole thing. I opened my eyes. "I *have* to do this."

"All right." Dr. Lee grabbed his discarded notepad. "Take me back to the beginning. What's the last thing that happened before it all fell apart?"

Emotions pulled at the already-frayed edges of my heart. There were too many of them. Each memory flashed through my head as fresh as the moment I experienced it. Reliving them was going to suck, but anything was better than letting them fester inside me.

I bit my thumbnail and tried to pinpoint the exact moment everything changed. "It all started with a text."

CHAPTER ONE

THREE MONTHS AGO

The buzz of a cell phone jolted me out of a dreamless sleep. Frantic, I grabbed for it but knocked over my bottle of pills instead.

"Regan!" my mom shouted from the hallway. Her sharp voice dug into my brain like shards of glass. "I expect you sitting at the kitchen table in five minutes. We have things we need to discuss."

Awesome. Because on my list of fun things to do, lectures from my mother rated just below being stabbed in the eye with a fork. I gave up fumbling for the phone or the pills—I wasn't sure which one I needed more—and blinked at the ceiling until my room slid into focus. I couldn't have gotten more than four hours of sleep, judging by my zombielike reflexes. Not good. I couldn't let my mom get to me. It was too important of a day to be off my A game.

My phone buzzed again, and I managed to snatch it from the nightstand. A text from Payton screamed at me in all caps.

OMG DID YOU SEE CHRISTY HOLDER'S FB POST???!!!!

Christy was the captain of this year's varsity cheerleading squad. I could only assume, given the number of exclamation points in Payton's text, that Christy's post had something to do with the previous day's tryouts—the same tryouts I'd completely bombed when I fell ass-backward out of a full extension.

Nausea rolled through my stomach. I tried to focus on my phone as I scrolled through my Facebook updates. It only took a second to find Christy's post.

Tryouts were amazing, but due to the overwhelming number of girls hoping to make this year's squad, not everyone is going to make it. How will I choose?

I dropped my phone into my lap and chewed on my thumbnail. Would Christy cut me? I'd screwed up the extension, but she *owed* me. I'd gotten her into Jason Spear's party last spring. She'd remember that, wouldn't she? I *needed* to be on the squad, or I suspected my mom would kill me.

Pain lanced through my thoughts. I pulled my thumb

from my mouth and stared at the blood beading along the jagged line where I'd chewed my nail to the quick. Again.

I grabbed a tissue from the box on the nightstand and wrapped it around my thumb. If my mom saw it, she'd add nail biting to her list of topics to cover every morning.

I hauled myself out of bed and across my room. Carrot, my childhood stuffed bunny, watched me from his place of honor on the shelf over my desk. His black button eyes seemed to stare at me with sympathy, as if saying, *Remember when you were a kid and we lived in a house half this size? And even though the backyard was smaller than the driveway is now, we'd have the most fantastic adventures there. And the best part was that none of this stuff mattered— not cheerleading tryouts or student council, and especially not your mother's politics.*

That was a lifetime ago, I told myself as I turned away. Everything was different back then—*I* was different. But now? I didn't have time to waste on wishes, memories, or stuffed toy rabbits. Nothing could change the fact that I was seventeen, and no matter how much I hated it, cheerleading, student council, and my mother's politics *did* matter.

Not making the cheerleading team wasn't an option— at least not according to my mom. And I hadn't worked so damn hard getting where I was only to lose it because of a stupid botched extension in tryouts.

I grabbed my phone off the down comforter. As any athlete would tell you, a team needed both a stellar offense and a stellar defense. Thanks to the lessons I'd learned from my politician mother, I was my own all-star team. First up, damage control.

I clicked on Christy's Facebook post and composed a quick comment.

Christy, you're such a fabulous captain, I'm sure whatever decision you make will be the right one. Here's to the best cheerleading squad this school's ever seen. Go Royals!

While the public suck-up post was a good start, it certainly wouldn't hurt my cause to send another, more personal message. Last month, Christy's boyfriend had cheated on her with a girl named Mia, who also just so happened to show up at tryouts with the same Gucci purse Christy had last year.

I found Christy in my phone's contacts and typed out a text.

Can you believe Mia showed up at tryouts? Saw her carrying what looked like your old Gucci purse. Poor Dumpster diver has to shop thrift for both purses and secondhand boyfriends. I say let the trash keep her trash. You're too good for that shit.

Christy responded a minute later with:

RIGHT? Thanks, girl. I can always count on you for a smile :)

I knew it was stupid, but my mother taught me to never underestimate the significance of flattery to put you on someone's good side. At the same time, I also knew the importance of a good offense, so I clicked back on Payton's text and added my other friend Amber to the conversation. My request was simple.

I NEED ALL THE DIRT YOU CAN GIVE ME ON CHRISTY HOLDER

Payton was the first to text back with:

You got it!

Amber responded a minute later with:

OMG Regan. A little early in the morning for a freak-out, isn't it?

I rolled my eyes and tossed my phone on the bed. I should have known Amber wouldn't understand. As the most popular girl in the school, she didn't have to work for anything. She also happened to be the co-captain of the squad. If I could find something to take Christy out of the picture, Amber would be captain. And as one of her best friends, *of course* I'd make the squad.

I let myself relax a bit. With Payton on the hunt for reputation-ruining information on Christy Holder, I was free to schedule my volunteer hours for Honor Society, formulate a plan for my student council campaign, get started on my pre-SAT studying, and—

"Regan. Time's up."

I flinched. My mother. Damn. I'd almost forgotten.

I dragged myself to my closet and slipped on my school

uniform. It was a joke that the school thought requiring us to dress the same would promote some sort of equality among the students. What it really did was give us more creative ways to compete, like who had the best designer-label shoes or the most expensive jewelry—a title I was pretty sure I won thanks to the diamond necklace Daddy gave me for my sweet sixteen.

I fingered the necklace to make sure it was exactly where it should be—at the nape of my throat where everyone could see it. Next, I ran a brush through my hair, slid on a headband, and added a spritz of Marc Jacobs Daisy to my neck and wrists. I had just enough time to apply powder and mascara to cover up the dark circles under my eyes before my mom called for me again. My entire look was calculated to exert an air of perfectly sweet, all-American class.

I quickly zipped my makeup case and turned for the door. I knew better than to make her call me a fourth time. But as soon as I stepped into the hall, I paused. My pills. I scooped the pill bottle off my nightstand and zipped it inside my backpack. *Technically*, it was against the rules to carry prescription drugs in school. I didn't care. Every time I retrieved a pill from the school nurse, she emailed my parents, leading to unwanted attention from my mother, which brought more anxiety, more panic attacks, and the growth of an already-vicious cycle of stress. No one wanted that.

Besides, who knew? Maybe today would be the day the panic attacks stopped.

A vision of pigs flying had me smiling to myself when I

entered the kitchen, but the moment I spotted my mother glaring at me from a chair at the table, the smile died on my lips. She wore one of her many suits tailored to fit snugly on her slender frame. Her hair was pulled into a bun at the nape of her neck, revealing the lines of her face—angles sharp enough to deflect any argument.

"Regan," she said coolly while motioning to the empty seat to her right. "Let's have a chat, shall we?"

"Where's Dad?" I asked, ignoring her question. He'd taken on the job of buffering my mother's assaults, and I wasn't about to suffer through this one without him. This morning, however, Dad wasn't sitting at his usual chair beside Mom. I glanced around the room and saw he wasn't at the coffeepot pouring a refill, either.

A look of annoyance flickered across her eyes. "Gone," she answered. "He had to perform an early-morning root canal. It's just you and me."

Her words echoed inside my head.

Just you and me.

I had no idea what my mother was about to say, but I knew one thing: somehow, I was letting her down. Anxiety wove through my body, pulling my muscles tight.

Recalling my doctor's instructions, I sucked in a deep breath, held it for the count of ten, and slowly exhaled until the coils wrapped around my body unwound.

She narrowed her eyes. "What are you doing? Why are you breathing like that?"

I didn't bother answering, because she knew *exactly* what I was doing. She drove me to my appointments and held hushed conversations with my doctor after I left the room. God forbid she acknowledge my stress. I mean, why would she when it was so much easier to play dumb than admit something was wrong with her daughter?

"I think I'll make myself a bowl of cereal," I said, faking pleasantness.

My mom reached for the purse looped on the back of her chair, withdrew a protein bar, and tossed it onto the table. "Regan, dear, you should be cautious with carbs. Girls with curves like yours walk a fine line between flattering and flabby."

I pressed my teeth together so hard my jaw ached. Still, I didn't move. The last thing I wanted to do was sit at the table with *that* woman. I had a better chance of making it out alive if I covered myself in blood and dove into a shark tank. "Coffee, then."

I turned for the pot and tried to remember that my mother wasn't always this critical. She'd given me Carrot, after all. I knew the political arena—the constant fear that your enemies would spot an opening—had changed her. In fact, I knew *exactly* how she felt, but that didn't make being her daughter any less stressful.

"I threw out all the coffee," she said.

I froze. Her tone implied she didn't know she'd just tossed a live grenade in our kitchen.

A spark of anger burned through me, and I embraced it. Besides my pills, anger was the one thing that effectively kept my panic attacks at bay. I bit out, "Why would you do that?" She knew I needed coffee in the morning more than air. Without that extra kick, I'd be lagging in first period, and I had an exam coming up. Was this some sick test to make me stronger?

She paused before replying. "Coffee stains teeth. It's campaign year, Regan. There will be commercials and interviews. We all need to look our best."

I turned to face her, folding my arms across my chest. "You're worried about my *teeth*?"

Her eyes narrowed. "Must I remind you that image is everything in politics? Do you want me to lose the next election?"

Actually, the last thing I wanted was for her to lose the election. Typically she spent half of every week in Washington, DC. The 791 miles separating her from our house in Illinois was the only thing keeping me sane. But come on. My damn teeth? At her insistence, I had them whitened on a regular basis, so I knew that was not the problem. And I *needed* that caffeine if I was going to stay on top...

"I'm sorry," I said. "You're absolutely right. The economy is in shambles, people are out of work, but God forbid I have stained teeth."

Something almost resembling apologetic flickered in her eyes. "You know it's more than that. Your doctor says caffeine isn't good for your...nerves."

I knew I shouldn't push it. That was as close to an *I love you* as I was ever going to get from her. Still, I couldn't help but add, "You mean my anxiety disorder?"

She lifted her chin and leveled me with her stare. "Sit,

Regan."

Reluctantly, I trudged over to the table and dropped into the seat across from her. She motioned to the protein bar, and all I could think was, *Mmmm, chocolate-covered cardboard*, as I unpeeled the wrapper and dreamed about the cola I was going to grab from the vending machine at school.

I bit into the bar, but it took a minute to convince my throat I had actual food in my mouth and I should swallow instead of spitting it back out.

My mom watched me before shaking her head. "I just don't understand it, Regan. You're such a beautiful girl. Why won't you put more effort into your appearance? A little blush and lipstick would keep you from looking like you just rolled out of bed."

I frowned at her and kept chewing my cardboard. I *had* made an effort.

"Anyway"—she waved a hand dismissively—"that's a conversation for another day."

I swallowed hard. *I can't wait.*

"The real reason I want to talk to you," she continued, adjusting the small American flag pinned to her lapel, "is that with your senior year only a year away, we need to devise a game plan. This is your last chance to impress a college admissions board. Not to mention, with my upcoming election, the public will be watching, too."

I struggled to keep the protein bar from making an encore appearance. It was bad enough going down; I could only imagine how it would be coming back up. I swallowed several times before I was able to answer. "I actually already have a plan."

"Oh?" My mom quirked an eyebrow. "Please. The floor is yours."

I hated it when she talked to me like I was presenting a bill on the House floor rather than talking about my *life*. I fought to keep from rolling my eyes. "Well, I've been nominated to run for student council, so I'll have my own campaign to focus on."

"Wonderful." She smiled and laced her fingers together. "You simply *must* win. Student government looks fantastic on a college application."

"Right." There was little use pointing out the student body had to actually vote for me, and I had no say in the matter. "And I'm scheduling my service hours for school. I'll keep volunteering to walk horses at the stable, and I'll start serving dinners at the soup kitchen at church. And then there's cheerleading…" *Hopefully*.

"Good." She hiked the purse strap over her shoulder. "I've got a plane to catch. I'll speak with your father tonight to make sure you stay on target. It wouldn't do to have things fall apart while I'm away."

And there it was. The ever-present threat of my failure ruining everything. The invisible straitjacket pulled so tightly around my ribs, my lungs ached. Despite my best effort, the panic attack was upon me.

She paused in the doorway long enough to give me one final warning. Her mouth moved, only I couldn't hear her words over the sound of my pulse pounding in my head.

Either my mom didn't notice or she didn't want to notice my trouble breathing, because she turned and left the moment her lips stopped moving. The second she was out of view, I grabbed my backpack and pulled out the small orange bottle. My shaking hands rattled the pills together. This was nothing new. I'd shaken it on so many occasions that a film of dust coated the interior.

Fear twisted through me—the same fear that always manifested during my panic attacks—that maybe I wouldn't make it through alive.

I knew it was a stupid thought. My doctor and therapist both explained countless times that no one could die from a panic attack. Still, I couldn't breathe—and you needed to breathe to live, right? I also assumed you needed your heart to not explode out of your chest. Yet both of those things appeared to be happening to me. But I'd survive. Somehow.

I always did.

Chapter Two

I pulled into my assigned parking spot, slid out of my white Ford Escape, and shut the door behind me. Mom insisted our cars be American-made. "It's good for public image," she'd said when I asked for an Audi or something equally hot.

My phone chirped. A text from Payton.

I've got major dirt on Christy Holder. You're not going to believe it!

Perfect. Hopefully it was something I could use. After the texts I'd sent that morning, there was no way Christy would ever suspect me.

What is it?!

I imagined Payton hunched over her phone, her lips curled with evil glee as she typed. The longer it took her to respond, the juicier I knew it was going to be. For Payton, the delivery of a rumor was every bit as important as the acquisition. If gossip were an art form, she would be the master.

"Hey, Regan."

I turned in the direction of the voice. A dark-haired sophomore waved at me from several cars over. I didn't know her. At least, I didn't think I did. I tucked my phone away and waved back anyway. "Hey, girl." What if I'd blown the girl off and someone important saw? *You never know when you'll need someone's support.* That was what my mother always said. *You've got to be thinking three steps ahead at all times.*

I withdrew my sunglasses from my Kate Spade bag and put them on. I was sure some people thought it was a style thing—and that was fine with me. I'd never tell them I wore my sunglasses to keep everyone from seeing the fear in my eyes. Because I hadn't even been here five minutes and I already felt the staring—their eyes like gun scopes marking a target on my back.

When you're popular, someone is always trying to knock you down so she can step over you and gain your spot.

As if I was going to let that happen. Already I had my phone out, securing my social standing before I even stepped foot in the door. First up were several identical messages to some of the other girls on the cheerleading squad.

You looked great at tryouts yesterday. Seriously, everyone else's kicks were shit compared to yours. I'm sooo jealous!

It might have been a little lazy to send out the same text, but I needed to secure as many allies on the squad as quickly as I could. Besides, who was going to question a compliment?

My phone chirped. Payton.

> *Rehab. I heard straight from Christy's best friend's cousin that her parents sent her to California this summer. She has an eating disorder and stayed at some fancy clinic in Malibu. Nearly made her parents go bankrupt sending her there.*

Shit. That wasn't the kind of gossip I wanted. When I first read "Rehab," I was hoping for a secret Adderall addiction or something I could use as blackmail to secure my spot on the squad. But an eating disorder was technically a psychological disorder, right? Just like an anxiety disorder — like *my* anxiety disorder. Something like this could ruin a person. How far was I really willing to go to make my mom happy?

As if summoned, my mother's voice whispered through my mind. *Do you really think I worry about my opponent's mental state when I rip him through the mud? Do you really believe Christy would hold back if she knew your secret?*

My phone chirped again.

> *So what are you going to do?*

I tapped the side of my phone and considered my next move. I'd been going to school with Christy since kindergarten, and she'd never so much as said a mean thing about me. I didn't want to ruin her reputation or anything. Just…distract her a bit. But how? I couldn't just spread the rumor about her rehab stint. Everyone would rush to her side and fight over who got to be "most supportive." That wouldn't help me at all.

I'll think of something. We've only got to get her out of the picture temporarily, right? Just long enough for Amber to take over and make sure I'm on the squad.

Not that I had any idea how to make that happen yet. Or whether I actually wanted to use something as serious as an eating disorder against her. It didn't feel right.

Well, you better hurry. She's listing the squad in two days.

I pocketed my phone and sighed. Maybe I should let it go. I mean, how bad would it be if I *didn't* make the cheerleading squad? It wasn't like I lived and died for cheerleading or anything. In fact, I hated reciting those *stupid* cheers and the way boys flipped up my skirt when they walked by. If I didn't make the squad, I'd have more time to spend with my horse—a definite bonus—as well as more time to study instead of the all-night cram sessions I'd grown accustomed to because of my busy schedule.

No. If I didn't make the squad, I'd ruin my chances of getting into a good college. And if I didn't get into a good college, my career options would be limited. If I couldn't get a job, I'd be forced to live at home, with my *mother*, forever. And since my mother was a political figure, the entire world would bear witness to the failure of my life.

A sour taste burned the back of my tongue. I couldn't fail, even though I hated fucking with people's lives. I'd done it so often that you'd think I would have stopped caring at some point. I pretended I didn't. Hell, if Amber was around, I even pretended to enjoy it like she did. But it never got easier, never made my stomach hurt any less or stopped my palms from getting sweaty.

"Regan," a girl with short blond hair called from the entrance steps as I approached. I recognized her from cheerleading tryouts. If I played my cards right—and she actually made the squad—we could end up on it together.

"Hi," I called back and flashed a huge grin. "I can't wait for practice to start, can you?"

"It's going to be such a great year!" she answered before resuming her conversation with the boy beside her.

The way she'd said "great year" made me pause. Given the enthusiasm in her voice, I could tell she honestly believed it. I wondered what that was like. What kind of life must she have where that kind of optimism came naturally? Where she woke up eager to face whatever the morning had in store, instead of wanting to bury herself under the covers because she was sure *that* day would be the day everything came unraveled?

My smile wavered, but I quickly forced it back into place before anyone caught on. As far as they were concerned, I was Regan Flay, all-American, straight-A cheerleader and daughter of congresswoman Victoria Flay. I loved Jesus, my family, and horses—*in that order.* As my mother said, I was the embodiment of a child raised with firm boundaries and wholesome American values, and I must conduct myself as such. And I did—as long as you didn't count the anxiety disorder, pill usage, and a little social espionage here and there.

If I was raised with "American values" like my mom said, just how fucked up was this country, anyway?

Bracing myself for the inevitable wave of panic, I inhaled deeply, pushed my shoulders back, and pulled open the school's glass doors. Several dozen pairs of eyes turned in my direction. My muscles strained with the desire to spin around and run back the way I came. Instead, I concentrated on putting one foot in front of the other—to keep moving forward even though the farther I walked into the school building, the more the air thinned to an unbreathable level.

Several people called my name in greeting, but my sunglasses made it difficult to distinguish faces among the mass of students milling through the halls. Even so, I didn't dare remove them. With them on, I could pretend there was a wall between me and those around me. Still, I didn't want to be perceived as a bitch, so I widened my smile and raised my hand in a general greeting.

Honestly, I wasn't sure why I was popular. I was no different from anyone else; in fact, I was probably a lot worse than most of them. One of the many responsibilities my mother forced on me, I supposed. Not only did I have to constantly impress the media, but I had to put on a face every day for these kids, too. There was nowhere in the world I was allowed to just be average.

"Regan!" Payton pushed through a group of boys laughing about something on one of their phones.

At the sight of her, the weight bearing down on my shoulders lifted, and the lightness I felt in its wake was dizzying. I couldn't help but smile—for real this time—at my happiness and relief at seeing my best friend.

"You and those sunglasses." She rolled her eyes playfully. "It's like you think you're a fucking celebrity or something."

"Aren't I?" I pulled the glasses to the tip of my nose and gave my best *I'm a celebrity and better than you* look. "I've been on television practically my whole life. How many times have you been on television, Payton?" I slid the glasses off my face and tucked them into my purse. I didn't need them now with my friend here. The hallway that had been only moments from caving in on me suddenly opened up, allowing me to breathe. "Oh yeah—*never.*"

"Bitch." She laughed and looped her arm through mine as we wound our way to my locker.

Payton tugged on the hem of her sweater-vest, adjusting it over her hips as I spun the combination dial on my locker. As usual, the pleats of her skirt were ironed into lines so sharp they looked like they could saw through logs. The tie at the nape of her neck was perfectly even with her collar, and not a single strand of her straight blond hair had escaped the band of the ponytail on top of her head. "When you weren't at your locker earlier," she said, "I was worried you were going to be late."

"I almost was," I answered. "Mom wanted to have another one of her *talks.*"

"Oh, God." Her eyes widened in horror. "What was it about this time?"

"The usual shit."

"Ugh." Payton wrinkled her nose. "I seriously don't know how you deal."

I thought about the pills tucked away in my bag and shrugged. After zipping my first-period books inside my backpack, I closed my locker and sighed.

Payton leaned in and dipped her forehead against mine. "At least when she finds out you've made the squad, she'll have to lay off of you a little."

I paused. I didn't really want to bring up how badly I'd botched the tryout or the fact that even if I made the squad, my mom would only find some other fault of mine to obsess over, so instead I smiled and nodded.

Seemingly satisfied, she grinned. "Speaking of the squad, you're not going to believe the dirt I found on Christy. Come on." She didn't give me a chance to respond before grabbing my arm and guiding me through the throngs of students milling the hallway and waiting for first bell. Most of the people we passed glanced our way with a smile or wave of acknowledgment. A few even backed out of our path, giving us room to pass.

Or so I thought, until I collided face-first with a muscular torso.

"Well if it isn't little Regan Flay."

I jerked back, and my stammered apology died on my

lips. I'd know that deep, condescending voice anywhere.

Payton's older brother pulled out his cell phone and hit the record button, his eyes narrowing in concentration. They were the same color hazel as Payton's, but that was where the similarities between brother and sister ended.

Once upon a time in junior high, Nolan—like his sister—hung with the popular crowd. But something changed when he entered high school and started dating purple-haired Jordan from the drama club. After that, he only hung out with people in the AV and drama clubs as well as various other *artistic* crowds. It was almost like he wanted to become a loser on purpose. Even now, his shirttails hung out from under his sweater-vest like wrinkled flags, and the hem of his pants was torn and frayed. His tousled dark hair was longish, just brushing the collar of his shirt and falling across his forehead. He'd be supercute if he gave a damn what he looked like and kept his mouth shut.

Not that I'd ever tell him.

Payton stepped between us. "Watch where you're going, jackass."

"Where *I'm* going?" Still recording us, he arched an eyebrow. "If I'm not mistaken, little sister, Regan bumped into *me*. I guess your directional compasses are just as off as your moral ones."

I pulled at the hem of my blouse in an attempt to straighten it. "What's that supposed to mean?"

"It means that because I live with her"—he jutted a thumb at Payton—"and have known you practically your whole life, I'm immune to the innocent act you and my sister have going." He held up a hand before I could say anything. "Wait. Don't answer until I get a better angle. I want to capture the complete and utter lack of soul in your eyes when you reply." He adjusted the phone so the lens faced me head-on.

A flush of anger burned up my neck. "Who the fuck do you think you are, pretending to know *anything* about me?"

"Go away. Neither one of us wants to be in one of your stupid documentaries." Payton shoved her brother's chest hard enough that he stumbled back. "Stop being a dickwad, Nole, or I swear I'll tell Mom."

He smirked and pocketed the phone. "Oh no. Please don't tell Mom. When are you going to stop acting like a baby?"

She folded her arms across her chest. "Probably when you stop acting like an asshole."

"I'll stop acting like an asshole when you stop manipulating people into liking you." He turned to me and grinned, like maybe he really *did* know a thing or two about me.

And that was terrifying as hell.

I didn't know what *exactly* he knew or if he even knew anything at all. What I *did* know was I needed him to stop talking before people overheard. So I took another page out of my mother's book. When you found yourself backed into a corner, bypass the lesser insults and go straight for the jugular.

Forcing my face into a mask of cool indifference, I lifted my chin. "I can't help but notice your ex-girlfriend—Jordan, wasn't it?—doesn't go to school here anymore. You must really be a special kind of freak if she can't stand to be within a twenty-mile radius of you. Is that why you're still single?"

My insult had the desired effect, and Nolan's smile vanished. I wanted to celebrate my victory, but something in his eyes stopped me. It wasn't anger. Maybe… disappointment? Pain? Whatever it was held me captive, and I realized somehow, I'd crossed a bigger line than I'd meant to.

Payton laughed, and the sound snapped me out of my paralysis. "Good one, Regan," she said, tugging on the strap of my purse. "Let's get out of here. I don't want to find out if 'freak' is contagious."

She pulled me around him. Only after we'd made it several yards down the hallway did I finally feel the tension inside my chest loosen. We reached the end of the hall and were about to turn the corner when something compelled me to look back.

Nolan hadn't moved from the spot where we'd collided. The moment our eyes met, I inhaled sharply. I could practically feel the heat in his gaze.

"Just ignore him," Payton said, pulling me back around. "He might be an ass, but he's totally harmless."

I nodded even though "harmless" wasn't the word I would have picked to describe her brother. "Harmless" wouldn't make my breath hitch in my throat.

Before we reached the door to our homeroom, our bodies were wrenched apart and shoved aside as our friend Amber pushed through. As usual, the waistline of her skirt had been rolled down so her hem sat several inches above dress-code limit. Her tie hung in a loose knot below the gape in her blouse—a result of the conveniently missing buttons.

"I've been looking everywhere for you bitches." Amber's heart-shaped lips puckered. She tossed her long black hair over her shoulder and narrowed her almond-shaped eyes. "You weren't talking about me, were you?"

"What?" Payton asked. "We would never talk about you behind your back." She laughed, but the pitch was a little too high to sound natural.

I winced inwardly. The truth was, Payton and I talked about Amber all the time. I mean, yes, Amber was our friend, but she had the personality of a charging rhinoceros. One wrong move and she'd pulverize you. If Payton and I couldn't vent to each other about her, we'd probably go crazy—or in my case, crazier. The three of us had been friends since freshman year when Amber spread a rumor that Macy Simmons's mono was really gonorrhea in order to steal her boyfriend.

That was when I'd realized Amber was dangerous.

Keep your friends close and your enemies closer, Mom always said. Being Amber's friend enabled me to keep an eye on her and make sure she didn't stab me in the back. I suspected she was my friend for the same reason. Either way, over the years an unspoken agreement had passed between us. I kept her secrets and she kept mine.

"Where's Jeremy?" I asked in a pathetic attempt to change the subject. As the current fly ensnared in the black widow's web, he was never more than arm's length away from her—probably because he was always using those arms to slide his hands up the hem of her skirt. Seriously disgusting.

"The showers." Amber wrinkled her nose. "The entire wrestling team had weight training this morning. He was so sweaty; it was gross."

Yeah, it wasn't the sweat that made him gross, but I wasn't about to tell her that. As discreetly as possibly, I jabbed my elbow into Payton's side to get her to stop giggling like an idiot.

"Forget Jeremy." Amber placed a hand on her hip. "So, were you bitches talking about me or what?"

I remembered watching a therapist on *Dr. Phil* say how cheaters were the first to accuse others of cheating. I guessed the same held true for throwing shade. "No one's talking about you, Amber," I said. "My mom gave me another one of her *motivational* speeches this morning, and I was just telling Pay about it."

"Uh-huh." Her lips curved into a wicked grin. "I can't imagine how you'd have time to tell anyone anything with all the texting you've been doing." She held up her hand and counted down with her fingers. "First the kiss-ass text to Christy, then the generic text to half the squad. Nice touch saying the rest of us looked like shit, by the way."

I choked out a laugh to cover my gasp. "You're making it sound worse than it is."

Amber snorted. "Please. That Little Miss Innocent bullshit might work with everyone else in the school, but it sure as hell doesn't work with me. I know exactly what you said in those texts."

It took all of my strength to lock my knees and keep my legs from shaking. "How?"

Amber shrugged. "Because I'm co-captain of the squad, beyotch, and people tell me everything. I don't know whether to be really impressed or hurt that I didn't get my own conniving, kiss-ass text." She stuck out her bottom lip. "I'm the fucking co-captain. Do I not rate at all on the Regan give-a-fuck meter?"

"What?" I took a step back. "No. I mean, yes. I mean—" Honestly, I hadn't a freaking clue, because I didn't quite understand what was happening. My heart pounded like a fist against my sternum, and all of my fingers were tingly and numb.

"Oh my God." Her eyes widened, and she barked out a laugh. "You should totally see your face right now. You're totally freaking out, aren't you?"

I wanted to argue, but my throat was so tight that I couldn't squeeze out the words.

"Look at her, Pay." Amber spun me around so I faced Payton. "She's totally freaking out, isn't she?"

I wrenched my arm free from her grip. "Stop it. I'm not freaking out."

Amber folded her arms across her chest and smirked. "Obviously."

I clutched the straps of my backpack so she couldn't tell how badly my hands shook. "Look, I don't know who lit the fuse on your tampon this morning, but you need to back off."

The smile slid off her face, and her glare turned icy. "Or you'll what? Send nasty texts about me?"

"I would never do that. We're friends."

"Of course we are, which is why I'm totally fucking with you." Amber's icy expression melted into a grin.

I wanted to believe her, but there was a tension I couldn't explain hanging in the air between us.

Maybe I was imagining it. Maybe I was reading too much into a look that didn't exist in the first place. Anxiety had a tendency to do that—to warp the way I thought people perceived me, painting everything in a negative light. At least that was what my doctor was always telling me.

Amber grabbed my arm and pulled me toward our classroom door. Payton followed us while chewing on the bottom of her lip. She looked every bit as nervous as I felt.

"Don't worry," Amber whispered in my ear. "I'm not going to tell anyone about your texts. I only brought it up because I think you should be careful. I'm your friend, so I have to look out for you."

She paused outside the door, and I turned to face her. "Why do I have to be careful?"

"Aw, sweetie." She patted my arm. "We can't have people finding out that Little Miss Perfect is really a huge-ass bitch. What would happen to your pristine reputation then?"

Before I could respond, she snatched Payton's wrist and dragged her inside the classroom, leaving me alone in the hall.

What would happen then?

CHAPTER THREE

The next morning, I sat in my car for several minutes, clutching my steaming caramel macchiato. Mom might have thrown out all the caffeine in the house, but she couldn't stop me from making a pre-school Starbucks run. Sure, the caffeine didn't help as far as panic attacks were concerned, but it wasn't like I could function without it—especially after a night plagued by nightmares.

Sometime around three in the morning, I'd decided not to go after Christy. All I could think about was how I'd feel if everyone knew about my "stress problems," as my mom would say. Even if all I managed to do was make half the school feel sorry for her, they'd still *know*. When I thought about it that way, I decided I would have to make the squad some other way.

All around me, students exited their cars and filed inside the brick building. Some hurried toward the entrance with smiles on their faces, while others staggered forward looking like they'd rather be anywhere else. It didn't matter if we wanted to be here or not; we were all compelled inside, like insects drawn to the blue glow of a bug zapper.

"Today is going to be better," I said, as if by speaking the words out loud, I could make them so. "Today is going to be a good day."

I performed a quick makeup check in the vanity mirror. I'd slept a total of four hours last night, despite the fact that I went to bed around eleven. It never mattered how exhausted I was. Sleep was no match for the anxiety that wove through my body long after my head hit the pillow.

After rubbing away a smudge of mascara, my gaze settled on the eyes in my reflection. My lake-blue irises were a carbon copy of my mother's, and with the vanity mirror too small to show my face, it was almost like my mother was in the car with me, staring at me with an accusatory expression.

My throat tightened. I quickly flipped the visor back into place before slipping on my sunglasses. I so did not need my mother inside my head right now.

With coffee in hand, I exited my car and plastered on another fake smile. Just the sight of the school's double glass doors raised my blood pressure every day without fail. The second I passed through them, I flipped the switch and became a version of myself that didn't really exist.

I had this fantasy where, on the last day of my senior

year, I skipped through the halls with my middle fingers held high while I screamed, "Fuck you, I'm Regan Flay."

Okay, so I'd never do it—that was why it was called a *fantasy*—but the thought still brought a smile to my lips.

I climbed the concrete steps. As usual, the eyes of every student lingering outside the doors turned in my direction. *Showtime, Regan.* After double-checking my smile to make sure it hadn't slipped, I proceeded. I waited for the waves of greetings, but unlike every morning since the beginning of my freshman year, they didn't come.

Weird.

I paused at the top of the stairs and glanced around. A sophomore girl pointed in my direction before she and the girl beside her laughed. A senior guy sitting on the base of the flagpole behind me smirked, the gesture anything but friendly.

Unease trickled down my spine, and the smile slid from my face. Something was definitely up. I was used to people watching me as I walked through the halls, but this was different. It was like I was the punch line of a joke no one bothered to share.

I just stood there, clutching my coffee to my chest as if its meager heat would be enough to warm the chills coursing through my body.

What the hell is going on?

I pushed through the double doors, and every head in the hallway turned in my direction. Fingers pointed and mouths curled in wicked grins. A group of girls whispered behind cupped hands, like they were trying to be discreet, but come on. Whispering behind their hands only drew attention to the fact they were whispering. So in reality, they were fully aware I knew they were talking about me, and they just didn't give a shit. I understood this because I'd shared whispers that way myself.

My lungs seized. I would have run back to my car, but my legs refused to budge. Whatever the hell was going on, I couldn't deal with it alone. I scanned the hallway for Payton, but she was nowhere to be found.

While most students continued to stream around me, oblivious to whatever shift had occurred, another small group gathered nearby. The sounds of their hushed whispers twisted together into a loud hiss. What little latte I'd drank on the drive to school churned dangerously in my stomach. I had to move. It wasn't like I could stand in the entryway all day. And if I did get sick, I couldn't throw up in the hallway, not in front of everyone with their cell phones and Web access.

I took a step forward. Then another. And another. I continued this process until, miraculously, I was walking like each step wasn't a conscious effort. The halls were thick with students, their gazes following me as I passed. I started to wonder if there was some news announcement about my mother. Yes. That had to be it. My perfect mother had gotten herself wrapped up in something unsavory.

The gathering at the entrance pressed forward as I moved, following me, closing the distance faster than I could walk, until I was sure their bodies would lurch and collapse on top of mine, burying me alive.

Stop being so dramatic, Regan. I took a deep breath. Whatever political scandal was unfolding with my mom, it would pass soon enough.

Ahead of me, visible above the crowd due to his height, was Nolan. He was the closest thing to Payton I saw, and I felt myself drifting toward him, even though he was the last person at this school I should be going to for comfort. But then I spotted the damned cell phone in his hand, raised so he could film me walking down the hall.

Oh, hell no. I might not have had a clue what was going on, but I sure as hell didn't need someone recording my every move for replay on the five o'clock news. The anger flushed away some of the panic. I marched toward him until I reached two girls standing in the middle of the hall with their backs to me, blocking my path. I huffed in annoyance and twisted sideways to pass between them.

I slipped by and was nearly to Nolan when one of them called out behind me. "There's the bitch now."

Her words struck me like a fist to the gut, and I jerked to a halt. Surely I'd heard wrong. *Nobody* had ever called me a bitch before. I mean, nobody besides Amber, and definitely never in such a *you-suck-please-die* tone. I'd spent my life befriending everyone I could. Everyone loved me or wanted to be me.

Slowly, I turned on the heel of my ballet flat. Christy and her best friend, Sarah, stood in the hall, glaring at me like I'd cheated with their boyfriends or something. Even with the anxiety coursing through my blood, I managed to keep my hands from shaking. I placed one on my hip while balancing my coffee with the other and met Christy's cool stare head-on. I had been nothing but nice to her yesterday. "Excuse me?"

She raised her chin so her hair swung away from her eyes. "You heard me, *bitch.*"

Several onlookers gasped. The crowd surrounding us shifted as more people pushed through for a better view. The electricity from their excitement prickled along my skin. They wanted a show, and I'd be damned if I gave them one. Regan Flay was not some show poodle to be paraded around a ring.

Still, I wasn't about to let the girl off the hook. I'd put her in her place verbally for now, but later I'd really make her pay. Fuck being nice and my decision to keep her secret. I'd destroy her with whispered rumors about her eating disorder. About how she nearly ruined her parents by insisting on a ritzy clinic in Malibu. Another lesson from my mother: gossip was practically untraceable. And when you couldn't be blamed, the dirt on your hands came clean easily enough. It made it that much easier to exaggerate the truth.

When I spoke, I concentrated on my voice to keep it calm and my words even. "I really don't think you want to do this."

"Sure do." She took a step closer and, even though I tried not to show it, my heart leaped into my throat. From this close, she could touch me, *hit* me if she wanted. The thought made my mouth go dry, and I glanced over my shoulder, searching for Payton or Amber. Where the hell were they?

I scanned the crowd, but both my friends remained absent. Nolan, however, and his damned phone were still happily recording away. At least I'd have recorded evidence if I filed a lawsuit.

"Everyone deserves to hear what you really are, *Regan Flay*," Christy continued. "You're so phony I can't believe I never saw through your act. At least now the entire school does."

I racked my brain for anything I'd said to Christy that was fake. Maybe she wasn't the best captain the squad had ever had, but since when was sucking up a crime? "What are you talking about?"

She leaned in, and it took every fiber of strength I possessed not to back away. "You had the entire school tricked into thinking you were perfect. But in reality, you're the worst kind of bitch—the two-faced kind."

Amber. I needed Amber. She'd know exactly what to say. Again, I scanned the crowd, but the moment I took my eyes off Christy, she slapped the coffee cup from my hand. It hit the ground and the lid shot off. I gasped and scrambled backward as hot caramel macchiato splattered my shoes and tights.

The crowd responded with a mixture of gasps and *ooh*s. As much as I wanted to lash back with an attack of my own, shock kept me rooted firmly in place. I was vaguely aware of my mouth hanging open and how stupid that made me look, but no matter how many electrical impulses my brain fired, I couldn't seem to make my lips work.

"I take that back," she said. "There's one bitch worse

than you, and I think you just met her." When I didn't respond, she smiled. "Karma."

Christy smirked and stalked away, Sarah right on her heels. Several girls who usually said hi to me turned up their noses and followed behind them. The rest of the students gathered around us backed away and cleared a path for her to walk. Several guys high-fived her as she passed. The second she disappeared, the buzz of whispers exploded around me, filling my head like a hive of bees.

This couldn't be happening. Was it possible I was stuck in the middle of another anxiety-induced nightmare? I clenched my fists and dug my nails into my palms until the pain was enough to make tears well in my eyes. No. Not a dream. I relaxed my hands, and while the pain slowly drained from my palms, it didn't ease the quickening of my heart or the tightness inside my chest.

I searched for a gap in the crowd or some sort of distraction I could use to escape. There was nothing. I was surrounded. Trapped. I raked my fingers through my hair. What would Mom do? I'd watched her opponents back her into corners during debates, and she never once lost her cool. *So, deep breaths, Regan.* I pushed my shoulders back and inhaled deeply. After a few seconds, I felt…no different.

If Mom were here, she'd probably smile to throw everyone off. She'd make them think she knew something they didn't—that they were making idiots of *themselves.* But I was a far cry from the confident, unmovable force that was my mother. The only thing I felt like doing was fleeing the school, driving home, and burying myself under the covers until I turned eighteen and could leave this hellish place once and for all.

But first, I needed to figure out what the hell was going on.

My throat tightened, and I heard my breathing go ragged. I realized I couldn't stand here much longer, or the entire school would watch as my throat closed and I dropped dead in a pool of caramel macchiato. And while the words "breathe, Regan, breathe" played on a loop inside my head, they meant nothing.

I *couldn't* fucking breathe, and the cool I tried so desperately to hold on to slipped from my grasp.

I whirled around and glared at the first girl I made eye contact with. "Fucking move," I shouted. I half expected her to come forward and challenge me like the previous girl had, but I no longer cared. Right now, I'd risk a fistfight for a chance to get some air.

To my surprise, she backed away, along with several others beside her. A little path opened up in the crowd, and I took it. The words "fucking bitch," "evil bitch," and worse jabbed me as I passed. I had no idea who said these things as my vision swam with colors from my inability to draw breath, but I'd be damned if I let them know how terrified I was. So I retreated behind a look of indifference as I worked my way through the crowd. Every step I took, however, put another crack in the mask.

The whispers dogged me, even when I finally broke through the ring of people. They followed me down the hall, around every corner, and through the quad. Everywhere I went, students watched me, smiling knowingly at each other and laughing after I passed.

The coffee spots on my tights had grown sticky and pulled at my legs. I knew better than to pause and clean them off. I was an injured diver in a sea of sharks. If I stopped moving, I'd only give them a chance to attack again. I wasn't going to rest until I found Payton and Amber. They had to know what was going on and what to do about it. But where the hell were they?

I pulled my phone from my pocket and shot off a text to both Payton and Amber.

Where are you guys???

Someone bumped into my shoulder as I typed. I didn't bother looking up to find out if it was an accident or not. Instead, I stared at my screen as I walked, willing my friends to answer me so I didn't have to be alone.

Seconds turned to minutes, and my phone remained silent.

Reluctantly, I tucked it away and approached my locker. There I found numerous sheets of paper taped to the door. I stopped several feet away. I was definitely not in the mood for more surprises. Was it a list of insults? I glanced around the hallway to see if the note-leavers were lurking nearby, but it was impossible to tell with all the people staring at me. What I did notice, though, was my locker wasn't the only one marked. Several others had the same pages taped to the front. And in the hall all around me, people were reading them.

The freshman occupying the locker beside mine glanced up and gave a squeak of surprise when she saw me coming. She quickly slammed her locker door and scurried away with her backpack open and her books cradled in her arms. Until today, she'd always smiled at me when I approached.

I slid the backpack off my shoulder and let it fall to the ground. I needed to gather my books quickly, so I had enough time to stop by the bathroom and wash the coffee out of my tights before first period. Still, I was reluctant to go anywhere without my friends.

Where the hell were they? I couldn't remember a time since starting high school when I'd made it as far as my locker without Payton or Amber joining me in the hall and chatting away while I gathered my books. The only exception was when they were sick. But what were the odds that both of them were sick on the same day? Unless they were puking, being sick was still no excuse for not answering my texts.

They better be puking their fucking guts up.

I ripped the pages off my locker door, hoping for a notice about drug searches or an upcoming pep rally—not that I cared about anything so stupid. I started to crumple the papers when a name in bold letters caught my attention— *my* name.

A cord of panic wove through my ribs and pulled tight. Carefully, I smoothed the paper out and read the title:

HERE'S WHAT REGAN FLAY THINKS ABOUT YOU.

Pictured below were hundreds of screenshots of my private messages, IMs, and text messages, only everyone else's names had been blurred out, incriminating only me. Scanning through them, I saw they went back months, a year even, including the texts I sent to Christy and the cheerleading squad only yesterday.

And right at the top, the texts Payton and I had written about Christy and how I'd use her going to rehab to secure a spot on the squad.

My knees buckled, and I leaned against my locker before my legs gave out. No wonder she was so pissed. My fingers curled, crumpling the paper's edges. I wanted to throw it to the ground, to tear into it with my teeth and stomp on the remains. But it was like the paper had fused to my hand. As much as I wanted to, I couldn't let go and I couldn't look away. Practically every nasty thing I'd ever written about anyone was there. From implying hookups that never happened to shit-talking and ass-kissing.

Of course, the replies back were equally bitchy, but with the sender's name blurred out, I was the only one who could be held accountable.

My hands shook so violently that the words jumbled on the pages. I finally managed to drop them and tried to make sense of the situation. How the hell had this happened? These were *private* messages among me, Payton, Amber, and several others. Were we hacked? Or, even worse, had the messages been leaked on purpose? And if so, why? There were at least two dozen people I talked shit about on those pages—and now the entire school knew. What was I going to do? Normally, I'd deny the texts were mine, but the hacker screen-captured the messages. The proof was impossible to deny.

I tried to suck in a breath, but it was nothing more than a wheeze. I glanced around, and at least twenty people lurked nearby and watched me panic. A group of girls holding instrument cases walked by, glaring at me over their shoulders. Some girl from the softball team wadded up a piece of paper and threw it at me as she passed. The ball hit my chest and bounced to the floor. The girls beside her hooted loudly.

I wanted to scream at them, to flip them off, *something*. My muscles, however, refused to do anything but tremble.

Dark spots crept along the edge of my vision. I couldn't squeeze enough oxygen into my tight lungs, and if I didn't do something about it, I had no doubt I'd pass out. I needed a pill, and I needed one fast. But it wasn't like I could slip one out of my purse with everyone watching, so there was only one place I could go. I pushed away from my locker and nearly stumbled face-first onto the ground before I caught myself.

The warning bell sounded robotically over the intercom. The students watching me shuffled away to their respective homerooms. They cast reluctant looks over their shoulders as they left. They weren't ready to give up on their free entertainment so easily. And what would be better than to watch Regan Flay drop dead in the middle of the hall?

I pressed my hand to my chest and dug my fingers into my blouse, clawing my way to the skin as if I could rip through my sternum, into my lungs, and force air in that way. I half stumbled, half shuffled to the nurse's office.

Around me, the hallway spun into a whirling blur of different shades of gray—gray walls, gray floor tiles, gray lockers. The shades darkened the farther I traveled, making me feel as if I were walking deeper into a tomb, one that might seal up behind me at any moment.

"What the hell's wrong with her?" someone asked behind me.

"Who the fuck cares?" another answered.

That was the million-dollar lightning-round question. *I'll take Caring About Regan Flay for a million dollars, Alex. I believe the answer is, Who is no one?* I was completely alone as I stumbled down the hall. Amber and Payton hadn't bothered to show up or even text me. It didn't really surprise me that Amber was lying low, but Payton…she was supposed to be my best friend. At least, I'd thought so until now.

Again, I wondered how someone could have gained access to our accounts. One of us might have unintentionally left the computer lab while logged in, but I knew Amber and Payton, and we all knew how to cover our tracks. Maybe one of them had accidentally left her phone somewhere?

The tardy bell sounded just as I reached the nurse's office. My chest heaved with ragged gasps as I flung open the door.

Nurse Fuller set down the sudoku puzzle in her hand, her eyes wide as she looked me over. "What the—?" She pushed to her feet. Her glasses slipped from her nose and hung from the chain around her neck. "Already, Regan? Classes haven't even started yet."

With my hand still twisted into the front of my shirt, I shrugged helplessly.

"Okay. Just take it easy." She stepped around her desk and, despite her two knee surgeries, hobbled over to me. Wrapping an arm around my shoulders, she guided me to the hard, duct-taped puke-green exam table in the corner. Nurse Fuller, who was every bit as ancient as the table, pulled her glasses on and squinted at me through the thick lenses.

"Sit, sit," she ordered, helping me onto the paper-covered table. It crinkled in protest as I collapsed on top of it. Lines of disapproval creased the nurse's forehead. "Relax, Regan. You're not breathing."

I scowled at her. I *hated* when people told me to relax. It wasn't like I had any control over it, like I'd woken up that morning and thought, *Hey, you know what would be fun? Death by suffocation.*

"Hold on." She crossed the room to a small counter with a sink and a hand-sanitizer dispenser mounted on the wall. She opened the overhead cabinet and withdrew a small brown paper bag. After rolling the edges down, she returned to my side. "Here you go. You know the drill."

I took the bag from her, barely managing to hold on to it with my trembling fingers.

Nurse Fuller grabbed my elbow and forced me to lift the bag up to my face. "In and out. In and out."

With my lips pressed into the bag, I drew in a shaky breath, collapsing the bag with a crunch. When I could inhale no more, I exhaled, and the bag ballooned outward. I repeated this over and over until my chest no longer ached and the room fell into focus around me.

The nurse watched me with her lips pressed tight and her arms folded across her pink scrub top. "Are you good?"

Not by a long shot. Still, I nodded, because I didn't want her to suggest calling my dad. If he had to pick me up, he'd call Mom, and she'd fly in from Washington just to crawl further up my ass than she already was. No thank you.

The nurse's frown deepened, as if she could read the lie on my face. "All right then. Just lie there and focus on relaxing while I go get one of your pills. Okay?"

Still breathing into the bag, I nodded. The crinkling sound it made as it inflated and deflated nearly drowned out the sound of my heartbeat.

She snatched a pillow that felt like it was packed with cardboard and stuffed it under my head. "Hang tight. I'll be right back." Faster than a seventy-something-year-old woman with a knee replacement should be able to move, she spun on her heels and disappeared into the closet where she kept students' prescription pills and EpiPens locked inside a wire-mesh case.

A minute later, she returned with a pill in one hand and a paper cup of water in the other.

It took about fifteen minutes for my body to deflate against the table like a leaky balloon. I closed my eyes and continued to breathe. *In and out. In and out.* Like I could expel the entire morning as easily as I expelled my breath. *In and out. In and out.* The more I sank against the hard cushion, the more energy bled from my body. Maybe it was the panic attack or the nightmare-fraught, sleepless night, but I could feel myself begin to drift away. *In and out.* I didn't fight it. In fact, I welcomed it. I only wished wherever the darkness pulled me, it would be somewhere no one could find and drag me back from.

But no matter how much I wanted to stay here, I knew I couldn't hide forever.

Only two inches of wood and a pane of glass separated me from the rest of the world waiting to watch my downfall.

And I was going to have to face them soon enough.

CHAPTER FOUR

"Regan, honey? It's time to wake up." A hand grabbed on to my shoulder and gave a gentle shake. "You either go to class or I need to have your dad pick you up."

"No," I murmured as I squeezed my eyes shut. I didn't want either of those things. I wanted to remain in the protective darkness of my unconscious. But despite my best effort to cling to the comfort of sleep, Nurse Fuller's hand on my shoulder roused me awake. I blinked my eyes until a poster warning against the dangers of HPV slid into focus.

The nurse sighed. "I can't have students spending the entire day sleeping in my office." She gently gripped me under the arm and pulled me into a sit. "If you don't want to go to class, I have to call your dad. Do you—"

"No." I jerked out of her grasp, instantly awake. My

tights smelled like caramel macchiato. As annoying as that was, they were the least of my worries.

The nurse frowned and took a step back.

"I'm sorry." I forced a weak smile to my lips. "My dad is probably in surgery and Mom's in DC. We don't have to bother them with this, do we?"

She dipped her chin and stared at me over the rim of her glasses. "You know I have to email them about your visit, right?"

I nodded and slid to the edge of the table. "I know." With an email, they'd be concerned, but not as freaked as they'd be receiving a call from school asking them to come pick me up because I had a massive breakdown. I could only imagine how drastically my therapy appointments would increase. Or the tone of my mother's voice as she pointed out how pathetic I was to give in to weakness like this.

I dropped off the table. Nurse Fuller rushed to my side and held out a hand as if to catch me as I fell—a pretty bold move, considering she weighed about ninety pounds and I'd most likely break her hip if I did. I swayed but managed to keep my balance.

"Easy there," she told me. "That was the worst attack you've had in a while."

I'd say. My head felt like it'd been stuffed with cotton. Not especially awesome when you had classes to focus on, but at least it would numb the kids' stares.

"Here." She handed me a piece of paper, and I squinted down at it.

"It's a hall pass," she explained. "You're late for second

period."

My heart skipped a beat, but thanks to the numbing power of my medication, it barely registered as a tickle inside my chest. "I slept through first period?"

She nodded. "I shouldn't have let you, but you really looked like you needed it." She was quiet a moment. "This is the first time you've needed a pill so early in the day, Regan. Is everything okay?"

The way gossip traveled through this school, I had no doubt some of the faculty had already heard about—if not seen—the papers with my private messages. But because Nurse Fuller seldom left her cave, it was a safe bet she hadn't found out. That was a good thing, considering she had both of my parents' numbers on an index card pinned to her message board.

I shook my head. "I have a history test today. I guess it's got me a little stressed."

Her frown deepened. "You're still seeing a therapist, aren't you?"

I nodded before dropping my gaze to my shoes.

"Good. Make sure you talk to him about this."

I kept my eyes trained on the floor so she wouldn't see my irritation. Therapy was not a topic of conversation I ever cared to discuss.

She walked to her office door and pulled it open, revealing the hallway beyond. My throat tightened again, and I had trouble swallowing. I couldn't go back out there and face them. Not now. Not ever. For a split second, I considered asking her to call my dad so I could go home, but I knew that would only create more problems for me in the long run.

Nurse Fuller leaned against the door. Lines of concern pinched her forehead. I wondered if she could read the fear on my face, or maybe it was a sixth-sense nurse's thing.

"You know, Regan, you can talk to me if something's going on. I've been a nurse for almost forty years, not to mention I've raised six kids of my own. There's nothing you can tell me I haven't heard or seen before." She offered a smile.

"Thanks." I tried to smile back, but my muscles were slow to respond. I was pretty sure my smile came out as a grimace. "I'll keep that in mind."

I stepped into the hall, and she shut the door behind me. I was alone.

I hugged myself as I shuffled to class. I wasn't in a hurry. If they didn't take attendance each period, I'd be out the door and headed for the parking lot.

Unlike this morning when the hall felt like it was going to cave in on me, now it felt like a horror movie: dark, silent, and never-ending.

I approached my locker, which was along the way. None of the lockers I passed bore the taped sheets of paper responsible for my social ruin. Hopefully they'd been torn off by students and tucked inside lockers instead of being discovered by a teacher. A summons to the office was the last thing I needed right now. After all, more than one thousand students attended Saint Mary's, and I had no doubt that, if they hadn't read the pages, they'd soon hear about them. That meant one thousand students currently hated me. Well, one thousand minus my two best friends. But as the hours ticked by and my phone remained silent, I had to question even that.

I pulled out my phone and shot Payton another text.

> *Hey. I really need to talk to you. Just let me know you got this, k?*

I pressed send and then proceeded to stare at my phone, waiting. A minute went by. Then another. And still the phone remained silent. I told myself she wasn't answering because she was in class and didn't want to get in trouble—not that that had ever stopped us before. I waited one more minute until it became clear she wasn't texting back. A cord of unease pulled tight inside me, and I tucked my phone away. I refused to cry. In high school, tears might as well have been blood. Any wound, no matter how small, was a sign of weakness.

And high school destroyed the weak.

What I needed was to pull myself together and form a plan. I couldn't go on the defensive, since I didn't need anything else to further shred my *good girl* image. No, I needed to play the offense, to gradually win people back to my side. Right now, though, with emotions running so hot, I knew that was impossible. But maybe once people had a chance to cool down, I could begin to rebuild my reputation. Of course, I'd need my friends on my side to do that.

If only they'd text me back.

I continued walking. As my locker drew nearer, I noticed something on the door—a word written in what appeared to be black marker. A sick feeling washed over me, and I hurried over. The closer I got, the more the word fell into focus, until I stood in front of it, and it screamed at me in crystal clarity.

BITCH

My bottom lip trembled. I quickly bit down on it before my emotions got out of hand. I tried to wipe the writing off with my palm, but the letters wouldn't fade. I rubbed harder, my palm squeaking against the metal until my hand turned red and my skin burned. The asshole must have used a Sharpie. I stopped rubbing and sagged against the locker, resting my forehead on the cool metal.

"Excuse me."

Startled, I jerked back and found one of the school's uniformed security guards watching me with narrowed eyes. "You okay?"

I nodded, not trusting my words to come out with any sort of confidence.

He frowned, clearly not buying it. "Why aren't you in class?"

I held up my hall pass, and he examined it. "All right, then," he said. "Get your things and head on to class." His gaze drifted over my shoulder. His eyes widened in a way that told me he'd spotted the graffito. Immediately, his face softened. "I'll call maintenance and have that taken care of by the end of the day."

I should have told him it wasn't necessary. Chances were, my locker would be vandalized again the second it was removed. Instead, I murmured a barely audible "thanks" and tucked the pass inside my shirt pocket.

He nodded and turned away. As he disappeared around a corner, once again I found myself alone.

I opened my locker and pulled out my books for second period. The pill might have killed my panic attack, but it didn't touch how emotionally drained I felt. I was numb from the inside out, though all things considered, maybe that wasn't a bad thing.

I slipped my books into my bag and hoisted it over my shoulder. The second I closed the door, the word scribbled on the other side glared at me again.

Just this once, I wished I could be more like my mom. She wouldn't let something like a word scrawled in marker bother her. In fact, if someone dared to deface her property, she'd launch an investigation until the culprit was found, and then she'd sue him or her for defamation.

Not for the first time, I wondered how I could be the genetic offspring of someone so clearly made of stone, when my bones were as hollow as a bird's. Unfortunately for me, even with bird bones, I couldn't fly away.

I shrugged my backpack higher and started down the hall. I was almost to the door, my hand raised for the knob, when the bulletin board on the wall caught my eye.

Below the flyer for the model UN club and beside a clip-board with sign-up sheets for the school's fall musical *Grease*, another flyer announced the results of cheerleading tryouts. I held my breath. Making the team would fix everything.

I slid my finger along the page. The JV squad was listed

first, and I skimmed through the names until I came to the words "varsity cheerleading squad" in bold letters. I shuddered in apprehension as I drew my finger down the list. Christy Holder's name was at the top, followed by a dash and the word "captain." Next was Amber's, followed by "co-captain." Below her name was the list of everyone who had made the squad.

My heart climbed inside my throat as I slid my finger past each name until I came to mine, or at least what was left of it. My name was scribbled out with black ink, and a new name had been handwritten in: *Taylor Bradshaw*.

Ice shot through my chest. I squeezed my eyes shut and opened them, hoping the scribbles were a trick of light—that maybe if I blinked enough, the ink would disappear and my name would shine through. It didn't. Not even after I mashed the heels of my hands into my eyes and rubbed furiously.

My name had been on the list. Christy had picked me for the squad. But then my private messages were plastered across the hallways and she changed her mind.

Could I really blame her?

My stomach convulsed, and for the second time that day, I thought I might be sick. I yanked my backpack off my shoulder and fumbled in the front pocket until I found my Tums. I popped two in my mouth, grimacing as the chalky cherry flavor coated my tongue.

What really stung was that Amber, who was not only the co-captain of the squad but my *friend*, had done nothing to stop her from replacing me with Taylor—a sophomore of all things.

That still, however, didn't answer my question as to why.

"Sucks, doesn't it?"

I jerked upright with a gasp.

Nolan. He stood at the other end of the hall, leaning against a locker. He held his phone up and watched me through the screen. Anger burned through the numbness I'd taken comfort in. How long had he been recording me this time? Before I could order him to stop, he tucked it inside his book bag.

"What the hell are you talking about?"

He shrugged, pushed off the row of lockers, and walked toward me. When he stopped, he was so close I had to crane my neck up to look at him. His hazel eyes projected sadness behind the lock of hair that had fallen across his face. I refused to back up, even though his nearness made me nervous. His shit-eating grin proved he knew it, too.

He leaned down, his face drawing closer to mine. He smelled good. Irritatingly good. Like pine needles and oranges instead of the overpowering scents most of the guys at school wore. For one paralyzing second, I thought he might kiss me. I inhaled sharply, making his grin widen. But instead of kissing me, his mouth bypassed my lips and hovered above my ear. "Welcome to the other side, Flay. You won't last a week."

Before I could respond, he strode away, leaving me trembling in his wake. I wanted to shout after him, to tell him he was wrong, but the doubt he'd stirred sealed my lips. I didn't know how I was going to survive the day, let alone a week.

CHAPTER FIVE

The bell rang, signaling the end of third-period contemporary literature.

My heart hung in my chest as if strung from a line of tenterhooks. In class, sitting by a window, as close to freedom as I could possibly be, I was safe. Despite the hissed whispers and glares, the other students couldn't shout names at me, couldn't corner me or slam into my shoulder as they pushed past. In the hall, I was vulnerable, swimming in a sea of piranhas wanting to devour me whole.

"Miss Flay?" I looked up to find my lit teacher, Mrs. Lochte, standing beside my desk with her hands on her hips. "Where were you today?"

Two girls giggled to each other before walking out the door. The only student remaining in the class was Nolan, and he made a show of putting his books away with exaggerated slowness. For the first time, I regretted my decision to take a class a grade level above my own, my reputation as my mother's daughter be damned. It wasn't so bad back when we were content to ignore each other, but now the last thing I wanted was to be stuck in a classroom with him for an hour every day.

"Miss Flay?" Mrs. Lochte repeated.

I licked my lips. "Um…" I wasn't sure what she meant. Did she somehow find out about my first-period trip to the nurse's office? Even if she did, why would she care? "I was here." No lie there.

She frowned, and I knew I wasn't off the hook yet. "Were you, Miss Flay? Because every time I looked in your direction, you were staring at your shoes. Shoes don't teach contemporary literature, Miss Flay. I do. I expect your attention focused on me during class, do you understand?"

"Yes, ma'am," I answered in my most sincere voice. Another thing I'd learned from my mother—politeness and sincerity, even faked, went a long way when it came to getting out of trouble.

"Really?" Nolan asked. "How will you have time to concentrate on something as mundane as English class when you have reputations to ruin?"

Before I could respond, Mrs. Lochte turned her viperlike gaze on him. "Mr. Letner, am I to assume you don't have somewhere to be? If that's the case, I could always use help organizing my bookshelves."

To my pleasure, his smile withered. "Nope. I definitely have somewhere to be."

"Then *be* there," she said.

He gave a salute and sauntered out the door.

As soon as he was gone, Mrs. Lochte redirected her attention to me. It was all I could do not to flinch. "Now, Miss Flay, are you clear as to what I require from you?"

"Yes, ma'am."

"Good." She gave a curt nod. "Now you're excused." She returned to her desk and began typing on her laptop.

I slid out of my chair and snagged my backpack off the ground. While part of me couldn't wait to get away from Mrs. Lochte, another part was equally terrified of what awaited in the hall. I shuffled to the door, hoping if I lingered long enough, an invitation for shelf organization might be extended my way, but it never came. I had no choice but to enter the hallway. So I sucked in a deep breath, opened the door, and left.

I only managed five steps when someone bumped into my shoulder.

"Fuck." Whatever small part of me still cared about appearances crumbled. I dropped my backpack and whirled around, my fingers curled into fists. I'd never been in a fight before, and I'd probably get my ass kicked, but I knew I couldn't continue on like this. "Watch where you're fucking—"

The words died on my tongue.

Payton stood before me, her eyes filled with a hurt I didn't understand. "It's you…"

"Of course it's me." Gradually my shoulders loosened and my fingers uncurled. "Why haven't you answered my texts? Do you have any idea what's happened to me today?"

She pressed her lips together, her eyes shimmering with tears that refused to fall. "I know, all right? Amber told me everything."

Dread pooled in my belly. "What *exactly* did Amber tell you?"

She opened her mouth, but before she could answer, Amber appeared at her side and looped an arm through hers. "Yeah, um, sorry, Regan, but we can't be seen talking to you. It'd be social suicide."

I blinked, trying to make sense of her words. "I don't understand."

Students slowed as they passed, their necks craned for better looks.

Amber shook her head in mock sympathy. "You can drop the innocent act now. I told Payton what you told me—that you thought she was annoying and you were only friends with her because she was good at digging up dirt."

I reeled back as if I'd been slapped. "That's a lie."

"I told you to be careful, didn't I?" Amber continued. "I knew you'd get exposed eventually if you kept stirring up shit. I just honestly had no idea how far you'd fall. You've got to understand we have ourselves to look out for. We can't take the plunge with you."

My mouth dropped open. "But this is as much your fault as mine. You can't just *abandon* me."

She made a face. "Sweetie, think of it as self-preservation. It's not forever—just until this nastiness passes. Even animals know to steer clear of their own kind when one is wounded."

"You're such a bitch," I blurted out before I could stop myself.

Amber's eyes narrowed and her jaw tightened. "What did you call me?"

Payton slipped free from Amber's grip and glanced behind her at the growing crowd. "Guys, do we have to do this right here? Right now?" A look of panic flashed across her face, and she slowly inched along the lockers away from us.

Amber ignored her. "Better to be a bitch than a two-faced, backstabbing fake. At least with me, people know exactly what they're getting."

I looked at Payton. "You don't honestly believe I'd say those things about you, do you? We're best friends."

"How could she not believe it?" Amber responded. "You've talked shit about everyone else in the school. Why wouldn't you do it to your so-called best friend?"

Anger boiled through my veins. Why was Amber doing this? Why abandon me and lie to Payton about things I never said?

And then it hit me.

"*You* posted the messages." How had I not seen this coming? I'd kept her close, but obviously not close enough. Had she been cozying up to Payton all this time? I turned on Payton, the anger morphing into pain. "Why are you listening to her? You know what kind of person she is."

Before she could answer, the crowd shifted and Nolan pushed through with his cell phone in hand. A blond girl named Blake stood by his side. "What's this?" he asked.

"Friends turning on friends?"

"Nolan." Payton's voice held an edge of warning. "Stay out of this."

"Stay out of it?" He turned the camera on her. "What's happening needs to be documented. Years from now, you'll wonder how a lifelong friendship disintegrated. I mean, it must've been something really bad, because if something trivial broke you apart, how good of friends were you in the first place?"

"Nolan," Payton said again, "get a fucking life and stay the hell out of mine."

He ignored her and swept the lens over Amber and me. Amber raised her middle finger. I, on the other hand, froze like a rabbit caught in a rifle's crosshairs.

Nolan put the phone away, then he and the blonde turned and disappeared into the crowd.

"Fucking douche," Amber muttered. After a few seconds, she shrugged. "C'mon, Pay, let's go."

Payton stared at the ground, unblinking. I silently willed her to remember the fact that we were *best friends*. I'd never do this to her. Never.

"Come *on*." Amber huffed impatiently before turning and pushing through the crowd.

Payton wadded a fistful of her skirt. She glanced at me before quickly averting her gaze and hurrying to catch up with Amber, who was already halfway down the hall.

How good of friends were you in the first place? Nolan's words circled through my mind like buzzards over a carcass. Instead of a body, the dead thing was the friendship between my best friend and me.

If I didn't have Payton, I didn't really have anyone.

To my horror, tears pricked the corners of my eyes. But I couldn't cry—not in front of everyone. Wasn't that my mother's number one rule? Never show them you are weak.

I tried to hold back the tears, but I was too late. All I could do was scoop my backpack off the ground and run for the nearest bathroom.

When I reached the door, I pushed against it with my shoulder while wiping my cheeks with my palms. It didn't help. A sob clawed through my chest. I slapped a hand over my mouth to muffle it.

I headed for the stall farthest against the wall and locked myself inside. I heard the outside door squeak open and the sounds of several girls talking and laughing as they entered. I climbed on top of the toilet seat, praying they wouldn't try to push open the locked door.

"Oh my God, did you see her face?" a girl asked.

Several giggles answered.

"I think she was about to cry," the girl continued.

"Not like she doesn't deserve it," another girl replied.

"Totally had it coming," a third chimed in.

"It sucks to be her," the first girl admitted. "Her life is totally ruined."

The other girls murmured their agreement. I heard the whine of the bathroom door open. A second later, their voices faded, then disappeared entirely after the door swung shut.

Once I was sure they'd gone, I climbed off the toilet and

leaned my back against the stall door. Did I have it coming? Maybe. But why now? Why Amber? And why was Payton going along with it? *Why, why, why.* The word played on repeat in my head until I was wrung out, hollow and empty.

Eventually, I left the graffiti-covered stall and shuffled to a sink.

I stared at the red-eyed, defeated girl in the mirror. If my mom were here, she'd tell me to stop wasting my time with the pity party. I should be implementing a plan — trying to figure out how to rebuild my reputation that was taken from me. But the only plan I did have involved friends.

Something I didn't have anymore.

So I racked my brain for a new plan, something I could put into action on my own. But as I stared at my reflection for several minutes, nothing came to me. The longer I stood there, the more the possibility of salvaging my life felt like it slipped through my fingers like threads of sand.

How the hell did I fix this? I had no freaking clue.

So I did what I did best. I popped another pill.

Once the numbness settled through me, I left the bathroom and ventured into the hallway. Lunch was almost over, so I made my way through the scattering of last-minute students to class.

No one sat with me. No one talked to me. The silent treatment would normally freak me out, but after the hellish morning I'd had, being ignored was kind of a relief. It meant they were getting bored. At least, that was what I hoped it meant. The alternative was too ugly to think about.

When seventh-period Spanish let out, I pretended to be confused over the homework assignment so I could stay inside the classroom for an extra twenty minutes, just to be safe, while Señor Batey translated the noun list *twice*. When he finished, I glanced up at the clock, satisfied that the building and parking lot would be empty enough for me to make my escape.

In the hall, I fished my car keys out of my purse and headed for the exit. I needed my history book from my locker, but I was going to have to make do and prayed I'd pass the quiz without studying. No way was I going to stop long enough to be confronted. Besides, if anyone else had decided to "decorate" my locker, I didn't want to know about it.

The hallways were relatively empty as I walked, my footsteps echoing hollowly against the stained linoleum. An occasional student passed on his or her way to a club, but luckily, no one paid me any attention. I reached the front doors and breathed a sigh of relief as I stepped outside and into freedom. When I wasn't immediately assaulted by an angry mob, I figured the worst was behind me.

And then I saw my car.

It was parked behind a large truck so only the bumper was visible at first. When I passed the truck, I skidded to a halt. My backpack slipped from my shoulder and fell to the ground with a *thump*.

Empty soda bottles, chip bags, and wadded-up pieces of paper covered the hood and roof. The words "liar," "backstabber," and "two-faced" had been scribbled more than a hundred times in several different shades of lipstick on all of the windows. As I approached, I saw that a large scratch—most likely made by a key—had been gouged across the driver-side door.

I sank to the ground beside my backpack. I had a therapy appointment in twenty minutes that I wouldn't make if I didn't leave right then. But how could I? I'd have to go through the car wash at least ten times to get all the lipstick off. I knew because Payton, Amber, and I had lipsticked a girl's car last year after she hit on Payton's boyfriend. It had been Amber's idea, of course. We'd hid in Amber's car and laughed every time the girl went through the car wash then burst into tears when she pulled out and the pink and red letters remained.

Maybe Christy was right. Maybe I was finally getting what I deserved. I'd played my cards with karma and this was my payout. The only question was, after everything I'd done, did I ever deserve to be happy again?

That sounded like a question for my therapist, but talking about what was going on was the absolute *last* thing I wanted to do. Words were just that, useless sounds passed through lips that faded as soon as they were spoken.

Unlike texts, which could be captured, copied, forwarded, and saved.

There was no way out.

CHAPTER SIX

It took more than fifty dollars and a half an hour's worth of car washes to get off all the lipstick. Every time I pulled out to check, I half expected to look up and see Amber and Payton laughing at me from Amber's car. Maybe Christy would be there, too. I hadn't been able to go home afterward on the off chance Dad left the office early. He'd know I missed my therapy appointment, and I couldn't risk his calling Mom.

There was nothing my therapist could do for my mental state that some time with my horse couldn't do twice as well, so I went to the barn instead.

I unbuckled the girth and lifted the sweat-soaked saddle pad and saddle from Rookie's back. Rookie was a thirteen-year-old ex-racehorse I'd adopted straight off the track when he was seven. After only a couple years of training, he'd become an amazing hunter/jumper, and together we'd won enough ribbons and trophies to fill an entire wall. On weekends, the two of us worked in the barn's therapy program for children with special needs.

The volunteer work was actually—surprise—my mom's idea. After all, what was the point of doing anything if you couldn't use it to improve your image? For once, I didn't mind. Unlike building houses and picking up trash in the state park in the sweltering heat, horse therapy was something I actually looked forward to. I never got over the feeling of seeing a kid sit on top of Rookie, grabbing fistfuls of his black mane and grinning so broadly, it was like nothing existed but him and the horse. That was what made horses magical.

I leaned out the stall door to place my saddle on the wall rack while Rookie pressed his velvety muzzle to the back of my head. He chuffed softly, tickling the fine hairs along my neck. I smiled, but even alone with my horse, it felt forced. I wondered if I'd ever really smile again.

I twisted around and leaned my head against Rookie's, my forehead brushing the white star between his eyes. I combed my finger through his wind-tangled mane. Earlier, we'd spent an hour cantering around in the outdoor arena. As a former racehorse, Rookie would sometimes strain against the reins in my hand, and I could feel the desperation of his muscles beneath me, his desire to run farther than the fence allowed.

Before today, I'd never understood his urge. I'd always thought it was safer in the arena, where people were nearby and watching. But now, for the first time in my life, I wondered what it would be like to unlock the gate and fly with him, as fast and as far as he could go, without looking back.

My phone rang, pulling me from my fantasy.

"Sorry, boy. I'll be right back." Hope swelled through me as I ducked beneath the chain hooked across Rookie's stall door. Maybe Payton was finally returning my calls. Maybe she'd realized how stupid it was to be mad at me for something she did, too. Maybe she'd already figured out how to get back at Amber.

Ignoring Rookie's nickers of annoyance, I ran for the wooden picnic table outside the tack room where I'd left my phone and keys. I snatched the phone off the weathered wood and read the screen. My shoulders slumped. With a sigh, I answered. "Hey, Dad."

"Hey, honey," he said. "I just got home. Therapy go long?"

"No." My head throbbed, and I rubbed my fingers against my temples to ease the building migraine. "Sorry for not calling earlier. I decided to stop off at the barn after my appointment."

"How's my second mortgage doing?"

"Rookie's the same as he always is—hungry."

Dad laughed and then fell quiet. A couple seconds later, he cleared his throat. "Listen, Regan, when are you going to be home? I think we need to have a chat."

My stomach clenched into a knot. "Does this have anything to do with today?"

"The nurse called me at work."

I closed my eyes and swallowed past the lump in my throat. I so did not want to have this conversation right now. I needed to work on fixing my problems, not adding to them. And if Dad became involved, he'd bring Mom with him, and it would snowball from there. "It's not a big deal, Dad. I had a minor freak-out over a test."

"Regan." I could hear the worry in his voice. "The nurse said you hyperventilated."

"It was a really intense test."

Dad was silent. I could picture him sitting at his desk in his blue scrubs with the little crease pinched above his nose that he got whenever he frowned. Finally he said, "Why do I get the feeling there's more to it than that?"

"There's not," I said, maybe a little too quickly, because he didn't reply. I was sure he knew I was lying, and since I had no other choice, I decided to use another of Mom's techniques—throw him off the trail with a half truth. "Okay, maybe there is something else going on."

"Okay," he prompted.

"Payton and I kind of got into a fight at school."

"Really?" The concern in his voice shifted to surprise. "You two have been friends forever. What started the fight?"

I was certainly not going to tell him about the notes with all the horrible things I'd said about people being plastered all over the school. While my mind raced for a possible explanation, it hit me. Another one of Mom's tricks—throw your opponent off with a topic that made him uncomfortable. And I knew *exactly* how to make Dad uncomfortable. "You see, there's this boy — "

"A boy?" Panic laced Dad's words. "Since when have there been any boys? You've never mentioned a boy before. Who is he? Do I know his parents? What are — "

"Relax, Dad. It's nothing that serious. But I thought he liked me and it turned out Payton likes him and there was all this tension and — "

"You know what?" Dad cut me off. "This might be a topic better suited for your mother."

Thank God. I quietly exhaled so he couldn't hear my relief over the phone. "Okay. If you think that's best."

"I do." He paused. "Maybe you should give her a call tonight."

My mouth went dry at the thought. Talking wasn't exactly something you did with Mom. All of our "conversations" consisted of her lecturing me and not listening to a thing I had to say. "This can wait until Mom gets home. I don't want to bother her while she's in session. You know how stressed she gets."

"You're her daughter," he replied. "You always come first."

I was glad he couldn't see the face I made over the phone. "Yeah, okay. Look, Dad, I have to get Rookie cleaned and fed before I can leave. Can we talk about this later?"

He sighed. "Not tonight, I'm afraid. I have to head back into the office — emergency oral surgery. I won't be home until after dinner. There are leftovers you can reheat in the fridge."

"Sure," I said, masking my disappointment. While I was

happy to avoid family talk, I wasn't crazy about spending the evening alone in our large, empty house. Normally on nights when Mom was out of town and Dad worked late, I'd call Payton and Amber to come over and hang out. Didn't look like that was going to happen ever again.

"All right, Pumpkin. Just try to take it easy for the rest of the night, okay?"

"Okay. I will."

We said good-bye and hung up. I was about to slip my phone inside the pocket of my riding breeches when I noticed I had an email. I clicked on it to discover a Facebook notification alerting me I was tagged in a post— Amber's post. A sinking feeling slithered through me, and I dropped onto the nearby bench. My thumb hovered over the Facebook link as I reached for my necklace with my free hand and slowly slid the pendant along the chain. Whatever Amber had written about me, it wouldn't be good.

I chewed on my bottom lip, my feet tapping against the ground. I knew I shouldn't click on it, that I was better off not knowing, but I couldn't let it go. I had to know what I was up against.

I held my breath and clicked on the link.

My Facebook app opened and directed me to a fan page—at least that was what I thought it was until I read the title: The Regan Flay Abuse Support Group. The profile picture was of my face, though someone had altered it with one of those "turn yourself into a zombie" apps. My eyes were sunken and my skin rotted and peeling. Cracked lips stretched wide to display rotted and broken teeth. The announcement below said: *This is a page for anyone who's ever been abused by Regan Flay. Tell your story and find support.*

I wasn't sure how long the page had been live, but it already had more than a hundred likes and at least a dozen comments. While the page claimed to be a support group, given the nature of the comments, it was anything but. One commenter posted that I was so ugly she needed a support group for the trauma of having to look at me in the hallway. Her comment was liked by Amber and thirty other people. There were more, but tears blurred the words.

I pressed a button and the page disappeared. I jammed the phone into my pocket and dried my eyes on my shirtsleeve. I thought I'd be safe at the barn—that my problems wouldn't be able to find me here. Turned out I was wrong—I wasn't safe anywhere.

A wave of dizziness swept over me, but I shoved it back. I wouldn't have an anxiety attack over this. I *refused*.

The whole thing was so hypocritical. Like the people calling me names and throwing shit at me had never spoken an unkind word about someone else? They were just persecuting me because I got caught.

It wasn't fair.

Rookie snorted at me from his stall. I leaned across the chain and reached for him, desperate for a little of that horse magic to rub off on me. He stared at my hand but didn't bridge the gap between us. Great. My horse had turned against me, too? It was like he knew I wasn't the same little girl who used to climb on his back and braid his mane while he munched on grass. I was broken, and I didn't know how to fix me. And for the first time, I didn't think Rookie could fix me, either.

And so it happened. This was the day horse magic finally stopped working.

"It's okay," I told him. I withdrew my hand and used it to wipe my tear-streaked cheeks. "I'll go get your grain."

Later that night, after taking a shower so scalding it left my skin red and numb, I crawled into bed and pulled the covers to my chin. I wasn't really sure why I bothered. Sleep was the last thing I wanted. Sleep would only bring morning, and morning was something I never wanted to come.

Before crawling into bed, I'd made the mistake of checking Facebook one last time. I'd discovered a new comment on the Regan Flay Abuse Support Group page. That comment churned inside my chest like a ball of razor blades, ripping and shredding everything in its path.

Regan Flay should just do the world a favor and kill herself.

It wasn't so much the comment that hurt as the fact that it had seventy-six likes. *Seventy-six.* More than two football teams' worth of people agreed the world would be a better place if I didn't exist.

I glanced at the bottle of pills on my nightstand.

They were right there. All I had to do was reach for them, and then everyone would be happy. If I were gone, I couldn't possibly ruin any more lives. If I were gone, I wouldn't have to endure their hatred.

And it would be easy. So damn easy.

Panic jolted down my spine like an electric current. I snatched the pill bottle and flung it across the room, where it bounced off the wall and landed on the floor. Sure, it would be easy, but it wasn't what I wanted. The pills would only be a way out, and I wanted a way through. Out was final, but through at least held possibilities. These people couldn't hate me forever—and even if they did, I'd be done with high school in another year. If I could just hang in there and try not to draw any more attention to myself, things had to get better, right?

Not that they'd ever been great to begin with.

I curled my knees up to my chest and wrapped my arms tightly around them. I honestly had no idea what would make me happy anymore. My mom certainly thought *she* knew. But what if she was wrong? What if all the things she said would make me happy—admittance to an Ivy League school, a suitable husband, a successful career—left me feeling as empty and hollow as I did right now?

When I was younger, everything had been so much easier. Happiness was jump ropes and cotton candy. But now I couldn't remember the last time I'd truly felt happy. When did I lose it? And why had it become so difficult to find again?

Worse still, what if I never did?

CHAPTER SEVEN

The next morning, I sat in my car and watched students weaving around vehicles through the parking lot on their way to class. I gripped the steering wheel so tightly my knuckles turned white. I hadn't even stepped foot outside the car yet and already anxiety squeezed my ribs.

I reached for my purse and was searching for my pill bottle when a fist rapped against my window. I gasped and withdrew my hand. Nolan Letner smirked at me. As usual, his cell phone was in hand and pointed at me.

Crap. Just when I thought my day couldn't be off to a worse start.

I didn't bother to roll down my window. With my new plan to lie low in place, the last thing I wanted was to encourage his attention. Instead, I grabbed my phone and pretended to scroll through my nonexistent texts.

"You'd better hurry up. You're going to be late for class."

I clenched my teeth so hard, my jaw ached. "Go to hell, Nolan."

He glanced over his shoulder at the school building. "Well, it is high school, so close enough." When I didn't move, he knocked on the window again. "Are you coming or what?"

I fingered the keys still in the ignition. It would be so easy for me to start the car and just drive away. Unfortunately, if I skipped class, my mom would find out. If she thought I was in some kind of trouble that would reflect badly on her or the family, she'd tighten her hold on my already-choking leash.

I whipped around and glared at Nolan. He was only here to antagonize me, but if I tried to wait him out, I'd get a tardy. He had me trapped and he knew it. "I'm not going anywhere until you put that phone away."

He shoved it into his pocket and smiled.

Jackass.

With a sigh, I pulled the key from the ignition, triggering my automatic locks. Before I could stop him, Nolan grabbed my door handle and swung it open. "After you."

Obviously the last thing I wanted to do was go anywhere with him, but I couldn't afford to ditch school, which meant I didn't have much choice. I grabbed my backpack and climbed out of my car. As soon as I started walking toward school, he fell into step beside me.

"Go away, Nolan."

"Why would I do that?" he asked. "If I left, I wouldn't be able to bask in the warmth of your glowing personality. And do you really *want* me to go away? Before you walk *in there*?" He gestured to the doors. *"Alone?"*

I made a face. "You think I need your protection or something? I can take care of myself."

He laughed. *"Sure* you can."

"And so, what?" I placed a hand on my hip. "You're going to keep following me around so you won't miss a second of my misery? Is that your plan?"

He shrugged. "That's part of it."

I barely restrained a growl. We'd never gotten along, but I never knew he was that sadistic. No wonder his girlfriend broke up with him. I jabbed a finger against his chest. "Fuck off."

Before he could respond, I marched up the walkway and into the school.

Not even several heartbeats later, he was back at my side. "I have to walk this way, too, you know. You don't own the hallways, Princess."

What I wouldn't have given to ball up all the anger and sadness from the last twenty-four hours and unleash it on Nolan. But with my reputation in ruins, the last thing I needed to do was draw any more attention to myself. I needed an escape, so I detoured to the nearest doorway.

Mrs. Weber, the middle-aged school secretary and a longtime supporter of my mother, smiled at me from behind her raised desk. "Regan." Her two front teeth were smudged with bright red lipstick. "What can I help you with, honey?"

Good question. "Um…" Initially all I'd wanted was an escape from Nolan. I hadn't thought out my plan further than that. But then an idea came to me, a piece of advice straight from my mother's political playbook. *When hit with a scandal, the best course of action is to remove yourself from the public spotlight until heated emotions have a chance to cool.*

"I need to withdraw my name from the student election." The last thing I needed to do was remind the entire school how much they hated me by plastering posters of my smiling face all over the school. Mustaches, devil horns, and penises—it didn't take a genius to figure out the vandalism that would befall them.

Mrs. Weber stopped smiling. "Really? Are you sure about that? Politics runs in your blood."

I fought the urge to roll my eyes. I was used to people expecting me to look and act like a younger version of the congresswoman. Instead of seeing me as a unique individual, it was like they thought I was a clone manufactured in a lab. If my mother wasn't so right-wing, I wouldn't have put it past her to have considered it.

But the fact was, I wasn't my mother. Sure, she was going to be pissed when she found out I dropped out of the election, but I also knew a weight lifted from my shoulders the moment I'd spoken the words. Lying low felt like the right course of action for now. Remaining a candidate would only bring me more humiliation and ridicule. Not to mention if I handed out Vote for Regan buttons, the other students would probably use them to stab me.

I leaned across the counter. "I don't know if you've heard, but I've been...under a lot of stress." Of course my mother didn't want people to know her daughter suffered from an anxiety disorder—someone might think there was something wrong with her parenting. So instead, I'd been instructed to tell people I suffered from stress—a much more socially acceptable answer. After all, who wasn't under stress?

"Oh, honey." Mrs. Weber reached forward and patted my hand. Her skin felt like cold leather. "That's completely understandable. With your mother up for reelection, of course you'd be stressed."

It took nearly all of my strength to fight off the frown pulling at my lips. God forbid I had problems of my own, *stress* of my own that didn't revolve around my mother. "Yeah." I withdrew my hand from her grasp. "So you can see why I can't run for student council. I have too much on my plate. I need to focus my attention...elsewhere."

"Regan." Even though we were the only two people in the office, Mrs. Weber lowered her voice to a whisper. "Does this have anything to do with the graffiti on your locker?"

I jerked back, and my cheeks flushed hot. "You know about that?"

She gave me a sympathetic look. "Of course. But don't worry, so does the principal. She's going to launch an investigation to make sure the culprit is found."

My throat tightened. What if the investigation uncovered the messages taped to the lockers with my private messages and the awful things I said? "An investigation isn't really necessary. I'm sure it was just a random, onetime thing."

Mrs. Weber frowned. "Now, honey, you know we have a strict anti-bullying policy at this school. That includes name-calling."

My stomach dropped, and I thought I was going to be sick.

"We're going to find this person," she continued. "And he or she is going to get in a *lot* of trouble. So don't you worry. You're a good girl, Regan. I'm sure whoever did this is just a Democrat causing trouble." She made a face, as if the word "Democrat" left a bad taste on her tongue.

Right. Because once again, everything that happened in my life somehow related to my mother. I pushed off the counter and moved back toward the door. "So you'll take care of the ballot for me, Mrs. Weber?"

She sighed and tapped her manicured nails against her desk. "I sure wish you'd reconsider. But if that's what you really want, I'll do it."

I nodded. "That's what I want. Thanks."

She pursed her lips as if she wasn't quite through arguing with me. Before she could say more, I backed out of the office. I was in such a hurry to get away that I didn't notice the person standing outside the door until I slammed into his chest.

Just what I needed—another person to yell at me. "Look, I'm really sorry—" Before I could finish the apology, I looked up to find Nolan grinning down on me.

"We really need to stop meeting like this," he said.

"Seriously?" I threw my arms in the air and stepped

around him. "Are you stalking me just to piss me off?"

"Why?" He smirked. "Is it working?"

I flipped him off.

He laughed. "Is that any way to treat a friend?"

I stopped in my tracks. "You are *not* my friend."

"You're right." He looked around. "But I don't see anyone else vying for the position. Can't say I blame them. You're pretty cranky."

I let out a frustrated groan. "What the hell do you want from me? An apology? If that's what it takes to get you to leave me alone, *fine.* I'm sorry I was mean to you on Tuesday, Nolan. Now can you *please* go away?"

"What I want?" All traces of humor vanished from his face. "What I want can never be given back."

I folded my arms across my chest to shield myself from his icy gaze. "What the hell does that even mean?"

The five-minute warning bell rang.

Instead of answering, Nolan hiked his backpack higher on his shoulder. "I've got to get to class." He brushed past me and strode down the hall, leaving me blinking after him.

Jeez, and I thought PMS gave *me* mood swings. I'd never seen anyone like Nolan, someone who could laugh and smile one second—even if it was at my expense—and the next second look like he wanted to murder someone. "Psycho," I muttered. There was a reason Payton, Amber, and I used to make fun of him—the dude was a fucking nutbag.

As I walked to class, I couldn't help but wonder *why* he and his girlfriend broke up. They were essentially perfect for each other. Jordan was in my grade. Her hair was always dyed purple, blue, or some other equally crazy color. She dressed in black every day of the week and even wore a black veil on the death anniversaries of musicians like Kurt Cobain, Freddie Mercury, and Jimi Hendrix. Obviously she wasn't a typical cheerleader, but that didn't stop her from trying out for the JV squad last year. She hadn't gone through half of her tryout routine before Amber burst out laughing. I felt bad Amber reacted like that—even worse when I pretended to laugh along with her. She could never fit in with us.

Except now there was no *us*.

Look who was the freak now.

With only a couple minutes before the tardy bell rang, the halls were empty—well, except for a girl standing at her locker. As I approached, I noticed that the girl hastily shoving books into her bag wasn't just *any* girl. She was *Julie Sims*—the girl I'd accused of being too fat for the Heimlich in the posted private messages.

My heart stuttered against my ribs and I froze, not sure what to do. Julie was still pulling books, oblivious to my presence. I could easily turn around, but my classroom was only a couple of doors down. If I took another route, I'd be late for sure.

Crap. I so did not need another confrontation right now, but at the same time I couldn't be late, not when I was coasting on such thin ice. Maybe if I hurried, she wouldn't notice me. I ducked my head and quickened my steps. I was just about to pass her when one of the books she was shuffling through fell open and a folded sheet of paper decorated with tenth-grade geometry puzzles wafted out. It fell to the floor at my feet.

Julie turned around, and I stopped in my tracks, the air locked inside my lungs.

For a second, Julie appeared not to notice me. She bent over and grabbed the paper. But before she stood, her gaze drifted to the tops of my shoes, and she stiffened.

My throat tightened, and I swallowed hard. I waited for her to scream at me, to cuss me out, or at the very least to slam her locker in my face and storm away. She didn't. She just stared at me with her wide brown eyes, unmoving. For the life of me, I couldn't figure out why. I searched her face for the hate I was sure to find lurking there, but another emotion flashed in her eyes—*fear.*

The realization hit me like a punch in the stomach. Julie wasn't going to attack me. I was the monster here. Julie was afraid of *me.*

She swallowed. "I-I'm late for class and can't find my homework." I couldn't figure out why she was telling me this; it wasn't like she owed me, of all people, an explanation.

"Do you need help looking for it?" As soon as the words left my mouth, I took a step back, surprised. This was the second time in fifteen minutes I'd said something unexpected, and I wasn't sure what to make of it. After all, hadn't I wanted to get away from her as quickly as possible?

Julie eyed me skeptically. "Why would you want to help me? You hate me."

Her words caught me off guard, and I shook my head. "I don't hate you."

She laughed bitterly. "*Please.* I read what you wrote about me."

I fidgeted with the straps of my backpack. *Duh, Regan, of course she read it.* "Julie, I—" But I didn't know how to finish, so the word hung awkwardly in the air between us. I mean, why *had* I written those things about her? Really, I didn't hate her. In fact, I didn't know her well enough to have any opinions about her at all. So as far as why I'd written the things about her, I guess I'd done it to get a laugh out of Amber. Shame burned through me like acid, and I dropped my eyes to the floor.

"Why, then?" she said. I glanced up to find Julie's bottom lip trembling. "What did I ever do to you?"

My mouth flapped open and closed, but no words came out—because there were none to explain why I'd said the terrible things I had.

The late bell rang. Neither of us moved. Silence hung between us, heavy and thick. When I could no longer take it, I shook my head. "I don't have a reason. I guess I really am the horrible person everyone thinks I am."

For a second, she looked like she might say something, but then she shook her head and turned back to her locker. She resumed rooting through her books. She didn't need to tell me to fuck off. I could read the signals loud and clear. But instead of walking away like I'd intended, something kept me glued in place.

After a second, Julie glanced over her shoulder, her brow creased in confusion. "Is there something you want?"

My throat was dry, and it took me several swallows before

I felt I could answer. In politics and in life, my mother never apologized for anything. She always said apologizing made you responsible, and a politician never accepted the blame for anything. All my life I'd lived by my mother's rules. After all, they'd gotten her exactly where she wanted to be. I was starting to realize, however, that where she wanted to be and where I wanted to be were two different places. "Julie," I said, "even if you don't believe me, I want you to know I'm very sorry I said those things—I didn't mean them. I was just…being an asshole."

She blinked at me a moment, and I could tell she was questioning my sincerity. Even if she wasn't sure, I was. I'd meant every word I said. Not just because Amber posted my messages and I'd been humiliated. I was sorry I'd hurt her feelings. Sorry because I hated the way she looked at me, even now, with eyes full of apprehension that I put there.

Seconds passed, and still Julie said nothing.

I wasn't stupid. I knew an apology didn't undo the awful things I'd said about her—even if I'd never intended for them to be seen. I'd probably never make up for the pain I caused. Still, the knots in my chest loosened a fraction all the same. "I'd better go," I said, bobbing back on my heels. "I hope you find your homework."

"Yeah…" She watched me go. Her expression revealed nothing about what she might be thinking about me, my apology, or anything, for that matter. But then she added, "Thanks."

I nodded, then headed to class. That's when I spotted him, standing at the edge of the lockers with his phone in hand. Our eyes met, and he slowly lowered the phone to his side. I braced myself for another snarky comment but instead, he said, "I honestly didn't think you had it in you, Flay."

I folded my arms across my chest. "*What* in me?"

He grinned before slipping around the corner and disappearing from view. His answer, however, echoed down the hall after he'd gone.

"A heart."

CHAPTER EIGHT

After homeroom, I slipped into the hallways with my head ducked low. I managed to make it unnoticed to both my first and second period classes. Still, I should have known my luck wouldn't hold. I was halfway to my third period class when I spotted Amber's boyfriend, Jeremy, weaving toward me with two of his wrestling buddies in tow. My stomach dropped into my ankles. I quickened my pace, praying I could outrun him. I firmly believed testosterone occupied the empty cavity in his skull where his brain should be. If he loved one thing more than pummeling his opponents on the mat, it was pummeling other students in the halls.

I'd only made it five feet before his hand clamped down on my arm.

"Hey Rey." Jeremy lowered his head next to mine so his

breath tickled against my neck. I barely suppressed a gag. I should have known it was only a matter of time before he screwed with me. He loved messing with the most vulnerable people in school, and right now I was at the top of that list.

"Don't touch me." I shrugged out of his grasp.

He laughed and held up his hands. "Hey now. No need to get all pissy. I was just trying to be friendly. Last I checked, you were fresh out."

Not bothering to answer, I quickened my pace.

He sped up, matching me step for step. "I know you don't like me," he said. "That you've never liked me. But that's only because you don't know me." He put an arm around my neck and pulled me against him. His cologne was spicy and strong, burning my nostrils. I tried to push away, but he tightened his grip around my neck, nearly cutting off the oxygen in my throat. "Give me a chance. I bet you'll find I can be nice—*really* nice." His friends laughed behind us.

Bile burned up the back of my throat. I fought to free myself from his grasp, but his grip remained firm. I knew he wasn't stupid enough to try anything at school. Still, despite my attempt to stay calm, he'd gotten under my skin. "Get the fuck off of me, Jeremy."

He chuckled, his arm not budging. All around me, other students were making their way to class, none of them seeming to notice my discomfort—or caring if they did.

The bystander effect. It was a psychological phenomenon I'd learned about in psych class last year. Basically, a group of people would rarely come to the aid of someone in trouble because they assumed someone else would help, and so no one did.

Just like now.

Jeremy leaned down, his lips an inch from my ear. "C'mon, Rey. Spend a little time with me. If you lost the bitch attitude, I bet we could have a lot of fun."

A dull throb spread through my jaw from my clenched teeth. As much as I wanted to scream, I couldn't lose my cool. That was exactly what Jeremy wanted. "Let me go. *Now.*" Anger punctuated my last word, making it a growl.

"But we're just starting to get to know each other."

I was on the verge of telling him that getting to know him was the last thing I wanted, when a hand grabbed Jeremy's shoulder and yanked him backward, releasing me in the process. The suddenness of it made me gasp, and I stumbled, colliding into several people as I did.

"Well, that looked cozy." Nolan stepped in front of me, facing Jeremy with his arms folded. "How come I wasn't invited to the lovefest?"

My mind spun, trying to make sense of what was happening. Surely Nolan wasn't trying to help me? After this morning, I was pretty sure his sole purpose in life was to harass me.

Jeremy braced a hand on a locker to keep from falling back. His two friends rushed forward, but Jeremy stopped them with an outstretched hand. His jaw tightened, and he glared at Nolan. "No one invited you, because you're a *freak*. Now get the fuck out of here before I kick your ass."

Nolan grinned, but there was nothing friendly about it. He had a couple inches on Jeremy, so he had to duck his chin in order to meet his eyes. "Now, that's not very nice, especially after all your talk about having fun. That's a real shame, because I like to have fun." He cracked his knuckles.

I felt like I'd fallen into a strange nightmare. There had to be an angle—maybe Nolan set the whole thing up to humiliate me? But if it was an act, it was a damn good one. The threat of violence electrified the air, drawing curious students closer.

Jeremy's neck flushed red and his nostrils flared. "You actually want a go at me?" He snorted. "I always knew you were a fucking loser, but I just didn't know you had a death wish. Why do you even care? It's not like she's your girlfriend."

Nolan narrowed his eyes, the smile melting from his face. "I *care* because Regan told you to leave her alone, and you didn't."

A wave of shock barreled through me. This wasn't a setup after all. Nolan really wanted to help me... *Why?* Now that I'd been freed from Jeremy's grasp, I wanted so badly to run to the safety of my next class. My feet, however, refused to budge. I was rooted to the spot by some weird sense of loyalty to Nolan. Sure, he was an ass, but he was an ass who'd stuck up for me. I wouldn't abandon him.

"Since when are you a member of the cock-block police?" Jeremy asked.

Nolan drew his shoulders back, his fists tight at his sides. "Since assholes like you can't accept 'no' for an answer."

"No?" Jeremy's lips curled into a twisted smile. "How would a queer like you know the first thing about what a girl

wants? Regan didn't mean *no*. She was just being a tease. Everyone knows she's a slut."

My mouth dropped open. I could see why everyone was calling me a bitch, but a slut? I'd never even dated, let alone kissed a boy.

The tendons in Nolan's jaw flexed. When he spoke, his voice was low and dangerous. "Apologize to her."

Several voices rose in excitement behind me. I couldn't make out what they were saying, so I turned around and saw the school's security guard heading our way. My heart plummeted. Our school had a zero-tolerance fighting policy. While I couldn't care less what happened to Jeremy, I couldn't let Nolan get suspended for sticking up for me.

I edged closer to his side.

"You want me to apologize?" Jeremy laughed and shook his head. "Fuck you *and* fuck her."

"You're going to be sorry you said that." Nolan cocked back his fist.

I rushed forward. "No!"

The security guard pushed his way through the crowd. I jumped up and grabbed Nolan's raised arm. He was stronger than I thought. Instead of bringing his fist down, I remained suspended in the air, dangling from his biceps.

He whipped his head around. The look on his face clearly questioned my sanity, until he caught sight of the guard behind us. He slowly lowered his arm, placing me on my feet.

The guard frowned, his hand clutching his belt. "What's going on here?"

His question was all it took for the students surrounding us to disperse in all directions, like roaches scattering under a beam of light. Even Jeremy's two friends abandoned him without so much as a look back.

Jeremy didn't appear to notice. Instead, all traces of his earlier rage vanished, replaced with an easy smile. *Obviously* this wasn't his first tango with trouble. "What do you mean? We're just a couple of friends hanging out. Last I checked, that wasn't a crime."

"*Sure.*" The security guard pressed his lips together in a thin line. He turned to me. "Regan, is there something going on here I need to know about?"

I cringed. Of course he would know my name. And since I didn't want to get into trouble any more than I wanted Nolan to, I shook my head. "We were just…heading to class."

Jeremy's smile widened.

"Excuse me." Nolan pushed in front of him. "That's not what was going on at all. Before you so rudely interrupted, I was about to kick this guy's ass." He pointed a thumb at Jeremy. "Seriously, he had it coming."

Jeremy's smile disappeared.

The security guard sighed and tugged on his utility belt. "You think you're funny? Let's find out how funny the principal thinks you are with a visit to her office."

"She does find me delightful." Nolan tilted his head to the side as if considering the offer. But before he could say more, I kicked him in the shin.

"Ow." His head snapped in my direction. "Did you just

see that? I was assaulted." He pointed at the security guard. "Mace and cuff her. She's a menace."

A vein throbbed along the guard's temple, and I could tell he was losing patience fast.

"I'm really sorry about the disturbance," I told him. "It's all a big misunderstanding. We'll go to class now, and I promise there won't be any trouble." Before Nolan could say anything else stupid, I grabbed his arm and squeezed it as hard as I could in warning.

"Good idea." The guard narrowed his eyes. "Now clear out of my hall."

Jeremy ducked his head and jogged away.

Nolan opened his mouth, but I jerked his arm, giving him no choice but to stumble after me. I released my death grip only after we were out of the security guard's hearing.

"Jesus," he muttered, rubbing his arm where I'd squeezed. "I knew you were mean, but I didn't know you were violent, too. Have you ever thought about anger management classes?"

Un-freaking-believable. I spun around to face him. "Are you kidding me? What about you? Has anyone ever told you that you don't know when to shut up?"

He folded his arms across his chest and smirked. "Just because I refuse to be a kiss-ass is no reason to be mean. Honesty *is* the best policy, after all."

Usually, I went out of my way to avoid confrontation, but something about Nolan made my fingers strain with the urge to wrap them around his neck and squeeze. "You're a moron."

"Oh good, we're back to name-calling. I was worried we were starting to get along or something."

"As if that would *ever* happen." I spun on my heels and continued the trek to my next class. Nolan quickly caught up to me.

"Oh my God," I muttered. "Why are you so obsessed with stalking me?"

He shook his head. "I'm not following you. We're in the same English class. I *have* to walk this way."

Pressure built behind my eyes. Another trip to the nurse's office was definitely in my future—at least this time it would be for an ibuprofen. "Can't you at least walk, I don't know, over there or something?" I waved at the other side of the hallway.

He cocked his eyebrow. "Why? Are you scared your new social-outcast status will tarnish my stellar reputation?"

"Aren't you?"

He shrugged. "I don't worry about things like that, unlike *you*."

I pursed my lips. I didn't know how Payton had managed to live in the same house with him all these years without murdering him in his sleep. "Jesus, Nolan, I— "

He interrupted with a dramatic sigh. "*Fine*. If you're so worried about it, I'll clear things up right now." He stopped walking and cupped his hand over his mouth.

Panic rippled down my spine. Whatever was coming, it wouldn't be good. I ducked my head and quickened my pace.

Before I got very far, Nolan darted ahead of me, blocking

my path. "Attention, everyone!"

Oh, damn. I wanted to run, but with Nolan in front of me, there was nowhere to go.

"This is a public service announcement," he continued. "I am merely walking to class in the same vicinity as Regan Flay. This does not mean I am in any way associated or affiliated with her. Our close proximity during commute is merely a coincidence. Now carry on." He dropped his hands and looked at me—as did everyone else in the hallway. Half of them laughed while others rolled their eyes and shot Nolan annoyed glances.

My cheeks burned so hot I was sure my skin would melt right off.

Nolan smiled. "Happy?"

I glared at him. "Are you insane? If you want to make me happy, leave me the hell alone." I skirted around him and practically jogged to contemporary lit.

I dashed inside the classroom, and Mrs. Lochte looked at me with narrowed eyes. As nonchalantly as I could, I slowed to a stroll and took a seat in the front row, as far away from Nolan's usual spot in the back as I could muster.

When he entered the room, I dropped my eyes to my backpack and focused on pulling out my books and stacking them neatly on my desk with my pen tucked at the side.

"Pssst," a voice whispered.

My throat tightened at the sound, and I froze. *Please, God, no.* Slowly, I turned in my seat to find Nolan smiling at me from the next desk over. He waved.

I lowered my head and raked my fingers through my

hair, hoping to relieve the pressure pounding inside my skull. Even if I believed in karma, was everything I'd done really bad enough that I deserved Nolan's unending harassment?

"Pssst," he hissed again, louder this time.

Class hadn't started, but when it did, Mrs. Lochte wouldn't tolerate talking. I knew Nolan couldn't care less about getting in trouble, but I was willing to bet if I didn't acknowledge him now, he'd only keep pestering me until I did.

I curled my lips into a snarl. *"What?"*

He propped his chin up with his fist. "Call it a hunch, but I get the feeling you don't like me."

Directing my attention to the board, I opened my notebook and pulled the cap off my pen. "Thanks for the report, Captain Obvious," I muttered.

"Even after I helped you out earlier?" he asked. "With Jeremy?"

So that was his game? He thought he had a free pass to harass me because he'd helped me get away from Jeremy? I whirled around and glared at him. "I never asked for your help. I was doing just fine on my own."

He snorted. *"Yeah."*

Before he could say anything else, the bell rang. Mrs. Lochte rose from her desk and strode to the front of the room. She touched the Smart board, and a picture book with a puppy on the cover appeared on the screen. "Today we're going to discuss children's picture books and how most can be broken down into three parts."

I silently rejoiced. With class in session, there was no

way he could bother me without attracting attention from the teacher. I settled back into my seat and scribbled down *picture books* in my notebook. Mrs. Lochte began reading the book out loud. She got through two pages when a folded piece of paper was tossed onto my desk.

I tapped my pen against my notebook and exhaled slowly. So much for wishful thinking.

"Pssst," Nolan whispered. Since he was oblivious and had no volume control, his whisper attracted the attention of our teacher. She spun away from the board, her brow pinched in stern lines. Her gaze swept over all of us, and I couldn't help but squirm a little when it fell on me. After I endured several seconds under her cool stare, she finally turned around and resumed reading.

The threads pulled tight across my chest loosened. I looked over at Nolan to find him grinning at me. He pointed to the paper on my desk and mouthed the words "Open it."

I knew he wouldn't let up until I did, so I carefully pulled the folded triangle apart, smoothing it until it laid flat on my notebook. Written on the paper in sloppy handwriting was the question, Do You LiKE mE? Beneath it, two boxes were drawn with the words "yes" and "no" written below.

Oh my God, I was dealing with a kindergartner.

"Answer it," he whispered.

My jaw was clenched so tightly that my teeth ached. I clicked my pen and checked "no" before handing the paper to him.

Nolan scribbled on it and slid it back over. My urge to groan was overwhelming. I glanced down at the paper to find a new question.

WHY NOT?

Mrs. Lochte was still reading, so I jotted down, There's not enough room on this paper to list all the reasons. I placed the paper on his desk.

He glanced at it and smiled. After scribbling a reply, he handed the note back.

In large, bold letters were the words, *LET'S TALK ABOUT IT AT LUNCH.*

I almost laughed out loud. As if I'd spend an entire lunch period listening to him tease and berate me. Besides, if I had any hope of building my popularity back, the last thing I needed to do was damage it further by hanging out with the biggest freak in school. I wrote back, Let's not. I crumpled the paper into a ball and tossed it on his desk.

He unraveled the ball and stared at my response. A second later, he looked at me, but before he could say anything, Mrs. Lochte turned away from the board, asking if we could detect the metaphor between the puppy's lost mother and our current society.

Relieved, I relaxed into my chair and did my best to pay attention. Still, my thoughts kept returning to Jeremy's arm twisted around my neck. My pulse spiked at the memory, and Mrs. Lochte's words twisted together, forming an incoherent drone of sound. Had Amber put Jeremy up to it? Or had he decided to harass me because he thought no one would stop him?

But someone had.

When the bell sounded, signaling the end of class, I stood

and gathered my things quickly. I'd rather take my chances out in the hallway than be forced to endure any more of Nolan. As soon as I had my things zipped up, however, Mrs. Lochte appeared in front of my desk. She arched a thin red eyebrow. "Miss Flay? Mr. Letner? Please stay seated. I need a word."

A brick of lead sank inside my stomach, and I dropped back down in my seat. This was the second day in a row she'd asked me to stay after. Not good.

Beside me, Nolan smiled and gave a halfhearted shrug. "Sure thing. It's always a pleasure to spend more time with you."

Mrs. Lochte folded her arms across her chest. "Charming, Mr. Letner." She watched the door until the last students left the room. When we were alone, she walked to her desk and perched on the end of it. "I couldn't help but notice how much you two enjoy writing during my class."

The weight in my stomach expanded until I thought I might sink through my chair. How on earth had she seen us? I'd been so careful.

"And since you enjoy writing so much," she continued, "I've decided to give you two an extra assignment. You will work together on a picture book due on Monday. You will write the story, Miss Flay, and since Mr. Letner is so found of art"—she gestured to the doodles in his notebook—"he will draw the illustrations."

"No." My chair teetered backward before righting itself. "You don't understand. I can't work with him. He's... impossible."

"Oh?" Mrs. Lochte tilted her head. "You looked like you were getting along just fine when you were passing notes in my class." She slid off her desk and pointed to the door. "The project is due Monday. If you fail to produce the book by then, you will be assigned detention. You are dismissed."

"But—" I began.

"Dismissed," Mrs. Lochte repeated. She moved around her desk and sat, giving her attention to her laptop.

I glared at Nolan, who appeared on the verge of laughing. The anger building inside me since this morning built to epic proportions. "You…" There were about a million names I wanted to call him, but with Mrs. Lochte sitting only a few feet away, all I could do was repeat the same word. *"You."*

He continued to smile. I envisioned myself snatching him by the hair and slamming his head against his desk. The fantasy only made me feel slightly better.

"So, we're going to have to get together this weekend to work on the book," he said. "Do you want to call me or should I call you?"

I groaned and marched toward the door. I didn't have to turn around to see it—I could hear the damn grin in his voice. It would be a miracle if we actually finished the assignment. The odds were so much greater I'd kill him before we even started.

Chapter Nine

"Regan," a deep voice called from behind me.

Huh-uh. There was no chance in hell I was subjecting myself to any more of Nolan's abuse. And since it would take his long legs no time to catch up to my much shorter ones, I darted for the only place I knew he wouldn't follow.

"Regan. Wait up."

I was out of breath when I reached the girls' bathroom — the same one Payton, Amber, and I used to hide out in when we wanted to talk crap about everyone. The same one I'd hid in only yesterday. Because it was in the old wing and in desperate need of a remodel, most girls tended to avoid it. When I pushed open the heavy door, I was relieved to find no one else inside. I slowly made my way to the sinks and set my bag on top of the cracked porcelain. I was definitely going to need help calming down if I hoped to make it through today. I dug through my bag for the bottle of pills.

"There you are." A voice rang out, echoing against the ceramic-tiled walls.

With a gasp, I withdrew my hand from my bag.

Nolan stepped inside the bathroom and let the door swing shut behind him. He ran a hand through his hair and made a show of looking around before letting out a low whistle. "This is really...shitty. Not at all what I expected. Where are the velvet lounge chairs? And the guy in the tux who hands you a paper towel when you're done washing your hands?"

I pressed my back against the sink. There was only one way out of the bathroom and Nolan was blocking it. "You can't be in here. You'll get suspended."

He held up his hands. "Oh, no. Please don't ban me from a place I hate." He leaned against the sink beside mine and folded his arms across his chest. Leave it to Nolan to look relaxed in a girls' restroom. "How else was I supposed to get you to talk to me? We need to plan out this project."

"There's a reason I don't talk to you, you know. We hate each other." I licked my lips and looked at the door. All I needed was for one person to come in and distract Nolan long enough for me to escape.

"'Hate' is a really strong word. I think 'loathe' is more like it, don't you?"

Voices from outside the door interrupted me before I could answer. Hope swelled inside me at the thought of Nolan getting busted, but as the voices drew closer, they became clearer, and my excitement gave way to terror.

Amber.

Shit. Fear clenched my stomach. The only way I was going to survive my fall from popularity was to blend into the background until my social scandal became old news. Being caught in the bathroom alone with Nolan would kill any chance I had at staying out of the spotlight. Since we couldn't sneak out, we'd have to hide.

"Come on." I grabbed his arm and yanked him off the sink.

His eyes grew wide. "What are you—"

"Shhh," I hissed. I pulled him with me into the handicap stall and locked the door behind us.

His lips parted, but before he could say anything to give us away, I rushed forward and clamped my hand over his mouth just as the restroom door squeaked open. I pushed him against the wall next to the toilet and said a silent prayer no one bothered to glance under the stall.

"I can't believe she hit on your boyfriend," a girl said.

I leaned forward and peered through the crack of the stall to see if Payton was with Amber—she wasn't. The speaker was Taylor Bradshaw, the girl who'd been penciled in next to my scribbled-out name on the cheerleading roster. Apparently Amber had a new groupie.

"It just proves what kind of girl Regan really is," Amber replied. "Fucking skank."

My hand fell from Nolan's mouth, and my fear that we'd be discovered fizzled into a horrible, hollow feeling.

"I heard she practically threw herself at Jeremy before

third period," Taylor responded.

Amber laughed. "Pathetic, right? She probably thought she could regain her popularity or get back at me by hooking up with him. As if he'd want anything to do with her skanky ass."

My pulse thundered inside my head. As if I wanted anything to do with *that* douche bag. Obviously Jeremy had either told Amber a *very* different version of our encounter or she was too stupid to realize the truth about her sleazebag boyfriend.

I didn't realize I'd reached for the door lock until Nolan grabbed my arm and drew me back. I wanted to fight him, to burst through the door and launch myself at Amber, even though I'd get suspended and my mom would be furious. I didn't care. In fact, I was finding it harder and harder to care about anything.

I heard the sound of a lipstick top being popped off. "She's lucky I haven't seen her today," Amber said. "I'd fucking beat her skank ass to the ground."

Tremors ripped through me, growing in strength until my teeth started chattering. Great. Now was not the time for a panic attack, but I was powerless to stop it. Nolan grabbed my shoulders and pulled me against him, wrapping his arms and his heat around me. I should have backed away—his arms were the last place I should want to be—but I just didn't have the energy. And despite the fact that I couldn't stand him, his chest was warm and his strong arms were rigid. I felt safe for the first time in a long time.

Taylor giggled. "I would so pay to see that fight."

"Oh sweetie, you wouldn't have to pay." I heard the *click* as Amber's lipstick lid snapped back on. "I'd do that shit for free. I bet I wouldn't even get suspended. As much as the entire school hates her right now, they'd probably throw an assembly in my honor."

"Totally," Taylor agreed.

"I'll tell you one thing," Amber said. The sound of their footsteps moved toward the door. "If she so much as looks at Jeremy again, I'll rip her eyes out."

The bathroom door squeaked open, and their footsteps disappeared into the hallway beyond.

And yet, I remained inside Nolan's arms. I wanted to shove him away, to scream at him to let me go. But I also knew if he did, I'd fall to the cracked tile at my feet. His arms were the only things holding me up.

My cheeks flushed and my eyes burned. One blink was all it would take to make the tears fall. One blink and Nolan would get everything he wanted. He'd see Regan Flay break before his eyes. He'd have proof of how weak I really was.

My eyes blurred. I knew I couldn't keep them open forever.

So I blinked.

Using the last of my strength, I ripped free from his grasp. Burying my face inside my hands, I huddled against the corner opposite him. I couldn't—*wouldn't*—let him see me break.

"Regan." The way he said my name then was different. Softer. Unsure.

I shook my head. "Please, just go away."

He didn't move. Watching me fall apart must have been too irresistible. After all, wasn't this what he'd wanted all along? He'd told me I wouldn't last a week, and he was right.

I refused to turn around. He probably had his damn phone out so he could record my failure. "Please, Nolan. *Please* just go away."

He paused. "I don't think you should be left alone."

Despite the tears coursing down my cheeks, I actually laughed. "Really?" I wiped my wet cheeks with the back of my hands and turned around. "You're actually going to pretend you give a damn?"

His face was the most serious I'd ever seen it. Not even a hint of a smile played on his lips. "Just because you and I don't get along doesn't mean I want to see you hurting. I'm not a fucking monster."

This coming from the guy who wouldn't stop harassing me. "Whatever. Just go away, okay?"

He didn't move for several seconds before giving the faintest nod. "If that's what you want."

"That's what I want."

"Okay." He pulled the stall's latch open and swung the door wide. He stepped out, and his eyes darted to the mirrors. They narrowed, and his lips pressed into a thin line. He muttered something, but the words were a growl.

Curious what had him suddenly angry, I inched away from the stall and peered around him. On the center mirror, written in Amber's signature shade of red lipstick, were the words REGAN FLAY IS A SKANK-ASS WHORE.

A stifling heaviness settled on my chest. It took the

last of my strength just to breathe around it, and I sagged against the stall door.

"This is getting fucking out of hand." He stalked over to the paper-towel dispenser and cranked out a long sheet of brown paper. He took it to the mirror and wiped through the words until nothing remained but a bright red smear. When he finished, he crumpled the paper towel in his hand and stared at me, his chest heaving.

Without Nolan's warmth, tremors were back. No matter how tightly I squeezed my arms around myself, I couldn't make them stop on my own.

I didn't want to think about what that meant.

Nolan slipped out of his school blazer and wrapped it around my shoulders. It was warm and smelled like him, that same mixture of pine and citrus I'd smelled in the hallway. The warmth sank into my body and slowly, I stopped shivering.

Damn it.

I didn't understand. Nolan wasn't at all what I expected. "Why?"

He shoved his hands into his pockets. "You looked cold."

Before I could respond, he turned and walked away, leaving me alone in the bathroom, wrapped in the heat of his body.

CHAPTER TEN

That night, when my mom appeared in the foyer fresh from DC, it was all I could do not to throw up on her Louis Vuittons.

When Dad called me down for dinner, I fought the urge to burrow under my blankets. I knew hiding would only make him worried—he was already suspicious enough. So I trudged downstairs and plopped into my chair. My mom, already involved in conversation with Dad about some tax reform bill, barely glanced my way.

It should have made my anxiety lessen, but I knew it was only a matter of time before she turned her laser-beam stare on me. I didn't want to talk about my day, or the cheerleading squad, or anything else that would set Mom off on a tirade about how I was ruining my life and, by association, *hers.*

"Regan, honey," Dad said. "You've hardly touched your

food."

Mom looked at me appraisingly. "Maybe she's watching her weight, dear." She gave me a nod of approval. "Smart, Regan. With the election coming up, there will be more interviews, and the camera does add ten pounds."

And just like that, the barbed wire that felt like it was wrapping around my chest cinched tighter. I pushed away my plate. "May I be excused?"

"I don't think you need to lose any weight." Dad pulled his napkin off his lap and tossed it on the table. "In fact, I think you're looking a little too skinny. Why aren't you eating? Is something going on?"

Without looking away from her phone, Mom waved a hand dismissively, as if the very idea of her daughter having any problems was a ridiculous one. "She's an athlete, Steven. Athletes need to watch what they eat." She set her phone aside. "How is cheerleading practice going?"

"Um…" I bit the inside of my cheek and concentrated on breathing. *In, out. In, out.* Every excuse I could come up with for why I wasn't on the team sat in the back of my throat, jumbled in a knot I couldn't untangle.

Mom's eyes narrowed, and she leaned forward. "You *did* make the squad, didn't you?"

"Well…" A rush of sound crashed inside my head. The walls of the dining room felt like they were closing in on me. The air in the room grew thinner as the invisible barbs dug further into my chest, blinding me as I fought to breathe.

"Regan?" Dad pushed out of his chair so quickly, it slid several feet away from the table. He rushed to my side. "Are you okay, Pumpkin? What do you need?" He grabbed my hand and it felt like fire.

Mom took her time, folding her napkin into a square and placing it in the center of her plate before she got up. She left the room only to return a moment later with a pill bottle. She opened the top and placed a small pink pill on the table in front of me. "Take it."

I grabbed the pill, but my fingers shook so badly that it slipped from my grip and fell back to the table.

"For Christ's sake, Regan." Mom snatched the pill and pressed it into my palm. "Get it together."

I would love nothing more than to "get it together," I thought as I placed the pill on my tongue and swallowed it dry.

Dad pulled his cell phone out of his pocket. "I'm calling the doctor."

"No." My mother reached across the table and snatched the phone from his hand. "If we make an after-hours call, he'll insist we take Regan to the hospital. Is that what you want, Steven? Your daughter locked up in the same ward as dangerous schizophrenics and people who drool on themselves? And just imagine the field day the press would have if they found out. Poor Regan's reputation would be ruined."

I knew she was more concerned about her own reputation, but for once, I agreed. "Please, no," I managed through my chattering teeth. I curled my fingers into the tablecloth, hoping to hold myself steady as tremors coursed through me. School was bad enough. I could only imagine what would happen to me if people found out I suffered a breakdown. "It's just a panic attack." I attempted to shrug, but the movement was too jerky to appear natural. "We'll call the doctor tomorrow and schedule an appointment."

Dad's frown deepened. "This is more than just a panic attack."

"It's cheerleading, isn't it?" my mom asked. "Didn't you make the squad?"

There was no point denying it any longer. I shook my head.

Mom pressed her fingers to her temples and closed her eyes. "It's all right," she muttered, though I wasn't sure if she was talking to herself or me. "There's always the student election."

I glanced down at my plate and said nothing.

"Regan Barbara Flay." Her voice was low and dangerous. "Please tell me you're still in the election." When I didn't answer, she grabbed my chin and jerked my face toward hers. "It's drugs, isn't it? You're on drugs."

I almost laughed. Of course I was. In fact, she'd just fed me a pill a minute ago.

Dad inhaled sharply. "You're *not* on drugs, are you?"

I turned my head toward him as much as Mom's fingers allowed. I wasn't the least bit surprised she'd accused me of something so ridiculous, but I couldn't believe Dad would think so little of me. "Besides the anxiety meds, I'm *not* on drugs."

Mom released my chin. "Really? Then how else do you explain your behavior? Why throw your future away if not for drugs? You had plans, Regan."

"I did?" I pushed myself to my feet. I was still shaking, though I couldn't be certain if it was from the panic attack or anger. "Because I'm pretty sure all these plans you're talking about were *yours*."

She recoiled, her mouth open. She stayed that way for several seconds before snapping her jaw shut and straightening herself. "I see." She stood, grabbed my dad's wrist, and pulled him after her as she marched toward the stairs.

My muscles tensed. In all the years I'd known my mother, she'd never retreated from a fight. So whatever she was doing now, it couldn't be good. I climbed the stairs after them to find my bedroom door had been opened and the light turned on.

I approached the door slowly and peered inside my room. My breath caught in my throat. Dad had already ripped the sheets off my bed and was in the middle of sliding my mattress off the box spring. My mother knelt beside two empty dresser drawers. The socks and underwear they held were strewn across my room.

I was frozen in place, unable to do more than watch as they continued their ransacking of my room. My books were pulled from their shelves and thrown in careless piles as spines bent and pages creased. The contents of my makeup bag were spilled onto my vanity and my desk drawers overturned onto the floor. Dad even went as far as climbing onto my desk chair so he could slide his fingers along the rim of my light fixture.

I watched in silence, swallowing over and over, trying to

loosen the knot that had tied my throat shut.

My mother grabbed Carrot from his shelf and, after a quick examination, tossed him into a corner. He landed on his head with one ear flopped across his eyes. Seeing him like that propelled me into motion. I moved from the doorway, careful to step around the clutter. I gathered him in my arms and cradled him to my chest.

The memory of Nolan pulling me against him made me shiver. And *want*. That want shook me to my core. I didn't need him. I couldn't.

Except, after how he'd stuck up for me and kept me safe, maybe I did.

"Don't you dare make that face." Mom set my now-empty jewelry box to the side and rose to her feet. "This is for your own good. I'm trying to protect you."

I pushed the memory of Nolan from my mind. "From what?"

She scowled. "Don't be cute, Regan. From drugs. Where are they?"

Dad pulled the last pillow from its case and looked at me.

Exhaustion settled over me. The pill was kicking in. Unable to fight it, I backed against the wall and slid to the ground. "I told you, I don't have any drugs."

"Then how else do you explain your attitude lately? And your total lack of ambition? I will not let you jeopardize your future and everything you've worked so hard for." She wagged a finger at me. "First thing tomorrow, we're going to have you tested."

I squeezed the bunny tighter and shrugged. "Do what you have to do."

She dropped her hand to her side. Her lips pressed together so tightly they all but disappeared. "You'd better pray you're not positive. My entire campaign is based on family values. What would the public think of me if my own daughter is a drug addict?"

I didn't answer. I was afraid of what I'd say if I did. Of course she'd twisted everything around and made it about her. God forbid if I actually did drugs, she'd worry about my health instead of how it would make her look in the public eye.

Tendrils of hair had escaped Mom's tightly wound French twist. She pushed them back with her fingers. "I don't understand, Regan. If it's not drugs, then what? How can you be so selfish? Don't you understand how your actions affect everyone in the family?"

I didn't answer—not because I didn't want to argue, but because I no longer had the strength to fight.

She turned to Dad. "Maybe it's not too late. I could call the school and speak to the cheerleading coach. I could tell her you were having an off day and—"

"No." I jerked my head up. There was no way my mother was going to forcibly place me on the squad—especially a squad Amber was in charge of. "That won't help anything."

"Then what will, Regan?" She threw her hands in the air. "Because I'm running out of ideas. Should I call the school board? Hire a life coach? What's it going to take to get you back on track?"

I chewed my bottom lip. The last thing I wanted was to go back to a school that didn't want me and fight for things I couldn't care less about. "What if you hired a tutor and I was homeschooled? Or I could transfer to another school?"

"What?" Dad, who up until this point had been working on putting my bed back together, stopped and looked at me.

Mom just shook her head. "That's not funny, Regan."

"I'm not trying to be funny. I just thought…I could use a fresh start."

Mom dropped her head and pinched the bridge of her nose. "Regan, you're a junior in high school. *This* is the year colleges take into account when you apply. If you leave school midyear because you can't hack it, they'll assume you're ill equipped for college. Yes, it's hard. Nobody has an easy time in high school, but we suck it up and press on — just like you're going to do."

"Is this about the fight you had with Payton?" Dad asked. "Because these things blow over. You just have to give it time."

Mom's eyes fluttered wide. "All of this is because you had a fight with one of your friends? I thought we raised you to be stronger than that. You can't allow a little spat to ruin your life."

A spat. I bit my tongue to keep from telling her high school had changed in the several decades since she'd been there. Instead, I said, "It's getting late and my room is trashed."

"I'll help," Dad offered.

"That's okay." I grasped the corner of my nightstand and

pushed to my feet. "If it's all the same to you, I'm exhausted. I'm going to straighten just enough to go to bed, and I'll worry about the rest tomorrow."

He hesitated before nodding. "All right. What you don't get done tonight, I'll help with tomorrow."

"I'm still scheduling the drug test tomorrow." Mom picked up a toppled drawer. "If I find out you're lying to me, there will be hell to pay. In the meantime, we'll need to revise your action plan, since you've derailed the old one. You may be willing to sabotage your future, but I'm not." She slid the drawer into the desk and slammed it shut. I prayed that was the end of it, but her head whipped around and her eyes narrowed. "What is *that*?"

Before I could ask what she was referring to, she pulled Nolan's blazer off the back of my desk chair. After school ended, I'd skipped my locker and run straight to the parking lot to avoid any unwanted run-ins. I'd intended to return the jacket tomorrow—a decision I now regretted.

I placed Carrot on the shelf behind me and did my best to appear nonchalant, despite the pulse racing through my veins. I shrugged. "It's a blazer."

She sighed. "Thank you for pointing out the obvious. But perhaps you can tell me what it's doing here?" She turned it over, examining it from every angle. "It's certainly not yours."

"No." I grabbed the pendant at my neck and slid it along the chain. "Another student let me borrow it. I-I was cold."

"You have your own jacket," Mom said, her voice low.

"I didn't bring it."

Her eyes darted back to the blazer. "This is a *boy*'s jacket." She tossed it onto the chair. "Who is this boy? How do you know him? Are you dating? Why haven't you introduced him to us?"

Oh my God, this was exactly why I didn't date. There was no way I was giving her another aspect of my life to control. "Mom, please, it's not like that. I'm not dating *anyone*. It's just a jacket." I picked up a pillow and threw it onto my bed.

Her eyes narrowed. "Good. I'm not Sarah Palin. There will be no teenage pregnancies in this house."

The muscles across my chest pulled tight. "You can't get pregnant by wearing a jacket, Mom."

"I'm not talking about jackets." Her voice rose to a pitch just below a shriek. "I'm talking about *sex*—which you will *not* be having as long as you live under my roof. Understood?"

"Fine." I rolled my eyes. "I'll have my jacket sex outside the house."

A garbled choke burst from her mouth. She whirled around and pointed a finger at Dad's chest. "This is exactly why I think she's on drugs. She would never have talked to us this way before. I'm calling the doctor first thing in the morning."

He nodded but said nothing.

"And you." She turned her finger on me. "Go to bed. You'd better have a brand-new attitude in the morning, or else." Before I could ask what, exactly, "else" would entail, she spun on her heels and marched out the door.

Silence stretched between Dad and me. After several seconds, he sighed and walked to the door, careful to step over the clothes and books littering his path. He paused at the door and glanced at me over his shoulder. "We'll get this mess cleaned up tomorrow."

He left my room, leaving me to wonder exactly what mess he was referring to. My room or my life? Both were pretty disastrous.

I pushed shirts and books aside with my foot and crossed the room to Nolan's jacket. I pulled it off the back of the chair and slid inside it. While his warmth was long gone, his scent remained. I closed my eyes and inhaled deeply. Pine needles and oranges. Who'd have thought I'd like that smell so much? I could almost conjure his arms, feel them tighten around me and pull me closer.

Shuddering, I opened my eyes. God, what was wrong with me? I shook my head as if I could shake free of the memory of him.

I needed a distraction.

Thanks to Nolan, I had that picture-book assignment to work on. The sooner I finished it, the sooner I would be done with him—for good, I promised myself. I searched the floor until I found a notebook and pen. I grabbed them and sat down at my desk. It wasn't until I sat that the full force of the Xanax settled over me, heavy like a blanket. Sleep sounded awesome, but I couldn't let the lure of my bed stop me. I pulled the cap off the pen and opened the notebook.

I needed a protagonist. I glanced around the room until my eyes settled on Carrot. I smiled. That was easy; now all I needed was a problem for him to solve. I tapped my pen against my chin. What kind of problems did five-year-olds have? Losing a tooth? Being scared of the dark? Those kinds of books were done all the time, and they felt so trivial.

My thoughts returned to my own problems, to the endless whispering, name-calling, and locker graffiti. Did four- and five-year-olds get bullied? Even if they did, how was I supposed to write about a solution when I hadn't found one for myself?

I leaned back against my chair and sighed. This entire week had been a nightmare, and with Amber after me, I doubted it would get better. The only time I hadn't completely hated my life this week was when I'd apologized to Julie Sims for what I'd said about her in the note. True, she hadn't exactly forgiven me, but just saying the words had loosened the ever-tightening band around my chest.

And just like that, a story burst open inside my head. Without a single word written, I could see it unfold in its entirety. The beginning, the middle, the end, the whole thing was there, waiting to be let out.

A tremor of excitement broke through the medication in my blood and buzzed along my skin. I licked my lips and placed the pen against the paper, the words spilling out almost faster than I could write them.

Two hours later, I was finished. I tossed the pen onto the desk and traced my finger over the title:

Carrot the Bunny Says He's Sorry

A Picture Book by Regan Flay

For the first time in days, I smiled.

CHAPTER ELEVEN

I'd been sitting in front of the school for so long that the coffee in my hand had grown cold. The morning was cloudy, elongating the shadows surrounding the school, bathing it in darkness. More than ever, the brick building before me felt like a dungeon.

I hadn't been able to bring myself to leave the safety of my car. How long had I been sitting there, anyway? Several minutes? Half an hour? Time seemed to move differently now. In the beginning of the year when I had friends and clubs to keep me busy, there was never enough of it. Now that I was alone, the minutes dragged on into infinity.

More than ever, I needed a plan. I was tired of sitting and waiting for something to change. I knew from politics that time and patience were the only ways to deal with bad press. Well, that and a good PR firm. And since I was on my own, I'd have to create my own good press. But where to start?

I set my latte in the cupholder and thought of the small plastic cup the nurse had given me this morning before ushering me into a freezing bathroom with an even colder stainless steel toilet. Mom never even apologized when the drug test confirmed I'd been telling the truth. It was becoming all too clear that no matter what I did, I'd never measure up.

A black Toyota truck pulled into the empty spot beside my car. *Nolan*'s truck.

My pulse quickened as Payton opened the passenger-side door and climbed out. She paused, her gaze sweeping across the key mark on my car. Slowly, she met my eyes.

Still hurt over the way she'd treated me, I wanted to look away, to ignore her the way she'd ignored me. Instead, I opened my door and climbed out into the chilly, fall morning. Nearly ten years of friendship wasn't something I could so easily push aside. "Hey," I said.

She had shadows under her eyes, and wrinkles marred her uniform. I couldn't decide if I was pleased or pissed she was suffering.

"Hey." Payton nodded at my scratched car door. "That sucks."

"A lot of things suck," I replied. "And my car is the least of them."

She chewed on her lip. "Things haven't been so great for me, either."

Irritation washed over me. How could she even say

that? Her name was blurred out on the texts while mine was plastered across the school. She wasn't the object of ridicule in the halls, and she certainly didn't have her friends publicly turn on her. "You really had me fooled, Pay. Before this whole thing started, I honestly believed we were best friends."

"That's not fair." Her eyes narrowed. "You were the one who called me annoying—who said I'm only good for gossip."

I snorted. "If you believe that, maybe your brother was right, and we were never really friends at all."

Nolan slammed the driver's door and watched us from across the hood of his truck.

She glanced between him and me, a perplexed look on her face. "You guys have been talking?"

I folded my arms across my chest. No way was I answering such a loaded question. "So, what. You're just going to believe Amber over your *best friend* who you've known since grade school? That makes a lot of fucking sense, Pay."

She opened her mouth and closed it, her lips trembling like she was on the verge of crying. "Swear to it. Promise me you never said those things." She raised her right hand, pinkie finger extended the way we used to do when we were eight.

"If we were really friends," I said, "I shouldn't have to."

"I'm sorry, Regan. I thought we were best friends, too," she responded, raising her hand so her pinkie finger hovered inches away from my nose. "But sometimes even best friends need assurance. According to your logic, being best friends means I'm not allowed to have a moment of insecurity?" Her voice raised an octave. "I guess I'm also not allowed to be confused or have any doubts because high school is so easy and makes total sense all of the time? I'm sorry, Regan, I fucked up...but so did you."

I stared at her. I'd never seen her so worked up before. She stood staring at me, her eyes wide. A few strands of hair had fallen loose from her headband. Maybe I wasn't the only one suffering, after all. "Jesus, Pay, when you put it like that—" I looped my pinkie with hers and tugged. "You're my best friend. I never talked shit about you. I swear."

Her eyes shifted from our joined hands to my face. When she spoke, her voice was softer. "Listen, I admit it was wrong of me to not listen to you, but after those messages were posted, Amber was saying all this stuff about you, and I just...panicked. I'm sorry." After several shakes, she dropped my hand and tucked the loose strands of hair beneath her headband. "Can we please be okay again?" She smiled hopefully.

Even though the sting of her betrayal still throbbed deep inside me, I had to admit, she made a good point. We'd both made mistakes. How could I expect her to look past mine if I couldn't look past hers? I returned her grin with my own. "We're cool."

Nolan moved around his truck and stopped in front of us. I tried to ignore how his nearness loosened the rope woven through my ribs.

"So what do we do now?" Payton asked. "About..." She

jutted her chin toward the school.

"I honestly have no idea," I answered. "My only real plan is to lie low until this blows over."

Silence stretched among the three of us until Nolan cleared his throat. "What I don't understand is why you even care. Everything that goes on inside that building is bullshit. None of it will matter in a couple of years. Why waste a second of your life worrying about what people—who you'll never see again after you graduate—think? Fuck 'em."

Payton snorted.

I, on the other hand, appreciated he was trying to make things better for once. "But it matters *now*. Speaking of"—I turned to Payton—"you should go. You shouldn't be seen walking into school with me."

She narrowed her eyes. "I thought—"

"As much as it sucks to admit it, Amber's right about what she said the other day in the hallway. There's no point in dragging you down with me." I gave a weak smile. "This will blow over soon, right?"

Her brow furrowed. "Yeah, but—"

"*Please.*"

Nolan gave her a gentle shove. "Go on. I'll walk with her."

She gaped at him, but he only grinned. "C'mon. What are they going to do to *me*?"

Payton seemed to consider his words for a moment before turning to me. "I'll catch up with you later, though, okay?"

I nodded, and some of the weight lifted from my shoulders. While I knew our friendship was in no way solid, it still existed.

Payton scurried off toward the school and Nolan took her place, leaning against my car.

I bumped his shoulder with mine. Or, rather, his elbow. He was much taller than I thought. "You really don't have to do this, you know."

He looked at me, his hazel eyes devoid of their usual humor. "I *want* to."

I didn't know how to respond, so I said nothing. After a while, the silence grew thick and heavy between us. When I could take it no longer, I unzipped my backpack, pulled out his blazer, and held it toward him. "Thanks." I wanted to add, *And not just for the jacket*, but I wasn't ready to go that far yet.

He said nothing and took the jacket. I watched as the fabric of his button-down shirt stretched tight over his surprisingly muscular chest—the very chest I'd been pressed against only yesterday. Dear God. Since when did I notice Nolan Letner's chest? Sure, I'd thought he was cute, but not once had I thought about his cuteness in relation to *me*. I quickly shook away the thought.

After he slipped on the jacket, he remained at my side, not touching, not looking at me, and it was somehow exactly what I needed. "Are you ready to do this?"

I stared at the dark building, watching students trickle inside. "Not really, but I guess it's too late to run away and join the circus."

"Yeah. I think they like to train their trapeze artists early. It might not be too late if you wanted to be the bearded lady. I bet we could find you some steroids and—"

I couldn't help but grin. "Pass."

He cocked his head, his eyes serious again.

"What?"

"I think that's the first time I've ever seen you smile for real. It's a good look on you, Flay."

A blush warmed my cheeks, and I looked away before Nolan could see it. I was pretty sure I was too late, because he chuckled. "We're going to be late," I said. I pushed off my car and headed for the entrance; Nolan was at my side in an instant. For reasons I didn't dare think about, I felt better with him beside me. Somehow, something had passed between the two of us—an understanding that maybe we weren't so different after all.

"I finished writing the picture book," I offered, just to fill the silence between us.

"Cool," he said. "What time should I come over this weekend?"

I stopped. "What?"

He kicked at a loose rock on the ground. His discomfort was kind of…cute.

"You're the author, so you're going to have to give me artistic direction," he said, keeping his eyes on the ground. "Plus, the average picture book is around thirty-two pages. That's a lot of drawing. I'll definitely need help with coloring." When I didn't say anything, he looked at me and frowned. "Did you expect me to do it all on my own?"

"No." I knew we'd be working together—it just hadn't occurred to me where. My house made as much sense as his. After all, my mom wouldn't be able to complain about a boy coming over if we were working on an assignment.

But then a new thought occurred to me. If Nolan came over, he'd be *in* my house—possibly even my room. The thought of being alone with him made something flutter inside my stomach. "I-I guess that's okay."

He smiled. "Good."

We traveled the rest of the way to the building in silence. When we reached the doors, several people called out to Nolan in greeting. He nodded and smiled at all of them. It was like he and I had traded social statuses. Or maybe I'd been so sure he was a freak, I never noticed he actually had friends. More than me, at the moment.

"Nolan?" Blake peeled herself away from a group of people and made her way toward us. "What are you doing?"

He raised an eyebrow. "Going to class."

Her eyes flickered to me, and her mouth curled with disgust. The move made her lip piercing glint in the overhead lights. "With *her*?"

I flinched. The disdain in her voice was the same news anchors reserved for stories about puppy killers. As far as I knew, I'd never done anything to her, so I had no idea what her problem was.

Nolan opened the door. "If you're asking me if I am entering the school building at the precise moment Regan Flay does, then yes."

She opened her mouth to say more, but he cut her off.

"I'll talk to you later," he said, ushering me inside ahead of him.

I hoped the worst was behind us.

I was wrong.

"Look who it is," a shrill voice called out.

Amber pushed through the crowd with a wide-eyed, bouncy-haired Taylor in tow. Jeremy and his friends followed closely at her heels.

Nausea rolled through me in waves. I was hoping to at least get through second period before anyone tried to pick a fight with me. Eluding Blake hadn't been very hard, but we wouldn't escape Amber so easily.

Nolan moved to my side, his hazel eyes practically shimmering with excitement. The muscles in his shoulders tightened as he drew them back. He looked eager for... something. I wasn't sure what, or whether I wanted to know.

Amber swung her long black hair over her shoulder and placed a hand on her hip. "Isn't that adorable? Apparently rejects attract other rejects."

Nolan smiled. "Apparently the same can be said for douche bags—only it appears you guys travel in packs."

Several bystanders laughed. Amber scowled at them. Jeremy stepped up beside her, his hands already balled into fists.

I tensed. Either Nolan didn't realize he'd initiated a fight or he didn't care. After how much time I'd spent with him the last two days, I was willing to guess the latter.

Amber fixed her heated gaze on me. "Seriously, Regan? *Nolan Letner*? Can't say I'm surprised, especially when no normal guy will touch you. I heard how you threw yourself at Jeremy yesterday. You're pathetic."

Her sleazy boyfriend winked at me, and it was all I could do not to launch myself at him. "He wishes. Not only is he disgusting, he's a liar."

"Not as disgusting as you," she replied. "*You're* the dirty whore."

Amber held out her hand. Beside her, Taylor withdrew a plastic bottle of Mountain Dew and handed it to her. "You've had everyone fooled into thinking you're so innocent. Little Miss Perfect. Not anymore. Now you're going to look as disgusting on the outside as you are on the inside."

She started to shake the soda bottle.

I knew exactly where this was going. Last year, Amber had doused a freshman who'd bumped into her while she was applying her lipstick. For a split second, I considered pushing out the back door and making a break for it, but that would only make things worse. I'd be known as the girl who ran away. I lifted my chin and forced my face into an impassive mask. I wouldn't give her the satisfaction of seeing me afraid.

Beside me, instead of bracing himself as I'd done, Nolan held up a finger. "Just a sec. This is exactly the kind of scene I need for my documentary—raw high school hallway footage. He reached into his book bag and withdrew his phone. He pressed a few buttons, then settled into place. "Okay, go ahead." He motioned with his free hand for her to continue. "Just try to avoid the lens, okay?"

Amber hesitated, her eyes uncertain.

"What are you waiting for?" Taylor hissed, practically bouncing on her toes.

"I'm not going to get caught on camera. I'll get expelled and my parents will shit." Amber shoved the soda bottle into Taylor's hands. "You do it."

Taylor took a step back. "I-I can't get in trouble. I'll get kicked off the squad. This is my first year making it."

It was true. Taylor had tried out both freshman and sophomore years and hadn't made the team. Having been at the tryouts, I knew she was pretty good, too. If I were honest, I'd say she was even better than me. But being Amber's friend, I'd been given the preferential treatment that I now realized I didn't deserve.

Nolan snapped his fingers. "I don't care who does it, but you need to decide fast. The warning bell is going to ring soon, and I don't want to be late for class."

Taylor turned to Jeremy. "You do it."

He held up his hands and backed away. "Fuck you. I'm not doing your dirty work. I'm already on thin ice with the coach thanks to these two and a security guard who can't keep his mouth shut. I'm not getting kicked off the wrestling team. None of you is worth that."

The two guys with him laughed before erupting in a chorus of *Oooh*s.

Amber's mouth dropped. She must not have been able to think of a snarky comeback, because she just glared at him. He shrugged and backed down the hallway with his friends following close behind.

"So wait, are you telling me *nobody* is going to spray

us?" Still holding his phone, Nolan sighed. "That sucks. It would have been incredible footage."

"Fucking loser," Amber snarled. She grabbed the bottle from Taylor and threw it on the ground. The cap burst off, and a stream of Mountain Dew doused her and Taylor's ankles.

Amber shrieked and scuttled backward. When the bottle emptied, she raised her head and glared at me. "This isn't over." She flipped me off before spinning on her heels and marching down the hall. Taylor scrambled to keep up.

Nolan aimed the phone at me. "Regan Flay, do you have any thoughts on what just happened here?"

I blinked. "Homeschooling is underrated?"

He laughed and, to my surprise, turned off the phone and stuffed it inside his bag.

"That's it?" I asked. "No more prodding questions? Don't you want to see me squirm?"

"Meh." He shrugged. "I wasn't lying when I said the soda shot would have been great footage for my documentary."

Careful to avoid the river of soda, we walked down the hall. "So what's your documentary about?"

"It's nothing." He tugged on the straps of his backpack. "I'm applying to University of Florida, but my first choice is Duke. They have an amazing documentary studies program. I need to make a documentary as part of the application process."

"Wow." This information surprised me. For the reject in the back of the class, Nolan was surprisingly ambitious. "That's not 'nothing.' Duke's a great school. Do you really have to be sprayed by Mountain Dew to get in?"

He laughed. "No. I just need a really awesome documentary."

"So what's yours about?"

"Honestly, at this point I have no idea. Blake was helping me with something, but it…kind of fell apart. So I need to come up with another idea, and fast."

I wanted to ask him what it was that had fallen apart when a guy stepped in front of us, forcing us to stop. He had a mop of dark red hair that he pushed out of his eyes with the palm of his hand.

"You Regan?" he asked. He looked familiar, and I was pretty sure I had biology with him last year.

"Who wants to know?" Nolan asked.

The boy sighed. "Look, some chick paid me to give Regan a note. Are you her or not?"

Nolan and I exchanged glances before I asked, "Who gave it to you?"

He shrugged. "Didn't ask her name. Do you want it or not?"

My stomach churned. Anonymous notes were never good, but it wasn't like a piece of paper could hurt me. Even if the person who wrote it called me every name in the book, all I had to do was throw it away. I held out my hand. "I'll take it."

The guy handed me a folded-up square of notebook paper and left.

"Don't read it."

The nearness of Nolan's voice made me gasp. I glanced

up at him leaning over me, his face inches from mine. I wanted to argue, but my tongue felt thick and the words jumbled around my mouth.

"Just throw it away," he said. "Whatever it says, it won't be good."

The corners of the note bit into my skin. He was probably right. Did I really need to read about what a skanky bitch I was? I eyed the nearby trash can. All I had to do was toss it inside, and the venom on the page would be lost with it.

Still, I couldn't seem to let go.

"Regan?"

I looked up at him. "I need to read this."

He frowned. "Why?"

Another bit of Mom's wisdom ran through my mind: *Never be caught off guard.* "I'm sick of being ambushed," I told him. "Yesterday it was in the bathroom at lunch; today it was by the front doors before class. Whatever this note says, I don't want to be blindsided again."

His face hardened, and he stepped back. "Do what you need to do, then."

The warning bell rang. Obviously, Nolan wasn't happy with me, but his hurt feelings would have to wait. Slowly, I unfolded the paper and read the unfamiliar, loopy script.

If you want dirt on Amber, come to the old girls' locker room after school.

Hide in the farthest shower stall and don't make a sound.

I turned over the note, searching for a signature, and found none. Dirt was usually Payton's department, but this definitely wasn't her handwriting. So who wrote the note?

I gave the paper to Nolan to read. When he finished, he handed the paper to me and rubbed his neck. "Don't do it. I have a bad feeling."

I reread the words. Three stuck out above the rest—"dirt on Amber." With Amber determined to make my life hell, anything I could use to get her off my back would be worth going after. I knew Mom didn't hesitate to do whatever it took to bring down an opponent. On the other hand, whoever wrote the note chose to remain anonymous, which *was* suspicious. "You think I'm being set up?"

"Definitely. What better way to get you alone than in the old girls' locker room after school? Either Amber's setting you up or you're about to star in a teen slasher movie. You haven't killed any hitchhikers lately, have you?"

I made a face. "Be serious. I understand this might be a setup, but what if it's not? What if this"—I held up the note—"is my one and only chance to get Amber"—*and my mother*—"off my back?" For the first time since I'd found my private messages taped to the lockers, a new idea presented itself to me. If this note was legit, maybe my only option wouldn't be to blend in. A quiver of hope—a feeling so foreign I almost forgot what it felt like—pulsed inside me. If I could twist this whole thing back around to Amber, I might be able to take back everything she stole from me. "I could have a real shot at reclaiming my life."

"Wait." He raised his hands, his eyes wide. "You want

that joke of a life *back*?"

He thought I was a *joke*? Irritation fizzed through my veins, extinguishing my short-lived excitement. I crumpled the note into a ball. "Fuck you."

"Really?" He snorted. "So you miss being friends with the girl who's now hell-bent on ruining your life?"

"That's not what I—"

"And hanging out with guys like Jeremy?" His voice rose, attracting curious glances from students as they rushed past us on their way to class. "You want to climb back on your throne and write more notes about how much cooler you are than everyone else? Ruin a few more lives? Is that it?"

His words struck me like a fist. To the best of my knowledge, I'd never ruined anyone's life. I backed up until I hit the row of lockers behind me. Nolan followed, closing the distance between us.

"I've got news for you," he said. "Whether you see it or not, *that* Regan was a joke. She wasn't real. Or maybe I'm wrong? Maybe you're not the girl I thought you were. The intelligent girl, the compassionate girl, the girl who apologizes when she realizes she's hurt people."

Anger coiled through me, tightening my muscles. He barely knew me, so what the hell gave him the right to form any opinions on who I was? Screw him and everyone else who wanted me to be something I wasn't, and then freaked out when I didn't measure up. "Don't try to pretend like you know me. You don't know *anything* about me."

"You're absolutely right."

I watched him walk away, wondering what the hell had

just happened. A couple days ago, I wouldn't have cared what Nolan Letner thought about me. But now, every word out of his mouth sliced through me like a knife, and each step he took away from me left another cut from which I bled.

He stopped halfway down the hall, his shoulders bowing. My heart stuttered. Maybe he'd decided to give me a chance to explain?

But then he fumbled through his bag until he pulled out what appeared to be a small video camera. My heart plummeted straight to the floor, sure he would turn the lens on me. Instead, he stalked back to where I slouched against the lockers and held his phone out to me. "Take it."

I slowly lifted my hand but stopped just short of grabbing it. For reasons I didn't understand, I was afraid. "I don't get it."

"Take it," he repeated. He thrust the camera at me so I had no choice but to grab it or let it fall to the ground.

"I have a video camera on my phone."

"Yeah, well, even though this camera is a couple of years old, its video quality is better than your phone's. It has more frames per second and better color quality in low-light situations. That might come in handy." When I said nothing, he sighed. "The threat of video protected you once from an attack. Maybe it'll protect you again."

He strode away, leaving me frowning after him. All I'd wanted was a shot at getting Amber off my back, but instead all I'd done was get Nolan pissed at me. Now, alone with his camera, I couldn't help but wonder why whenever I tried to make things better, all I managed to do was screw them up more.

CHAPTER TWELVE

Nolan refused to acknowledge my existence during third period. He even returned to his usual desk in the back of the room. When class ended, he was out the door before I had a chance to gather my books. If he wasn't going to talk to me, I assumed our plans to work on the picture book were off, so during lunch, I slipped a copy of the story into his locker, praying he'd draw the pictures on his own. Then I spent the entire lunch period in the second-floor bathroom's handicap stall. No one bothered me, and I was able to eat my granola bar in peace.

Other than the confrontations with Blake and Amber, I'd only gotten the occasional snide comment from a passerby. There was a group of freshmen who whispered and giggled as they passed, but it wasn't enough to make me pop a pill. That was something, at least.

Pushing all thoughts of Nolan from my mind, I worked the rest of the day to avoid Amber, Taylor, and Jeremy in the hallways. Where was Payton? I hadn't seen her since that morning, and I had to wonder if she and Amber had gotten into a fight. If not, Amber had to be getting suspicious. With all the hype about me dying down, I suspected she didn't have much left to focus on. During seventh period, I watched the clock wind down with a growing sense of unease. As much as I tried to concentrate, I couldn't conjugate a single verb my Spanish teacher wrote on the board. I knew I should be taking notes, but all I could think about was the anonymous handwritten note in my pocket.

Who was it from? And why would he or she want to help me—especially when I was the most hated girl in school? And what was with the instruction to hide in the shower? More and more, I was beginning to agree with Nolan. I was being set up. Maybe Amber sent it as a way to get me alone?

I didn't realize I was beating my pen against my notebook at a frenzied pace until Señora Batey turned from the Smart board and glared at me with beady, narrowed eyes.

I dropped my pen onto the notebook and offered her a weak smile of apology.

She frowned before returning to the board.

I grasped my diamond pendant and slid it along the chain. If there was even a small possibility of getting dirt on Amber, I couldn't ignore the note. But I also wasn't going to be dumb enough to walk into a trap. I just had to figure out a way to protect myself—thankfully, Nolan's video camera was a good starting point. If someone did attack me, at least I'd have evidence.

The bell rang, and I leaped out of my chair so quickly, the metal feet screeched against the floor. Señora Batey scowled at me over her shoulder. I ignored her as I crammed my books into my bag and ran for the door.

I wove through the mass of students pouring into the halls until I reached the girls' locker room. If I was going to pull this off, I had to make sure I arrived first. I pulled open the heavy wooden door and nearly recoiled in disgust as the scent of damp mold and sweat washed over me. Like the bathroom I'd been spending my lunch hour in, the old girls' locker room was located in the wing of the school that was in desperate need of renovation. The once blue lockers were now chipped and rusted, and the calcium-encrusted showerheads still dripped no matter how many times you turned the faucet knobs.

As far as I could tell, no one else was there. Still, I performed a quick sweep of the fluorescent-lit room, making sure to peer around every corner, beneath every toilet stall door, as well as around every mold-streaked shower curtain.

I was alone.

Nervous energy hummed along my skin. The note told me to wait in the shower, but there was no way I was going to trap myself inside one of those disgusting concrete cells. Besides, if it *was* a trap, I wasn't going to allow myself to be found so easily.

I couldn't very well hide out in the open, either. So that left me with only one option. I walked to the row of toilet stalls and sighed. If I did manage to get dirt on Amber, hopefully my days of hanging out in bathroom stalls and ducking through the halls between classes would be over soon. All I needed was the *right* dirt. If it were strong enough, everyone in school would forget about me and glom on to her.

I picked the handicap stall because it was farthest from the door, and I locked myself inside. Graffiti covered every inch of the salmon-pink stall (why was that color ever popular?), declaring undying love as well as naming who was a bitch, a slut, or a bitch *and* a slut.

I traced my fingers over the words Delaney Hickler is a fucking whore. Years, if not decades, had faded their color, but like ghosts, the anger emanating from each scrawled letter refused to die. So many times I'd been inside a stall, surrounded by these hate-filled words, and never given a shit one way or another. But now that I had my own graffiti, I couldn't help but wonder if Delaney Hickler had ever sat in this stall and read the words written about her. Did they make her chest burn like they did mine? Did she cry like I did? And now that she was long gone from this place, did she still think about the words, or had time lessened their sting? Nolan had said none of this would matter in a few years. Maybe he was right.

The door to the locker room creaked open. I covered my mouth, as if I didn't trust myself not to make a noise and give away my location. Moving slowly, so as not to make a sound, I crouched and withdrew Nolan's video camera from my backpack, opened the view screen, and pressed the record button. If I was about to be jumped, I wanted the evidence on film.

The soft pad of rubber-soled shoes approached — definitely not the *clack* of Amber's high heels. I peered through the crack of the stall door and watched as Christy Holder stepped into the middle of the room.

The camera shook in my hands. Christy was the last person I'd expected to see. If she had dirt on Amber, why give it to me?

Judging by the way she kept adjusting her ponytail and fiddling with her uniform, she was nervous. Seeing her nerves lessened my own. With the camera still in my hand, I reached for the stall lock. What was the point of hiding? Christy was obviously alone. If she wanted to talk, the least I could do was hear her out. I started to slide the rusted bolt when I heard the groan of the decades-old locker room door being pushed open, followed by the sharp *clack* of high heels echoing off concrete.

I gasped and backed away from the door. My heart beat like a fist against my ribs. Careful not to make any noise, I retreated to the back of the stall and climbed onto the toilet seat. Even though I could no longer see outside the stall, I kept the camera recording.

"What the fuck, Christy?" Amber demanded, her footsteps drawing close. "I had to hear secondhand you were back at school today. Why didn't you tell me?"

Christy gave an angry laugh. "Why the hell would I tell you anything? From what I hear, you were responsible for nearly getting me hauled back to rehab. Do you have any idea what it's like to be interrogated by your parents and held prisoner in your own home?"

"You can't blame me," Amber said. "Regan was freaking out about not making the squad, so she told Kiley Porter to tell the counselor that she heard you puking in the bathroom to get you thrown out."

My mouth dropped open, and I had to slap a hand across my face to keep myself from gasping. I hadn't told Kiley Porter anything. She was one of the sweetest girls I knew, always willing to help someone in need.

Which would have made her a perfect target for Amber.

"But I'd already given you the squad list. You could've just *told* her she made it instead of letting her almost ruin my life. Why didn't you stop her?"

Amber said nothing for several seconds. When she finally spoke, her voice was low, almost apologetic. "I didn't stop her because I wanted her off the squad. I was worried she was starting to figure things out."

The anger surging through my veins nearly toppled me off my perch. My supposed *friend* had set me up to take a social swan dive on purpose.

"You know," Amber continued. "About you and me."

"You think she knows?" There was a pause, and then Christy added, "You could have told me. I wouldn't have put her on the squad. Do you have any idea how much my parents are on my case now? I can't fucking *pee* without my mom listening outside the door."

Amber's heels clicked along the concrete as she paced. "I had no idea your parents would threaten to send you back to rehab. I just thought if we put some distance between us, it would throw people off. Do you have any idea what would happen if anyone discovered the truth? We'd be kicked out. Our reputations would be ruined."

"My reputation *is* ruined."

Amber scoffed. "Your reputation is solid, thanks to me. Do you know how popular you're going to be now that people think you went to rehab? I made you a fucking celebrity."

"That's insane, Amber. An eating disorder is not a popularity perk."

"I know that. *You* know that. But welcome to our fucked-up world." She paused. "How are you dealing with all this shit, anyway?"

"You would know if you answered my calls and texts," Christy said. "I'm doing okay, I guess. Every day is a battle, and this stunt you helped pull did *not* make things any easier."

"I'm sorry," Amber said, sounding more sincere than I had ever heard her before.

"But not sorry enough to dump that prick Jeremy."

Amber sighed. "Jeremy's just for show. You know I couldn't care less about him."

"But that's not what he thinks," Christy countered. "Or what everyone else thinks."

"Fuck what everyone else thinks. We only have to do this for one more year, and then we'll be in college and able to do whatever the fuck we want. *One year*."

My fingers gripped the camera so tightly my knuckles

turned white. *Oh my God*. Amber and Christy? A thing? She was right that if our Catholic school found out, they'd be kicked out. But she was wrong about me knowing anything about it — until now. And that left the question: Who sent the note? Obviously whoever it was knew about them and wanted me to know as well. But why?

Christy was quiet a long moment. "I guess. The Snowflake Ball is coming up. I just wish — "

"Look," Amber said. "We can't risk being caught together like this — especially not at school. Next time you want to talk, don't send me a note. Text me, okay?"

"But I didn't send you a note," Christy said. "You left a note for *me* in my locker."

"No I didn't." Amber inhaled sharply. "Fuck. I bet it was Regan. She really *does* know. Fuck. Fuck. Fuck."

"Maybe she won't say anything?"

Amber laughed. "Yeah, right. With how the last two days have played out, she'll destroy me the first chance she gets."

Silence filled the room before Christy asked, "Why do you do it, Amber? Why do you go after people like you do? It's not who you are."

"That's the point," Amber said. "I'm not *allowed* to be who I really am."

Despite everything she'd done, I actually felt bad for her. I knew exactly what it was like to live a life you didn't want. How would things have been between us if we'd been honest with each other? With so much in common, we might have been *real* friends.

"Listen," Amber said. "I've got to go. It's only a matter of time before that annoying leech Taylor finds me. She totally freaks if she's not by my side every second of the day." There was a pause and she added, "We good here?"

"Yeah," Christy replied flatly. "We're good."

"Okay. I'll call you later."

I heard the sound of heels clacking back toward the door. A second later, the door squeaked open and Amber's footsteps faded into the hall beyond.

I didn't move for several heartbeats. If I hadn't been holding the camera in my hands, I wouldn't have believed my own ears. I waited another minute, straining for any sounds that would indicate I wasn't alone. The locker room remained silent. Satisfied, I climbed off the toilet, turned off the camera, and tucked it inside my backpack. I still couldn't believe I had an actual sound recording that would get Amber kicked out of school.

My heart raced at the thought. Forget turning the school against her. If I could get rid of Amber completely, I could concentrate on rebuilding my reputation. But even as I had the thought, a knot wedged its way inside my throat. Would ruining someone else's life *honestly* make mine better? I unlatched the door as I considered the question—only to stop dead in my tracks.

I wasn't alone after all.

Christy sat on a wooden bench between two rows of lockers, her head in her hands. She looked up when the stall door smacked against the wall. She jumped to her feet, her blue eyes impossibly wide. "What are you doing here?

Wait—" Her eyes widened. "How much did you *hear*?"

"Um…" I racked my brain for an answer—*any answer*—and came up blank.

Christy covered her face with her hands. "Fuck."

Unsure how to respond, I edged toward the door. My movement caught her attention, and her head snapped up.

"Please, Regan." She laced her hands in front of her. "I know I said some awful things the other morning, but you can't say anything. I'm begging you. We'll get kicked out of school. She'd never forgive me for that."

The old part of me that cared solely about self-preservation wanted to say, *Not my problem*. But a different part of me choked the words back because of the tears brimming in Christy's eyes—tears that conveyed it wouldn't be just Amber's life I destroyed if I posted the video, but Christy's as well.

It would be so easy to post it online, sit back, and wait for Amber's world to fall apart. I wouldn't even have to get my hands dirty. Just like that, I could have my old life back.

But even as the thoughts stirred through my mind, Nolan's words echoed inside my head.

*Whether you see it or not, that *Regan was a joke. She wasn't real.*

My gut clenched and I closed my eyes. Nolan stared at me from the darkness, his face full of disappointment. I wrapped my arms around my stomach.

Christy took a step back. Like maybe she thought I'd throw up on her. "Are you—are you okay?"

Not even close. But maybe, if I could figure out who the

real me was, I would be. "I won't say anything."

Christy sucked in a deep breath. "Are you serious?"

Apparently the real me was all about sacrificing my social standing based on the opinion of a boy I'd hated until very recently, because I nodded. I hadn't completely lost my mind, though. I was at least going to give myself some insurance. "I have a condition," I told her. "You tell Amber I promise to keep your secret so long as she and her band of assholes leave me alone. That means no Facebook posts, no hallway threats—hell, I don't want them to even *look* at me. Tell her that."

Christy bit her lip. "She's going to be so pissed once she finds out you know. She's going to blame me."

I didn't know what to say to that, other than to ask the question that had been plaguing me since I figured out what they were talking about. "Why are you with her? If things go bad between the two of you, or Amber thinks someone might find out, she'll destroy you. She's already proven she has no problem hurting you for her own gain."

"She wouldn't really hurt me." The uncertainty in Christy's eyes told a different story. "She cares about me."

I shook my head. I wasn't trying to be cruel, but I had to tell the truth, even if she didn't want to hear it. "Amber only cares about herself."

I expected her to argue. Instead, Christy's shoulders slumped and her chin dropped to her chest, defeated. "I keep hoping…" she murmured. She didn't have to finish her sentence for me to understand. Wasn't I hoping for the same thing, only with my mother? To be loved for who we were instead of what we provided?

Before I could stop myself, I reached out and touched her shoulder.

She flinched but allowed my hand to remain.

"I'm so sorry that I ever thought about hurting you, Christy. I can't imagine what it's like having to hide who you are because you go to a school like this. Good job, by the way. I totally had no idea."

She smiled weakly.

"Anyway," I continued, "that doesn't mean settling for less than you deserve. And you deserve a whole lot better than Amber."

She eyed me skeptically. "It's because you're unpopular now, right? That's why you're being nice to me? You want back on the cheerleading squad?"

"No." I dropped my hand from her shoulder. "I'm not even trying to be nice, really. I'm just trying to be…" I paused, searching for the right words. "I'm just trying to be who I think I am—or at least who I wanted to be, before everything got so damn confusing, you know?"

"Yeah." A sad smile pulled at her lips. "Fuck this high school bullshit."

I smiled back. "Fuck it."

"Well, I guess we should get going." She inclined her head toward the exit.

"You go on ahead," I told her. "There's something I have to do."

She gave me a questioning look. "All right. I guess I'll see you around."

"Hey, Christy?"

She paused by the door. "Yeah?"

"For what it's worth, I had already decided not to tell anyone about you going to rehab when those messages were leaked. I wasn't the one who told Kiley. Think about what that means, okay?"

She frowned, then nodded. I waited for her to leave the locker room before rummaging through my backpack for a pen. Once I found one, I returned to the handicap stall and scribbled over DELANEY HICKLER IS A FUCKING WHORE until it was a mass of black lines. When I finished, I wrote a new message above it.

Christy Holder is fucking awesome.

It was a single line amid a wall of hate. It barely made a difference.

But it was a start—and that was all that mattered.

CHAPTER THIRTEEN

If I closed my eyes, I could almost convince myself the soft sand in the arena was actually a cloud beneath my feet — that the horse I led around in circles was a Pegasus, come to fly me away to adventures untold.

As if he could read my thoughts, Rookie snorted. I smiled and opened my eyes. While my life was far from perfect, there were moments I didn't need to escape from, and this was one of them.

I looked up at Tamara, the little girl clinging to Rookie's mane. Black curls spilled out from beneath her riding helmet. Her eyes glistened with excitement, yet her mouth was tight with concentration. I didn't know her background, but it didn't matter to me if she struggled with a disability or came from a broken home. All that mattered when I volunteered my and Rookie's time was that the kid on his back wanted to be there. And I could tell from Tamara's face there was no place she'd rather be.

We approached a piece of PVC tubing on the ground. "Two-point," I called out.

Tamara complied. She braced her hands on Rookie's neck and rose out of the saddle as I guided Rookie over the pole. Pretty soon she wouldn't need me on the other end of his lead rope—she'd be taking small jumps all on her own. I wondered if she'd close her eyes and pretend to be flying like I used to do.

The thought startled me. I couldn't remember when I stopped.

"Do you ever pretend the horses are unicorns or have wings?" I asked as we rounded the corner and began another lap.

Tamara made a face. "I'm not a baby. That stuff isn't real. I like regular horses. They're real."

Rookie chuffed as if in agreement.

I couldn't help but smile. "You're right." I gently pulled back on the lead rope and Rookie came to a halt. "I think we're all done for today, Tamara."

"Aw." Her face crumpled. "But we just started."

"An hour ago." I laughed. "Tell you what, how about you dismount, I'll take his saddle off, and then you can brush him for a bit, okay?"

Her face lit up. "Okay."

I held my hand out to her, and she fell into my arms. I lowered her to the ground. Looking past me, she asked, "Who's that?"

"Who's who?" I turned and found Nolan standing outside the arena gate. The shock of seeing him was so sharp, I nearly tripped over my own feet. He wore faded jeans that hung low on his hips, and his tattered gray T-shirt hugged his arms and shoulders in all the right places. His hair, never tame on any day, looked even wilder in the breeze.

I had the horrible urge to run my fingers through it.

I cleared my throat, as if that would purge the disturbing thought from my mind. I blinked to make sure I was seeing clearly through the arena dust. He held a different video camera, larger than the one he let me borrow. What was he doing here? I thought he didn't want to talk to me—especially after the way things had gone between us at school.

The lead rope slid from my hand and fell to the ground. Rookie immediately set his nose to the sand in a hunt for loose hay. I grabbed a brush from a bucket beside the wall and handed it to Tamara. "You can brush him until your mom gets here. I'll keep an eye on you. Just remember to stay away from his back legs." In all the years I'd owned Rookie, he'd never once tried to kick me, but it wasn't too early for her to learn to be cautious.

"*Duh.*" Tamara rolled her eyes and snatched the brush from my hand.

"I'll be right over there if you need anything." I pointed to Nolan.

She ignored me and began brushing Rookie's front legs. "You're such a good pony, aren't you?" she cooed.

I dusted my hands on my breeches and made my way

across the arena. Nolan followed my trek with his camera lens. My steps faltered as I became suddenly conscious of the barn grime beneath my nails and the helmet hair from my earlier trail ride. "What are you doing here?"

He kept the camera trained on me. He grinned. "Nice pants."

A blush warmed my cheeks and I self-consciously ran my hands along the skin-tight fabric of my breeches. "You came here to discuss fashion?"

"No. I want to know what you're doing here."

I frowned. "This is a horse barn." I nodded to Rookie. "And that's my horse."

"That's not what I mean. What are you doing here *today*?"

"I volunteer for a horse-therapy program every Saturday."

His camera didn't budge. "Why?"

I sighed. Apparently I was dealing with the old, annoying Nolan again. I glanced over my shoulder to check on Tamara. She giggled while stroking Rookie's nose. I couldn't help but smile. "That's why. When she first started the program, she was so angry, but Rookie worked his horsey magic and now she's actually laughing." I hugged myself. "I never thought I'd see her smile, much less laugh."

Nolan lowered the camera. "What happened to her?"

I shrugged. "I don't know and I don't want to. Some of the kids in this program have backgrounds bad enough to keep you awake at night."

He was quiet a moment, his jaw tight. "God," he said

softly, "that's awful."

"Yeah." I continued watching Tamara and Rookie. "That's why the program is important." And then another thought crossed my mind. I turned back to Nolan. "How did you know I was here, anyway?"

He tucked the camera into the messenger bag strapped diagonally across his chest. "Your dad told me."

I jerked back. "You were at my house?"

"Yeah. I thought we made plans to work on the picture book. Apparently you decided it was more important to stand me up so you could help kids. You can be such an ass sometimes." He winked.

"But you weren't talking to me after what happened yesterday. I didn't think you wanted to work together anymore."

He leaned across the gate and folded his arms over the metal bar. The amusement left his eyes. "Look, I'm sorry I was an asshole. You frustrate the hell out of me, Regan Flay. I just can't figure you out."

"Me?" I laughed sharply. "What about you? You're in my face one minute and then you're…" *Grabbing my shoulders and pulling me against you.* My throat tightened, and I pushed the image from my mind. "You gave me your jacket."

His eyes hardened. "I guess neither one of us is who the other expected."

I licked my lips, suddenly unable to speak. It was no wonder, with how intently he was staring at me.

His fingers dangled from the gate, long and lean. For

a brief moment, I could feel them on my arms, tightening while drawing me in. I inhaled sharply and looked away.

"How did it go after school?" he asked. "In the locker room? You're still here, so I'm assuming Amber didn't get the drop on you?"

"No."

"Did you get ammunition for your revenge scheme?"

I dug a hole in the sand with the toe of my boot. "Yes and no."

His brow furrowed. "What does that mean?"

I stopped digging and shrugged. "I caught her on film making an admission—something that would get her kicked out of school. She doesn't know about the video—no one does—and it will stay that way as long as Amber stops harassing me."

"What?" Nolan pulled back from the gate. "You're not going to upload it to YouTube or something?"

I kicked up a cloud of sand. "If I post the video, someone else could get hurt in the process."

"I'm really impressed, Flay. Way to be the bigger man."

Warmth spread through my stomach, and I made a point to keep my eyes locked on the tops of my boots. "Whatever. Can you please not make a big deal about it? Besides, it's not like I'm a saint. I'm not going to delete the video or anything stupid. I'm keeping it for insurance. I was going to upload it onto my computer last night, but I don't have the right size cord. I was hoping you'd upload it and send me a copy? First, you'd have to promise me to not share the video with anyone." I knew it was a big decision to trust Nolan with the video that could ruin Amber's and Christy's lives, but I also knew he'd been nothing but honest with me from the start. While it was startling for me to admit, I trusted him.

"Scout's honor." He held up three fingers. "Does this mean your grand schemes for revenge and social climbing are over?"

I didn't answer him right away, because I didn't know how to. It was high school, after all. It was only a matter of time before someone else did something equally awful, and while the wrath of the school fell on them, I could fade into the backdrop. Without the spotlight of popularity, I would become just another faded graffiti name on the bathroom stall—forgotten. But was that what I wanted? To be remembered as the girl who said horrible things about people and then disappeared?

No.

Before I could say as much, a woman's voice called out.

"Tamara?" Behind Nolan, Tamara's mother approached the gate. Exhaustion hung in dark circles around her eyes, and ketchup and mustard stains decorated the Steak 'n Shake apron still tied around her waist. "You need to come right now. I only have an hour to get you to Gi-Gi's before my shift at Home Depot."

"Aw!" The brush fell from Tamara's fingers onto the sand. "But I don't want to go to Gi-Gi's. Her house is so boring. She doesn't even have a TV." She wound her small fingers into Rookie's mane. "I want to stay at the barn with Rookie."

"Tamara, please!" He mom sighed, her shoulders slumping. "I don't have time for this. Say good-bye to the horse and let's go. I have to work."

Tamara held fast to Rookie's hair, her eyes welling with unshed tears. "But you always have to work."

Even though our lives were different, I knew what it was like to have a mother working all the time. My heart bled for both the woman and child, and I racked my brain for a way to help. "I'll tell you what, Tamara, if you go with your mom right now, I'll give you a two-hour lesson next week."

Her mom shot me a grateful look.

Tamara's mouth twitched. "Why can't you let me ride for another hour now?"

"Because your mom needs to get to work."

The gate squealed as Nolan opened it and entered the ring. "You can't have another lesson right now because Regan promised *me* a lesson, and it wouldn't be fair for you to cut into my time."

"Wait, what?" I asked.

Tamara folded her arms. "The riding program is for kids."

"One could argue I'm very childlike," he replied.

"Kids who have problems," she added.

"I have problems," he said.

She made a face. "Like what?"

"Girls are really mean to me."

Tamara cracked a grin. "Where's your helmet?"

"Uh." Nolan looked around the barn and pointed to a pink helmet hanging on the wall. "Right there!" He strode over to it and fastened it to his head. "I'm all set. How do I look?"

Tamara giggled.

"That boy really does have problems," Mrs. Wells said, laughing.

I'd known Mrs. Wells for several years, and in all that time, I'd never seen her crack a smile, let alone laugh.

"Okay, so we're all agreed I look fabulous," Nolan said. "What next?"

Tamara let go of Rookie's mane and pointed to the saddle. "You have to get on the horse."

"Right, the horse." Nolan rubbed his hands together and started toward Rookie, the pink helmet bobbing on his head.

I brought my hand to my mouth to muffle a giggle. "You don't have to do this, you know."

He paused. "It's my first lesson and you're already giving up on me? What kind of teacher are you?"

The kind that's about to laugh her ass off in five seconds, I thought. I waved him forward. "You're right. Please mount the horse."

Mrs. Wells, who'd been so eager to leave only moments ago, leaned against the gate. "That boy's going to hurt himself."

"We could only get so lucky," I said.

She laughed in response.

"Okay." Nolan grabbed the front of the saddle while Rookie continued to search the ground for hay. "Here goes nothing." He grabbed the front and back of the saddle and pushed himself up only to slide off the leather and land on his butt in the sand on the other side.

Rookie jerked his head up and snorted while Tamara, Mrs. Wells, and I burst out laughing.

"It looks a lot easier in the movies," Nolan muttered, picking himself up and dusting off the back of his jeans. "Should I try it again?"

"No," I answered when I could finally breathe. "I think that's enough of a lesson for one day. We'll work on actually getting on the horse next time."

As if in response, Rookie flicked his ears back and wandered to the far end of the arena, dragging the lead rope beside him.

"Hey." Nolan pointed after Rookie. "The horse is leaving. That's a bad sign, right?"

"It's not a good one."

Tamara shook her head. "You're really, really bad at this."

Mrs. Wells chuckled. "Lord, I haven't laughed like this in years. C'mon, Tamara. I'm going to be late, but boy was it worth it." Meeting my eyes, she lowered her voice and added, "He's a good one." Her eyes flickered to Nolan. "There aren't many of them left. Remember that."

Stunned, my cheeks flushed fire-hot.

Tamara paused just outside the gate. "Will you be here next week?" she asked Nolan.

"I'm not sure." Nolan turned to me with his eyebrows raised. I pretended not to notice as I quickly looked away.

"I hope so," the little girl said.

"Me, too," he replied.

Smiling, Tamara took her mother's hand, and they left through the sliding barn door.

Once Nolan and I were alone, my heart sped up.

He closed the distance between us, stopping so close that I had to look way, way up to meet his eyes. He still wore the helmet, and I had to admit, pink was a good look for him. The color made his hazel eyes practically glow gold. The effect was dizzying, and it wasn't until he chuckled that I realized I'd been staring.

"You look ridiculous," I said in an attempt to save myself.

He grinned as he unfastened the helmet. "Yeah, well, I'll do almost anything to make a girl smile." Once he removed it from his head, he shook his hair until it fell across his face in a mass of waves that he had to shove back.

He handed me the helmet, and our fingers touched. A spark of electricity jumped from where his skin met mine and I jerked, startled.

If Nolan noticed, he didn't say anything. Instead, he moved closer, making my pulse thunder even harder. Despite the smell of dirt and hay, his pine-needle-and-orange scent wrapped around me, warm and earthy, filling my lungs like a balloon until I was ready to fall over from the rush of it.

"Uh…" I licked my lips, desperate to fill the space between us even if just with words. "Weren't we talking about something?"

"Revenge," he answered.

"Right. I don't want revenge." I tried to focus on the

bales of hay, the pigeons perched in the rafters, *anything* but the twin hazel pools of his eyes that I was dangerously close to falling into. And it wasn't just his eyes that held me captivated. I couldn't stop thinking about the way he'd made a fool of himself to help Mrs. Wells and to make Tamara laugh. Maybe Mrs. Wells was right. Maybe Nolan *was* one of the good ones.

"Okay. If you don't want revenge, what do you want?"

"I have no idea," I answered, and it was the truest thing I'd ever said. "Originally my plan was to lie low until things died down, but that wasn't solving anything. I did some shitty things. I can't ignore that anymore."

He nodded, his face giving no indication as to how he felt about what I'd said. "What are you going to do?"

I had no clue—not about school, not about salvaging my reputation, and especially not about these fucked-up feelings I had for Nolan. I tried to focus on the least confusing parts of the situation. If my mom were me, she'd post the bathroom video with no hesitation. She claimed to advocate family values, but I'd watched her destroy families to get what she wanted. I'd tried doing things her way, but I simply couldn't be that girl anymore. At the same time, I had no idea how to be anyone else.

"Don't you think it's sad some people are only remembered by the graffiti about them on bathroom stalls?" I asked.

Nolan quirked his eyebrow. "You want to get rid of the bathroom graffiti?"

"Not the graffiti, but the legacies they created."

His brow furrowed. Before he could ask another question, I waved a hand in the air. "Sorry, I'm getting really off topic. Once I get Rookie put away, you and I can work on the picture book."

"So let's forget the picture book," Nolan said. "We can work on this new idea of yours."

I made a face. "I don't have an idea; I was just thinking out loud. Besides, we *have* to get the picture book done—it's due on Monday."

Nolan smirked. "Just because you blew me off doesn't mean I didn't get anything done."

"What are you talking about?"

Without another word, he grabbed his messenger bag off a post and withdrew a manila folder stuffed with papers. He handed it to me. "I was playing with a new illustration software program and, well, try not to be too intimidated by my genius."

I rolled my eyes and prepared to make a snarky comeback. But as soon as I opened the folder, all thoughts of insults disappeared from my mind. "Nolan...oh my God."

He grinned and jammed his hands into the back pockets of his jeans. "Genius, right?"

I laughed out loud as I flipped through the computer-illustrated drawings of the most adorable bunny I'd ever seen. Nolan had drawn Carrot as a round, fat yellow fluff ball with tall pointy ears and a pink triangle for a nose. I wanted to pull him from the page and squish him against me like the real Carrot in my bedroom. "He's perfect."

With his hands still in his pockets, he shrugged. "Perfection's what I do."

Smiling, I rolled my eyes. "Cocky much? I'm glad you didn't wait for me to help. I probably would have ruined it."

"Doubtful. The only reason I didn't wait for you was because I wasn't sure you would want to work with me." His eyes darted away. "Not after yesterday, anyway."

I flipped to a page of Carrot handing a ball back to the teary-eyed puppy he'd taken it from. I traced my finger over the words "I'm sorry" written below. On the next page, the puppy and bunny were hugging.

"If only it were that easy," I muttered.

"Why does it have to be hard?"

I thought about all the awful things I'd said in my messages and the way people had looked at me afterward. "It's like bathroom graffiti." I handed the stack back to him. "Some things can't be wiped clean."

He tucked the folder inside his bag. "I think you're underestimating people, Regan. You do that a lot."

I folded my arms. "I don't—"

"You'd be surprised how forgiving people can be when you're sincere. They care. Julie Sims cared when you apologized to her in the hallway. I saw it on her face. That's what I don't understand about you. You're so smart, and yet you can't seem to figure it out."

I frowned. "Figure what out?"

He leaned forward until his face was so close to mine, all I would have to do was lift up on my toes and our lips would touch. My stomach quivered at the thought, and yet, I forced myself to not look away.

"I think you're onto something really amazing with this graffiti idea," he whispered.

"I don't have an idea," I whispered back.

"You do." He smiled. "And it's amazing. But the only way you're going to convince other people is to prove they can trust you. You're going to have to show them the *real* Regan, not the girl you pretend to be."

I still had no clue what idea he was talking about. But my tongue was so thick, I couldn't form the questions to ask him. He was so close that his breath left a trail of shivers along my skin.

"Do you know what you have to do?"

I shook my head dumbly.

"Apologize."

I blinked. He still wasn't making sense. "To the people I talked about in the messages?"

"No." He straightened, and suddenly I could think again, breathe again. "To everyone. You know the hurt you've caused didn't start or stop with the people you insulted in those messages."

Shame burned up my neck, into my cheeks, and all the way to the tips of my ears. I glanced over my shoulder, pretending to check on Rookie, but the real reason I turned away was because I could no longer look at him without guilt pinching my insides. "You think I should go up to everyone in the hallways and say I'm sorry?" I gave a little snort. "Not only is that ridiculous, it would take forever."

"Of course it would, if you did it that way." Nolan reached into his bag and held out his camera. "Instead, how about this?"

I eyed him skeptically. "I'm really not following anything you're saying."

"You record an apology," he said. "Open yourself up. Think about it." He turned on the camera.

Reflexively, I took a step back.

"If you willingly expose yourself," Nolan said, aiming the lens at my face, "if you come clean, nobody—including Amber—can hurt you. Plus, you have the chance to make a real difference here—not just for you, but for everyone."

I still wasn't following. How could one little apology change anything? Baring my soul to my classmates was enough to make me want to hurl. Still, wasn't this the kind of positive press I was looking for? Besides, owning my mistakes and apologizing was something my mother would *never* do. That alone made me want to try.

"So, what." I walked up to his camera and placed my hand over the lens. "You want me to do this now? At the barn when I'm covered in dirt and sweat?" I gestured to my tangled ponytail and mud-covered boots.

Nolan chuckled and turned off the camera. "Your appearance doesn't matter, even though I think you look great, by the way."

Heat washed through my body, and I attempted to tuck the loose strands of hair behind my ears.

"I do think we could stage it a little better," he continued. "Why don't you come over to my house tonight around seven. I should have everything set up in my room, and we can get to work."

"Your house?" My voice came out a pitch too high. It wasn't like I hadn't been to his house a million times before to visit Payton, but I'd never once been inside Nolan's room—I'd never been inside *any* boy's room, especially not alone.

"Well, yeah," he answered. "Unless you've got a green screen at your place."

I shook my head.

He grinned. "Then I guess it'll have to be my place. Seven. I'll see you then."

Despite the panic flooding my veins, I managed to squeak out, "Okay. Seven."

His grin widened. He winked at me before opening the gate and leaving the arena. He paused in the barn long enough to pat the nose of a curious horse as he moved past.

After he'd gone, it took me another couple minutes before I could move. *What did I just agree to?*

"Regan." Mary, the barn owner, approached the gate with a horse in tow.

"Yeah?" My voice was breathless.

"I was thinking about a trail ride. You in?"

It had only been a couple of days since I'd fantasized about opening the gates, hopping on Rookie's back, and riding off to wherever he took me. But now, things were different—Nolan had a plan, and though I didn't quite understand it, I trusted him.

"Thanks for asking, but I think I'm done for the day," I told her.

For once, I was pretty sure I knew exactly where I was supposed to be.

CHAPTER FOURTEEN

Nolan's room wasn't anything like I'd expected. True, I'd never been inside a boy's room before, but the ones I saw on television were piled with dirty laundry and decorated with posters of half-naked women.

If it weren't for the full-size bed tucked into a corner, I wouldn't have guessed it to be a bedroom at all. A large desk sat against another wall. On top of it, two computer monitors showed various video clips. A third monitor displayed video-editing software. The camera Nolan had brought to the barn sat on top of a tripod in the middle of the room, its lens facing a green sheet draped from the ceiling. A single stool had been placed in front of it.

I hesitated in the doorway. I knew exactly who that stool was for. I could almost hear it whispering my name, daring me to rip open my chest and reveal the soul beneath. I rubbed my suddenly sweating palms on my jeans. Suddenly, I wished Payton were here. When her dad answered the door and said she was out, I was disappointed. I still didn't know exactly where we stood. It bothered me.

"You look nervous."

I spun around to find Nolan at the door behind me, blocking my path. Even though he wore the same outfit he'd had on earlier at the barn, it was still so strange to see him in clothes other than our school uniform. I couldn't help but stare at how his gray T-shirt showed off the muscles of his chest. His hair looked different—instead of loose across his forehead it was brushed and tucked behind his ears. If I didn't know better, I'd think he tried to style it for me.

I wanted to mess it up with my fingers. The thought was enough to tighten my insides.

"I've changed my mind. I can't do this."

"Of course you can do this." He gripped my arms and squeezed. As I'd come to expect, his touch eased the tendrils of anxiety winding through my body. "I have faith in you."

At least one of us did. With him blocking my escape, I had no choice but to back into his room.

After shutting the door behind him, he moved past me to the computer. He leaned over the desk, grabbed the mouse, and began opening several windows on one of the monitors. "Can I get you anything? Something to drink?" he asked without looking up.

"That's okay." I doubted anything could loosen the knot of fear forming in my gut, not even Nolan himself. And with my stomach already queasy, I didn't want to risk upsetting it further.

He continued clicking windows and opening and closing screens. With Nolan distracted, I decided to check out his room. His walls were painted silvery gray, and his bed was made with a plain black comforter. While there were no posters of athletes, above his headboard were framed posters of documentaries I'd never heard of — each decorated with award banners for winning one film festival or another.

"You sure like documentaries." I turned away from a film poster about a man who'd lived with wild horses for a year. Other than the videos shown in school, I couldn't think of a single documentary I'd watched.

"Oh, yeah," he answered, still clicking away. "Did you know that before they were called documentaries, they were called 'life caught unaware'? I love that. So much so I was going to call my own documentary *Life Unaware*. There's nothing like a well-made, compelling film about life. They're so much better than movies, because they're *real*. That's what makes them so great. Feature films try, and they come really close, but you can't fabricate *real*."

I'd never thought about it like that. I set my backpack on his bed, careful to keep plenty of distance between the stool and myself. Anxiety buzzed inside me, like a jar of angry hornets, at the thought of baring my soul to the entire student body. *Relax, Regan,* I told myself. *This is the plan you've been looking for — the one that's finally going to repair the damage you've done. And really, it's no different from the apologies countless PR firms organized for celebrities and politicians who slipped up. Right?*

I swallowed hard. It wasn't that I doubted the plan—or even Nolan—but every second that had passed since he left me alone at the stables, I lost more faith in *myself*. Could I hold it together long enough to pull this off, or would I walk away leaving Nolan the most incriminating thing of all—me having a massive mental breakdown on camera? The thought had sent me scrambling for my pill bottle more times than I cared to admit.

The bottom line was, for all my fear, I *needed* to do this. I was sick of hiding from my problems—sick of hiding from life. After spending time alone in the graffiti-covered bathroom stall, I realized some scars never healed with time. This was no longer about hiding or regaining popularity— this was about fixing the damage I'd done. Even if I had to ball my hands into fists to keep from reaching for my pills, I'd do the video. Maybe that's where the real me had been all along—buried at the bottom of a pill bottle.

He glanced at me over his shoulder as I approached and smiled.

Something pulsed inside me, but I did my best to ignore it. "How's *your* documentary going?" I asked.

"Yeah…" His smile disappeared, and he turned his attention back to the monitors. "I thought I had this great idea to film a documentary about life in an American high school, but…" He shrugged. "It didn't work."

"Why not?"

He licked his lips. "Sometimes things can get *too* real."

"Is that why you were filming me in the halls?"

"Yeah...my attempt to capture unfiltered high school footage didn't go as planned." He rubbed the back of his neck. "My friend Blake was helping me. I don't know if you knew this or not, but she gets bullied a lot."

Actually, I knew that firsthand, because Amber did most of the bullying. She'd constantly teased Blake and Nolan's ex-girlfriend, Jordan, calling them both dykes. Now that I knew Amber's secret, it didn't make a lot of sense—unless she was bullying them to draw attention away from herself.

"Anyway," he continued, "Blake and I came up with the idea together. The focus of the film was popularity in high school. I was trying to capture both sides of the hierarchy and, like I said, it didn't work. I'm much more excited about our project."

"*Our* project?" I asked.

"Yeah." He looked at me. "That is, of course, if you're okay with me filming it. It would make an amazing documentary. We could call it *The Graffiti Project*, *The Bathroom Stall Experiment*, or whatever you want. But if the project is going to work, we have to make you credible again. That's why we're doing this." He pointed to the monitor.

I snorted. "But I still don't understand what bathroom stalls have to do with apologizing."

He grinned. "You'll see. You're going to love it." He returned to the computer and opened another program with various graphs and dials.

It didn't take long before my eyes glazed over and I was forced to look away. That's when I noticed the picture frames on either side of the monitors. In one, Nolan looked barely thirteen. His hair hung to his ears and his limbs were all joints and angles. He stood in the middle of a row of boys, each of them with a skateboard underfoot. In another photo, he had Payton in a headlock. His fist was pressed to her head while she shrieked in obvious delight. "Where's Payton tonight?" I asked

"Shopping with Mom. I think they're picking out her dress for the dance." He rolled his eyes. "As if she doesn't already have a closet full of dresses."

The Snowflake Ball. I'd completely forgotten the dance was only a couple of weeks away. Fat chance of me going now. I turned my attention to the last picture frame, a photo of Nolan and his ex-girlfriend, Jordan. They were dressed in all black, her hair dyed a pretty shade of blue. Nolan had his arms wrapped around her shoulders and his lips pressed to her cheek. Her mouth was open, frozen forever in the middle of a laugh.

I couldn't think of a single time I'd seen her laughing or even smiling at school. I'd always assumed she was just another moody emo chick. But now that I'd suffered Amber's abuse firsthand, I understood her so much better.

I turned from the photo to find Nolan watching me with a strange expression.

"What happened between the two of you?" I pointed to Jordan. "You look so happy there."

"That's the funny thing about pictures." He reached past me and set the frame facedown on the desk. "They only show what's on the surface."

I understood. The walls of my own home were decorated

with dozens of photos of my parents and me smiling and looking like the perfect family. But in real life, I couldn't remember the last time we'd smiled at each other when there wasn't a camera around to capture it. "So you weren't happy."

He returned his attention back to the computer. A muscle in his jaw flexed, like he was pressing his teeth together. "*She* wasn't happy. I tried so hard to hold everything together — to keep *her* from falling apart." He swallowed hard. "I might as well have tried to bottle the entire ocean inside a jar."

Before I could ask him what he meant, he pointed to the monitor. "With the green screen, you can choose from a bunch of different backgrounds." He clicked the mouse, punctuating the end of our previous conversation.

Several images appeared on the center monitor. One looked like the inside of my grandpa's study. A large mahogany bookshelf stacked with leather-bound books sat next to a brick fireplace. Another image looked like a school hallway. Two rows of silver lockers lined either side of a glossy tiled floor. A third was a picture of football stadium bleachers. Nolan pointed to the lockers. "I'm leaning toward this one, but if you have something else in mind —"

"How about a guillotine?" I offered. "Or a firing-squad block? Because I kinda feel like I'm going to be executed."

He laughed and shook his head. "Like I said, I like the lockers." He clicked the mouse, and an image of the lockers enlarged, taking up the entire screen. He clicked again, and the stool behind me appeared in front of them as if by magic.

"That's amazing," I said.

"Movie magic." He winked before leaving the computer and walking over to the camera on the tripod. He adjusted the angle until the stool was centered between the rows of lockers. When he finished, he patted the seat. "It's all yours."

My stomach churned. Biting my lip, I hugged my arms around my chest. Maybe this wasn't such a good idea after all. Wasn't I just opening myself up to more humiliation and ridicule?

Nolan's eyes softened. "Are you okay, Flay? I know I kind of rushed you into this. You don't have to do it if you don't want to."

Of course I *wanted* to, but wanting and doing felt like planets in different solar systems with an abyss of black space between them. I bit my lip. What was it Dad was always saying? Something about a thousand-mile journey having to begin with a single step? I was ready for that step. Even if Amber left me alone and Payton and I patched our friendship, even if the school gradually forgot what I'd done, I never would. I swallowed hard, and then sat. "I have to do this."

Nolan hit a wall switch off and his room went dark, except for the soft glow of light from the computer monitors. With his foot, he flipped a switch on a power strip. Instantly, I was nearly blinded as two bright lights on either side of the camera turned on. I squinted for several seconds until my eyes adjusted to the light and the spots left my vision.

"Sorry." Nolan adjusted the light stands, lowering them so they no longer shone in my face. "You're shorter than I am."

Feeling awkward and unsure what to do with my hands, I laced them together on my lap. "You filmed yourself?"

Even though I couldn't make out his features in the dark, I could see the black outline of his body behind the camera. He shrugged a shoulder and returned to the camera, adjusting the angle for the hundredth time. "For the old documentary—the one I scrapped."

"Because it wasn't working."

"Exactly."

Again, I wanted to ask why it wasn't working, especially now that I knew it was about popularity, but I didn't get the chance. He hit a button and a red light above the camera lens blinked on. I inhaled sharply.

Nolan chuckled. "Relax, Flay. Pretend the camera isn't here."

Easier said than done. The red light felt like a laser burning into my flesh, and I fidgeted. "What do I do now?"

He grabbed another stool from the corner of the room and perched on the edge with one foot on the boot rung and his knees splayed wide. "Pretend it's just you and me."

That wasn't any better, but I wasn't going to tell him that. Nervous energy pulsed through my body. I pulled my hands inside my sleeves and twisted the fabric around them. "I don't know how to start."

Nolan leaned forward just enough to illuminate the edge of his face. "How about this—I'll ask you some questions and you answer them. You just have to repeat the question in your answer so I can edit myself out later, okay?"

I nodded. My pulse beat heavily against my chest.

"Okay."

He clasped his hands together. "Tell me about the day you walked into school and found your private messages posted on the lockers."

I gave a small laugh, not because I found the subject funny, but because if I didn't laugh I might cry instead—something I definitely didn't want to do on camera. My throat tightened, and I reflexively touched the pill case in my pocket. I liked knowing they were there, even if I was trying my damnedest not to take any. It would probably make Nolan's video a lot more interesting if I dropped dead on camera anyway. The thought made me giggle.

"You're nervous," Nolan said.

"That obvious?" I tapped my fingers against the pill case. If I popped a pill now, I might be able to prevent a panic attack before it could start.

"What do you have in your pocket?" he asked.

My fingers froze, my throat tight. For a moment, I considered lying. I could tell him there was nothing but a tube of lip gloss. When I went over my apology earlier in the afternoon in front of a mirror, never once did I consider mentioning my anxiety disorder or my pills. And yet I found myself withdrawing the small silver case from my pocket and opening it for the camera. "This is my Xanax." The trembling of my hands caused the pink pills to rattle together. "They help pull me back from the edge when I start to fall."

"What do you mean?"

I closed the pill case with a *snap* and slid it back inside my pocket. "I have an anxiety disorder." After spending the last couple years working to keep my secret from everyone, spilling it to Nolan and his camera felt like inhaling after an eternity of holding my breath. I hadn't realized how exhausting it was holding it in until the words left my mouth and ribbons of pressure unwound from my ribs. "When I was a freshman, I was up late one night studying for finals when my chest started to hurt really badly. My arms tingled and I couldn't breathe. I almost passed out. I thought I was having a heart attack, so my dad drove me to the emergency room. Turns out it wasn't a heart attack but a panic attack."

I spoke faster, scared I might chicken out and swallow the words spilling off my tongue. In this moment, it didn't matter if Nolan thought I was fucked up for needing drugs just to function. What I was doing, the on-camera purge of truth woven with regret, felt right in a way nothing in my life ever had before. Like maybe if I laid myself bare, I could rid myself of the secrets and regrets buried like botflies deep within my flesh.

"High school was a little more than I expected. Everyone thinks I have this perfect life. They don't know that I'm barely holding it together—actually, I'm *not* holding it together. That's the problem. And then there's my mom—the congresswoman." I tried to make out my shoes in the darkness so I didn't have to look at the camera. "She's mapped out my entire life, set this standard that's impossible to live up to."

Even though I couldn't see Nolan, I could hear his steady breathing in the silence following my words. Finally he asked, "What kind of standard?"

"Perfection," I whispered. A small voice inside my head, the old Regan, screamed at me to shut up, that I'd said too much. *You made yourself look weak,* the voice hissed. Maybe. But I'd opened myself too wide to pull back now, displayed all of my many scars. And who decides where to draw the line between vulnerability and strength? Because in this moment, I couldn't decipher a difference. I'd come here tonight to apologize to the many people I'd wronged, but it took me until this moment to realize that maybe the biggest wrong I'd committed was to myself.

I fingered the tin of pills again and shrugged. "I have to be perfect. So *fucking* perfect all the time. Not just at home but at school, at church, at the fucking *grocery store* because everyone's watching. Like the entire world is just waiting for me to screw up. And I've been holding my breath for years because I knew it was only a matter of time before the day came when I slipped up and everything fell apart."

I stared into the camera lens. The darkness within seemed to grow larger, like a black mouth gaping wide to devour me whole. I felt my strength draining. I gripped the sides of my stool, trying to root myself to the chair when all I wanted to do was sink to the floor. *Just make it thirty more seconds,* I told myself. *Thirty more seconds and you can take a pill.*

I wouldn't die in the next thirty seconds, no matter how much the silence of the room made my skin itch and the sound of Nolan's breathing made me squirm. I opened my mouth and spoke, just to fill the emptiness. "Some days I think the only thing holding me together are these pills."

life unaware

I shook the tin and laughed a little. "It's so pathetic. Even more pathetic than the pills, though, are the horrible things I said about other people—the awful things I did. I'm not trying to make excuses because there are none. I just wanted to say I'm sorry for everything—just *everything*. High school is hard enough without other people making it worse, and I'm really sorry I was one of those people."

Exhaustion crept over me, and my shoulders sagged under its weight. *Almost done.* "I don't expect to be forgiven for the things I've done. I just wanted everyone to know. I don't want to be the person I was. I want to be me—whoever the hell that is." I shrugged. "Guess I'll find out."

I paused and searched for Nolan's dark outline beside the camera. "I don't know what else to say."

The camera's red light blinked off. A second later the lights on either side of it went dark. It took my eyes several seconds to adjust to the darkness. When they finally focused, Nolan stood in front of me.

I nearly fell off the stool. "Jesus."

He didn't apologize for scaring me. In fact, he didn't say anything at all. He just stared at me with a peculiar look on his face.

"Oh God." I shrank against the stool. "Was I really that bad?"

"No." Before I realized what was happening, he slid his hands along my cheeks. The tips of his fingers brushed past my ears and wound into my hair. "I had no idea you were going through all that. God, I'm such an asshole."

Unsure what was happening, I couldn't think, couldn't

breathe.

Nolan dropped to his knees. His eyes practically glowed in the dim light of his computer screens. A stray lock of hair had fallen across his forehead, a reminder of how uncontained everything about Nolan was. He was so close I could feel his breath tickling my lips. Every breath I took felt like I was breathing in a piece of him. My eyes drifted closed and my body turned to mush, his scent overwhelming my senses.

"Regan, I have no idea what to do here." His voice was lower than usual, husky even. "I only know what I want to do."

He wasn't making sense. "What's that?"

"I'm going to kiss you."

"What?" My eyes fluttered wide and I nearly choked on my heart, which felt like it'd leaped halfway up my throat. "Why?"

I cringed the second the question left my mouth. Asking a guy why he wanted to kiss you wasn't exactly encouraging him to do it. And it wasn't like I *didn't* want him to kiss me, did I? I mean, obviously I'd developed some feelings for him over the last couple of days. I couldn't deny the way my heart had trembled when he showed up at the barn that morning, or the way heat flooded my veins whenever he was near, or —

"Crazy, right?" Nolan laughed softly. For reasons I didn't understand, the sound of it held notes of sadness. "I'm going to kiss you because you're amazing, you're beautiful, and because I *want* to."

He leaned closer, and I got so dizzy, I knew I'd have fallen off the stool if not for his hands keeping me centered. He was less than an inch away when he paused and looked at me through heavy-lidded eyes. "Do you want me to kiss you?"

The heat from his palms seared into my skin. This was *Nolan*, the guy who'd annoyed me in the hallways for years. But he was also the guy who'd let me cling to him in the bathroom when I would have otherwise fallen to pieces. The guy who'd wrapped me up in his jacket because I couldn't stop shaking. Nolan, who, in a weird way, stuck by me when everyone else abandoned me. Still, I'd never kissed someone before. What if I did it wrong? What if it changed things between us?

"Regan?"

The breathless way he said my name made my own breath catch inside my throat. "Yeah?"

"In this moment we have everything going against us. Can we maybe just hit pause on all the outside world bullshit and not overthink this?" His fingers twisted deeper into my hair. "For just tonight, let's pretend that we have no past history—good or bad—and the only moment that's existed between the two of us is this one. With that in mind, give me the first answer that pops into your head and I'll be satisfied with the answer. Do you want to kiss me?"

Only one word came to my mind—the same word that had been there all along.

"Yes."

Chapter Fifteen

onsidering that everything about Nolan was lean and taut, the softness of his mouth caught me off guard. His lips brushed mine lightly before settling into a rhythm that made me feel like we were two puzzle pieces coming together. I leaned forward, and he pressed closer so my legs straddled his. His mouth explored every inch of mine, kissing both corners before tugging gently on my bottom lip.

His fingers curled into my hair, pulling ever so slightly. I gasped. The moment my mouth parted, Nolan deepened the kiss, and a warm wave of what could only be lust crashed through my body. The heat of it spread throughout my limbs, searing the tips of my fingers and toes. I reached up and grasped his shoulders to keep from melting away.

He pushed the kiss further, deeper, until I met him

halfway, drinking in the taste of him. Sweet and soft like sugar melting on my tongue. With Nolan's hands in my hair and his lips on mine, the world fell away until nothing else existed except him, me, and our kiss. I slid a hand down his neck to the hardness of his chest, just to confirm we were still separate people. Because with my eyes closed, with all the heat inside me and the fire burning through my veins, I was sure we'd somehow melted together. He groaned at the contact, skimming his hands along my sides until he reached the hem of my shirt. At the first touch of skin on skin, the last threads of anxiety in my system went up in flames.

I pulled away with a gasp. My cheeks felt like they'd been burned, but I wasn't sure if it was from the lingering effects of Nolan's kiss, panic that Nolan had gotten me mixed up with someone else, or fear that I'd done everything wrong. The mix of emotions twisted inside of me, rooting me to the stool and rendering me speechless.

Nolan pressed his forehead to mine. "That was… Wow. You okay?"

"I think so," I managed, but it was hard to stay calm about the whole thing with him touching me. Making me want to kiss him all over again, mistakes and doing it wrong be damned.

He cupped my cheek and frowned. "This week has been complete hell for you, hasn't it?"

"Pretty much." I attempted a small smile. "But there were some good parts."

"Yeah?"

He grinned, and my breath caught in my throat. I was

sure he was going to kiss me again, and my entire body quivered in anticipation.

But just as quickly as it appeared, his smile melted. Nolan leaned in and brushed his cheek against mine. The simple gesture, the feel of his hair and his smooth skin, broke something inside me. His lips were so close to my ear that I could feel them graze against my earlobe when he spoke. "I've been horrible to you, Regan. The things I've done—"

"Can't be any worse than what I've done to you," I interrupted.

He sighed. "I wouldn't be so sure of that."

"I thought we weren't bringing up the past tonight."

"Yeah," he responded, "but there are some things you need to know."

"No." I didn't want to throw more ugly words in the space between us. This moment felt too fragile, like threads of spun sugar so delicate the slightest touch could shatter everything. And the way he looked at me just now—like he could see through all the bullshit and find the me that actually mattered, the vulnerable parts I'd kept hidden for so long—I wanted to hold on to that for as long as I could. "I don't need to know anything. At least not tonight."

He opened his mouth, but whatever words he wanted to say stayed lodged inside his throat. After several moments, he finally said, "Stay with me, Regan. Please."

He sounded...vulnerable. Scared, even. The complete opposite of how I thought of him, but exactly how I felt unless he was around. I found myself nodding before I realized what I was doing.

His fingers trailed down my arms to my hands, where he grasped the end of my fingertips. One by one, his fingers slipped away as he walked to his bed and perched on the edge of his mattress. There was something dangerous about being alone on a bed with a boy. My pulse grew louder with each step toward him until it was a deafening roar inside my head. I managed to stand, shaky as my legs were, and cross the room, stopping in front of him. He glanced up at me and smiled, and it was unlike any smile I'd seen from him before.

How had I not noticed before now how gorgeous he was? The idea that someone like Nolan could have a secret smile just for me did strange things to my heart. I held out my hand, because in that moment, I desperately needed to close the distance between us. He pulled me beside him on the bed. After propping pillows against the headboard, he swung his legs onto the mattress, leaned back, and drew me against him so my head rested in the curve of his neck.

I was drowning in a sea of Nolan—his scent, his skin, his heat. My mind swam with the headiness of it all, every neuron pulsing with unfamiliar electricity. I placed my hand on his chest, and he shuddered beneath my touch.

"You're not who I thought you were," he whispered. A burst of pleasure washed over me, but it quickly fizzled out when he added, "I really like you," with a distinct note of regret.

I frowned. "I'm sorry that's such a problem for you."

Nolan ran his hand down my cheek. "It's not like that. It's just…" He sighed. "There are things you don't know about me—things you wouldn't like. Before…" His voice trailed off. But I didn't need him to go on to know what he was going to say. *Before* my messages had been posted on lockers, *before* we'd been paired up for the picture-book assignment, *before* he'd taken me in his arms in the bathroom stall, we'd both thought and said some pretty terrible things about each other.

"Don't." I laced my fingers with his. "I already told you we don't have to talk about this tonight. Things were different before."

"I know. I'm sorry for bringing it up again. It's just—" He shook his head, the top of his jaw tickling the hair at the top of my head. "I was so stupid."

"We were *both* stupid."

He swallowed. "You don't understand. What if I'd been too late? I was too late with Jordan."

I traced the faded writing on the front of his shirt. "I thought she moved. How was that your fault?"

He didn't answer right away. The more seconds that ticked by, the more I became convinced he wasn't going to. But then he sighed, and it was like his chest deflated beneath my head. "She *did* move, but it was more than that. I let her down. I wasn't there when she— *Fuck.*" He tipped his head back against the wooden headboard and stared at the ceiling.

"Nolan—"

"Things change," he said. "There's no way of knowing what the future will bring. I'll tell you what happened between Jordan and me. I promise you I will. But for tonight, can we pretend I never said anything? That the world outside this room doesn't exist?"

My protest melted on my tongue. How could I argue with that? "Okay. We won't talk about it tonight." Whatever his secrets were, they would still be there tomorrow.

His body gradually relaxed beneath me.

"Not tonight," he repeated. He lifted a lock of my hair and twirled it around his finger. The moonlight streaming through his window created a soft glow over our bodies. His room was heavy and silent, and it was almost as if Nolan and I were the only two people in the world.

Almost.

I couldn't get his words to stop running through my head. *What if I'd been too late?* The question pinged back and forth in my mind until my temples throbbed.

Too late for what?

CHAPTER SIXTEEN

Sunday came and went without so much as a text from Nolan. As much as I didn't want it to, it bothered me. It wasn't like I was his girlfriend or anything. Hell, we'd never even gone on a date. I'd just assumed Nolan was the kind of guy who'd call a girl after she spilled her darkest secrets and spent several hours tucked in the crook of his arm—even after he'd fallen asleep. I guess I was wrong.

The worst part was that I had *liked* watching him sleep—studying the rise and fall of his chest while listening to the soft thump of his heart beneath my ear. I now knew his eyelashes trembled when he dreamed and that the corners of his lips pinched into a frown. He murmured, too. Soft, unintelligible words. Part of me was looking forward to teasing him about it, but a bigger part of me was ashamed

I'd stolen moments I wasn't supposed to have.

Apparently I was right.

After showering to make sure every last trace of pine needles and oranges was scrubbed from my skin, I checked Facebook, scrolling through status updates and checking to see if anyone had posted something nasty about me in the group. There were a few new likes (apparently I only *kind of* needed to commit suicide now—how refreshing), but no new comments. The status updates were pretty quiet, too. I mean, there were the regular posts about parties, a handful of selfies, and even a couple updates from Taylor about her and Amber going to the lake with Jeremy and his friends. I rolled my eyes when I saw a picture that made it look like Amber *loved* hanging out with Taylor.

Poor Taylor. She'd never see it coming when Amber decided she was done with her. I could only hope Jeremy kept his disgusting hands to himself. I liked the photo to let Amber know I was watching. No harm in that. Especially since before leaving Nolan's house I'd left the small video camera on his desk with a note to please send me the video I'd taken.

Eventually, I forced myself to look up Nolan. He'd posted another link to a documentary, this one about some uprising in a town down south that happened before we were born, but that was it. I tapped the side of my phone, debating whether to like the post. On the one hand, I liked that he posted serious things. On the other, he was ignoring me. After Saturday, liking the post would be petty, but come on. He'd had time to watch videos and post links but not call me?

I hit like.

On Monday, I was in the school parking lot, locking my car door, when a shadow fell over my shoulder. I froze with my thumb on the key chain.

"Hey," Nolan said.

My muscles coiled, and I fought to keep my movements relaxed. The last thing I wanted was for Nolan to realize how much he'd gotten under my skin. I turned to face him, once again glad for my dark sunglasses. No way was I letting him see the hurt in my eyes. "Hey," I said, my voice flat.

"So…" He shifted his weight from foot to foot and tugged on his rumpled sleeves. I wasn't used to seeing Nolan uncomfortable, and, as much as I hated to admit it, it made him look absolutely adorable. "You, um, left without saying good-bye the other night." He scratched the back of his head and frowned.

I blinked. It never occurred to me I might have hurt *his* feelings by leaving the way I did. "I have an eleven-thirty curfew. You fell asleep, and I didn't want to wake you."

"You should have," he said. "I would have driven you home."

I quirked an eyebrow. "I drove to *your* house."

"So?" He folded his arms across his chest. "I could have followed you home in my car, or at least walked you outside or something, but you just *left*." Hurt flashed in his eyes, and he clenched his jaw.

Ouch. The disappointment in his voice was almost worse than seeing twenty pages of texts plastered all over the halls.

I cleared my throat and tried to calm the tremors starting in my hands. "I'm sorry. I would have woken you if I thought you were going to get upset." I cleared my throat again. "So, um…you really wanted to drive me home?" The hope in my voice was embarrassing, but there it was.

He sighed and grabbed my hands. "Look. Saturday was…heavy. I don't want things to get weird between us, and I'm not into head games, so I'm just going to say it. I like you."

Heat burned my cheeks. "I like you, too."

He smiled. "Good."

We stood there for a moment, Nolan holding my hands while neither of us said a word. I watched him lace his fingers with mine, pressing our palms together. Despite our admission, an awkwardness settled between us like a wedge. I didn't know if it was from the secrets I told him Saturday, the ones he still kept from me, or the fact that we'd blown each other off for no apparent reason. Whatever the reason, it felt like something thick and heavy pressed between us.

"Still weird, huh?" he asked.

I laughed. "Yeah, a little."

"Don't worry." He released my hands, his face serious. "I can fix that."

I eyed him skeptically. "How?"

"We're going to play a game." He guided me toward the school entrance. "Let's pretend we live in a world where we don't have to attend an institution filled with judgmental assholes. Let's pretend we can do whatever we want without any social repercussions, and every time we do, we get a point. Sound good?"

I looked up at him. "Uh…"

"Good. Glad you're on board. I'll go first." He sucked in a breath. "Right now, this very second, all I want is to be with you."

His words came at me so fast, I could barely catch on to them, let alone make sense of what he was saying. "Be with me?"

We climbed the stairs toward the school entrance. "I can understand your confusion," he said. "Basically what I'm saying is this: if you are going to be somewhere, I would like to occupy the same generalized area, preferably in close proximity. You know, as long as you're cool with it. I figured we could start with the school hallways and see where it goes from there."

I couldn't help but grin. "I'm very cool with it. Though I think I might have to add one addendum."

"Oh?" He quirked an eyebrow.

I stopped outside the glass front doors. "How about we draw the line at restrooms? Occupying the same stall and all that. It was cute the first time, but I think it would get old fast."

He laughed and opened the door for me before following me inside. "Duly noted: bathrooms are off-limits."

Unlike Friday, Amber and Taylor were nowhere to be seen. Christy must have held up her end of the deal. I'm sure my popping up in Amber's feed only reinforced the threat. Nolan placed his arm around my shoulders as we made our way to our lockers. The last of the knots in my stomach unwound for the first time in days. Maybe even weeks.

"So if we're keeping score," Nolan said, "right now you're losing zero to one. And it's about to get worse because there's something else I want."

I grabbed the straps of my backpack. "What?"

"This." He pivoted in front of me so suddenly I nearly tripped. Before I realized what was happening, his lips were on mine, soft, warm, and oh so much gentler than I wanted them to be.

I was only vaguely aware of the gasps and giggles echoing in the hallway. They'd seen people kissing in the hallways a million times before, but I could only imagine what kind of spectacle Nolan and I made, the freak artsy guy and the once-popular bitch hooking up between the science and computer labs. For once, I didn't care what other people thought.

Nolan pulled away, his cheeks red. "You're now down zero to two. If you want to catch up, you have to do something right here, right now, with pure abandon."

"What?" I made a face. "I kissed you back. That has to count for at least half a point."

He waved a hand. "Yeah, but it was *my* idea. That's cheating."

"Cheating, huh? How about when I do it like this?"

I grabbed him by the lapels of his blazer and hauled him into the slightly more private alcove between two banks of lockers. The second I pulled him against me, using his body to pin mine into the corner, his eyes went wide.

Then I *really* kissed him.

He groaned against my mouth. "Jesus, Regan. What are you doing to me?"

I smiled and bit his bottom lip.

"Never mind. Just don't stop."

He swallowed my laugh with a searing kiss that stole the breath from my lungs and the strength from my legs. If he wasn't careful, I'd need a Xanax to calm down when we were done—which I'd probably have to take while sitting in detention, since I was pretty sure where his hands were violated the school's code of conduct handbook.

"Hey, Nolan, I thought I'd stop by to see if you wanted to work— *What the actual fuck?*"

We broke apart on a gasp. Nolan's friend Blake stood not ten feet away, her eyes widened and her lips parted in horror. Her eyes zeroed in on Nolan like I wasn't standing there, still clinging to his chest. "Please tell me I didn't just see what I think I saw."

He turned to face her, carefully tucking me behind him. "I know what you're thinking," he said. "But you need to hear me out."

"For fuck's sake." She raked a hand through her short blond hair. "You know who she is, don't you? She's one of *them.* You know what they did to Jordan. Have you forgotten everything?"

I edged around him, my legs still weak, and looked at Nolan. "One of *them*?"

Students were slowing, drawn to Blake's raised voice. Just when things had started to die down, here I was giving everyone something new to use against me.

Nolan placed a hand at the small of my back. It was a small gesture, but enough to ease the anxiety that had begun building in my chest.

"Listen, Blake," he began. "I told you things changed. We talked about this. That's why we decided —"

"*You* decided." She jabbed a finger in the air. "Don't forget that. You never once asked for my opinion. God, I can't believe you'd betray Jordan like this."

Nolan tensed beside me. When he spoke, his voice was almost a growl. "I did everything I could for Jordan."

Blake's eyes hardened. "Apparently not enough."

His hands curled into fists that shook at his sides. "I think you should go now. Before either one of us says something we'll regret. I'll call you later when we've both had a chance to cool down."

She put her hand on her hip. "What's the problem, Nolan? Can't handle the ugly truth? I bet half the people here know what happened. Does *she*?" She scoffed. "God, I don't even know who the fuck you are anymore."

Without giving him a chance to respond, she stalked away.

"Fuck," he muttered. The muscles in his shoulders grew rigid, and he slowly turned to me. "I'm really sorry, but I need to talk to Blake. Can we catch up later?"

"Yeah, sure." Despite all the questions I had, I was glad to be dismissed. Blake's obvious hatred for me as well as the tension between her and Nolan was so thick, it made it hard to breathe.

He pressed a quick kiss to my lips, slung his bag over his shoulder, and ducked through the crowd after Blake.

My phone chirped. Payton.

Meet me at my locker?

I sucked in a shaky breath. It had been weird being at her house last night and not actually talking to her. When I sneaked out of Nolan's room, the last thing I wanted was to burst the happy haze I was floating in, so I didn't stop by her room. I had no idea if she'd be happy I'd hooked up with her brother or if she'd wake up the whole neighborhood screaming at me.

Guess I was about to find out.

Payton spotted me the second I turned the corner. She jogged toward me, her blond hair in a ponytail that fanned out like ribbons behind her. Judging by the big smile on her face, I guessed she didn't know about Nolan yet.

"Hey." I smiled and gave her a friendly bump with my shoulder. "Long time, no see."

"Yeah." She grinned and bumped me back. "So what's Blake's problem?"

I exhaled loudly. "So you saw that, huh?"

"Yeah." She shook her head. "Of all of Nolan's friends, I never liked Blake. She's always been so…bitter."

"Good word." I nodded. "She seems really hung up on his ex." I knew I should wait for him to tell me, but I couldn't help myself. "You wouldn't happen to know what happened between Nolan and Jordan, would you?"

"Not really." She shrugged apologetically. "He's always

been really weird about their breakup. Like, he'd get really pissed when I brought it up. I do know that before they broke up, Jordan's parents came over and talked to our parents. They kicked me out of the room, but not before I heard something about Jordan being in the hospital. So maybe she got sick?"

I bit my lip. "That doesn't make sense. Nolan's not the type of guy to break up with a girl because she's sick."

"Oh?" Payton arched an eyebrow. "So how is it you've come to know what kind of guy my brother is?"

"Um." I quickly dropped my gaze to the tops of my shoes before she could read the guilt in them.

To my surprise, she laughed. "I'm just messing with you. I already know you and my weirdo brother are into each other. I think it's disgusting, but I'm cool with it."

I stared at her. "You are?"

"Meh." She rolled her eyes. "He's actually been tolerable the last couple of days, so if his new attitude has anything to do with you, I'm all about it. That doesn't mean I don't find it a little gross. He's…weird. You used to agree with me."

I didn't say anything. I couldn't explain how, or even the exact moment, my feelings for him changed. All I knew was that when my world was crumbling underneath my feet, Nolan never wavered.

"Anyway." She waved a hand in the air. "Can we not talk about my brother anymore because, ew."

A group of girls gave us a dirty look as we passed. Their eyes bored into my skin and I reflexively hunched my shoulders. My fingers itched to fish my pill bottle out of my bag, but then I thought of Nolan and reminded myself that I was done hiding behind my pills. It was time to be the real me.

Still, I had no intention of subjecting Payton to my hell. "While I appreciate you being here for me, Pay, I'm not so sure talking to me is such a good idea," I said. "You know what people think of me. Being seen with me will not be good for your image."

"You know what? Fuck that." She smirked. "Last week when Amber told me you didn't like me, that was one of the worst moments of my life, and I'm so sorry I believed her. I think we've wasted enough time on this bullshit. For nearly ten years we've shared everything from clothes, makeup, to *secrets*. We can share this, too. *You're* my best friend, and yes, I know you've said some awful things, but I know that's not really who you are. Plus, I miss you. So fuck everyone and what they think." She shrugged.

Even though I knew she was being stupid, my heart swelled at her words. "I don't expect you to martyr yourself for me. We can hang out again after this whole thing dies down."

She looped her arm through mine. "Nope. You're stuck with me. Besides, according to my brother, this isn't going to die down any time soon. He hasn't shut up about this video you made and some bathroom stall project he wants to make a documentary of."

"He hasn't?" Even though I tried to fight it, a big, stupid grin pulled at my lips.

"Yeah." She nodded. "So *annoying*. Something about

how your project is going to revolutionize the school."

"Did he tell you *how* exactly?" I asked. "Because he keeps calling it *my* idea, and yet I have no idea what the project is about."

She laughed. "Typical Nolan. Nope. He didn't give me any details. Or if he did, I wasn't listening because it's, you know, Nolan."

We turned another corner, and that's when I saw her— Amber. She stood beside Jeremy, staring vacantly at the ceiling as Taylor yammered in her ear.

"Shit." Payton's arm tightened around mine. "Should we go another way?"

As much as I wanted to, I knew I couldn't spend another day running from my fear. "You can if you want," I told her. A jagged lump wedged inside my throat. "I won't be mad. But I have to keep going forward."

"Okay. Then I'll go with you."

I shot her a grateful smile, and together we continued down the hall. Taylor was the first to notice us. Her lips curled into a smile and she whispered something in Amber's ear. Amber snapped her head in our direction, her eyes locking with mine. Normally, this would be the moment an invisible band would tighten around my chest, rendering me unable to breathe. But not today. I wasn't sure if it was Payton's presence, the fact that I knew Amber's darkest secret, or that I simply didn't care what people thought anymore, but I stopped directly in front of her. "Hey, Amber."

Taylor's mouth dropped. "You think you can actually just *talk* to her now?"

Amber scowled at her. "Shut up, Taylor." She grabbed Jeremy's arm. "Let's go." Before he could respond, she dragged him down the hall with Taylor scrambling to keep up.

"Wow." Payton watched their retreat. "Is it just me, or was that *really* weird?"

Not so weird if she knew the secret I was keeping for her. "C'mon." I pulled Payton to my locker. I couldn't help but feel a pang of regret. I'd really wanted to talk to Amber—to let her know I understood what it felt like to pretend to be something I wasn't. Not that I thought she would listen, or believe me, for that matter. I didn't know why I cared in the first place—she was the one who'd tried to ruin my life, after all. Little did she know that by exposing me, she'd actually freed me.

I only hoped someday she would get to stop pretending and live her life how she wanted. Each time I forced myself into the mold of what my mother wanted me to be, I felt myself break. If Amber kept up her act forever, it would only be a matter of time before the broken pieces of her real self were too small to ever be put back together. I didn't know what happened to people once they were unfixable. I only hoped I never had to find out.

CHAPTER SEVENTEEN

I stepped inside the cafeteria. My stomach rolled in nauseous waves that had nothing to do with the smell of grease and processed cheese permeating the room. I grabbed Payton's arm. "I don't think I can do this."

"You'll be fine," she said. "Just straighten your back, keep your head up, and pretend you own this bitch."

I shook my head as acid burned up the back of my throat. The voices of nearly five hundred talking and laughing students blended into a buzz that reverberated through my body. "There are so many people—and they all hate me." My muscles tensed with the desire to flee from the room.

"They're more afraid of you than you are of them."

I made a face. "You're not helping."

"Wait. I was supposed to be helping?" Payton laughed. "Relax, Regan. You're not alone. Nolan said he'd meet us here and—look." She pointed to a table in the corner of the room where her brother stood waving. "Let's go."

She pulled me across the cafeteria. Tables of girls ducked their heads together and began whispering feverishly as we passed. I did my best to ignore the glares and murmurs. Several times I felt something hit my back, but I didn't dare stop to investigate.

When we reached Nolan, he wrapped an arm around my shoulder in the guise of a hug, while his hand swept along my back, brushing away whatever had been thrown at me. He gestured to the chair beside him. I sat, and Payton took the chair opposite me.

She sighed loudly. "I never dreamed I'd see the day when I'd spend my lunch hour with my brother."

"That just goes to show you, Pay," he said, "dreams really do come true."

She snorted and pulled several plastic containers out of her bag. She opened the first one and pulled out an apple slice.

Nolan had several pieces of pizza piled on his tray. He rolled one into a tube and bit into the end of it.

"God." Payton wrinkled her nose. "You're such a freak. You can't even eat pizza like a normal person."

He frowned at her while he chewed. After he swallowed, he turned to me. "You don't think I'm a freak, do you?"

"I think you're cute—but I never said anything about not thinking you're a freak." Smiling, I bumped his shoulder with mine.

He grinned back in such a way that my stomach quivered.

"I'll take cute." He slid his tray over. "Want a slice?"

I shook my head. "I better not. Nerves."

Payton glared at me and pushed a small container of hummus. She held out a cracker. "Eat."

"Yes, *Mom*." I took the cracker from her. I guessed something little wouldn't hurt. But no sooner had I bit into the hummus-dipped cracker than Blake appeared and set her tray down on the other side Nolan.

"Oh hey, Blake's here," Nolan said cheerily.

"Hey," she muttered. She sat and glared at me over his shoulder, turning the cracker I'd swallowed into lead as it slid down my throat.

"So guess what?" Nolan smiled. "I told Blake all about our project, and she thinks it's a great idea."

Blake rolled her eyes and turned her attention to the salad on her tray. She speared a cucumber with enough force that her fork shook the plastic container.

Payton and I exchanged frowns.

"Anyway," Nolan continued, his smile wavering. "Once I finish editing the video, our next step is going to be deciding the best way to reveal it. Afterward, we begin phase two of Operation Bathroom Graffiti."

"Which is what, exactly?" Payton asked.

His grin widened. "I can't ruin the surprise. All I can say is that it's going to be *amazing*. Which brings me to my next order of business." He laced his fingers together on the table. "Regan, I need to talk to your mom."

I laughed, sure I'd heard him wrong. "You're joking, right?"

"I'm dead serious. I would love to have a congresswoman's endorsement before I talk to the principal about our project." He tore another chunk out of his pizza roll.

No longer hungry, I set the remainder of my cracker aside. "That's a really bad idea. Mom doesn't really do *support* that well."

Nolan swallowed and waved a hand in the air. "Once she hears about our project, there's no way she won't be crazy about it."

Payton snickered. "Oh, I'm sure the word 'crazy' will come up."

I ignored her. "You keep calling this *our* project, but I don't see how that's possible, as I don't know the first thing about it."

"Pshh. It was your idea." Nolan took another bite of pizza.

I opened my mouth to argue when I was kicked beneath the table. I jerked back against my chair as pain jolted up my shin. I turned from Nolan to face Payton. "Ow. Why would you—" I stopped when I noticed her pointing over my shoulder. Her lips were pressed tight and her eyes held none of their earlier amusement.

With a sinking feeling, I turned very slowly in my chair.

Amber stood behind me with a water bottle in hand. What little hummus I'd eaten recoiled in my stomach out of fear of an altercation. Then I realized she hadn't seen me yet. She was too busy scanning the cafeteria, searching for—I had no idea. Possibly looking for a place to sit or watching for people to avoid. She nervously chewed on her lip, and it tugged something inside me. I knew exactly what it felt like to be alone. Before I could stop myself, I called out, "Hey, Amber, want to sit with us?"

Another jolt of pain rocketed up my leg as Payton issued another kick. I jerked upright in my chair but managed to smile through the pain. Nolan stared at me as if I'd just announced I was actually a member of an alien race and was awaiting a spaceship to return to my home planet. Blake's lip curled in disgust, and she stabbed her salad with even more ferocity.

I couldn't blame any of them for not wanting her to sit with us. In all actuality, I wasn't even sure why I asked—she was the reason my whole life fell apart.

Her head snapped in my direction, her eyes darting between Payton and me. "So you two are in it together? Is that it?"

"In what together?" Payton asked.

Amber opened her mouth, only to snap it shut again as she shook her head. "You know what? Just leave me alone—*both* of you." Before we could respond, she set off across the cafeteria. The clip of her heels punctuated every angry footstep.

Payton pushed her box of apple slices aside and leaned across the table. "Okay, just what in the hell is going on?"

I rubbed my leg. "I'm going to have two really nasty bruises. *That's* what."

"That's not what I meant." She narrowed her eyes. "You know just as well as I do that Amber does not retreat from a fight. Right now, you're her number one enemy and she just…ran away." Payton pointed a finger at me. "You have dirt on her. That's the only thing that makes sense."

I looked at the table. It wasn't that I wanted to keep a secret from my best friend, but it wasn't just Amber's secret—it was Christy's, too. And I'd promised Christy I wouldn't say anything as long as Amber backed off—and new Regan kept her promises.

"Oh my God. You totally do." Payton smacked her hands against the table, rattling the silverware on Blake's tray. "Tell me. Tell me now."

"Jeez, Pay, calm down." Nolan dropped his pizza onto his tray. "Maybe Regan has a good reason for not saying anything."

She rolled her eyes. "You're an idiot. Amber practically destroyed Regan's life. Of course she's going to spill." She turned to me. "You're just waiting for the right moment, right?"

Blake leaned around Nolan, watching me expectantly, as if also interested in my answer.

"I…uh…" I swallowed, wanting so badly to tell her. Just last night Nolan had sent me the video I'd taken from the bathroom stall. Payton's feelings would be hurt if she thought I was keeping secrets from her, and I didn't *want* to keep secrets from her. And it would be so easy to forward the video to her, just a couple swipes on my phone and it'd be done. The old me would have done it without question. But the new me, or at least the me I strived to be, couldn't. That video held secrets that weren't mine to tell. "I'm sorry, Pay, I can't."

Nolan smiled and Blake frowned.

"What?" Payton pushed back from the table, her eyes wide. "You're kidding right? I thought we were best friends."

"We are," I told her. "I-I just don't want to be that person anymore, the girl who ruins lives—and this secret would ruin two of them. You can kind of understand that, right?"

"I guess so." She stuck out her bottom lip in a pout. "I just hate not knowing."

"I don't know." I shrugged. "Sometimes I think knowing is worse."

"Unless you're suffering in silence," Blake added.

Payton and I turned to face her. I actually couldn't believe she'd said anything that wasn't an insult to me. "What do you mean?"

"I'm thirsty." Nolan pushed his tray away. "Blake, want to come get a drink with me?" Apparently, Nolan felt the same way. Maybe that's why he wanted to usher her away, before she had the chance to say something nasty.

Instead of leaving, she waved a hand dismissively. "All I'm saying is when you hold things in, they can start to eat at you—which is why I'm totally in support of your video."

I tried not to let the surprise show in my voice. "You are?"

"Oh, yeah." She nodded. "I'll admit, I've always thought you were a bitch." Nolan coughed loudly, but she ignored him. "That was until Nolan told me about your project. I'm so on board. In fact, I was thinking about ways to unveil it. Of course there are the obvious channels, YouTube and Facebook. But not everyone has accounts, and it won't be seen by the entire school—that's what you want, isn't it?"

Even though the thought of the entire school watching me admit to my wrongdoings and anxiety disorder made my stomach roll, I nodded. This video was, after all, my only real chance of putting my past behind me.

"Okay," she continued. "So I was thinking, you guys know that as a member of the broadcasting club, I produce the morning announcements, right?"

Payton and I both shook our heads. I'd never paid much attention to the morning announcements. All I knew was they were recorded live in the broadcasting club room and played every morning during homeroom—and they were boring. Since I didn't really care about the golf team's tournament scores, I typically used the time to text back and forth with Payton and Amber.

Blake sighed. "Doesn't matter. Mr. Jensen usually sits in on the morning show to make sure things run smoothly. Tomorrow he has a dentist appointment and asked me to oversee things. With him gone, I could easily get your video shown after the announcements are read. The entire school would see it."

The entire school.

The words buzzed inside my head like wasps ready to sting.

"I don't know." Nolan sat back down and placed an arm on the back of my chair. "The video still needs editing. I don't think it will be ready in time."

"I could help." Blake smiled brightly. "You know I'm an amazing editor."

"This is true." He tapped a finger against his chin. "Regan, what do you think?"

"Uh…"

The entire school.

The cafeteria around me blurred, and I blinked several times to bring it back into focus. That was what I wanted, right? To come clean in front of everyone, to start over, to not be remembered as the horrible girl who talked shit and spread rumors.

Nolan leaned toward me, leveling his lips with my ear. "You don't have to do this," he whispered. "We can forget this whole thing. I can delete the video."

Seeing the sincerity in his eyes, I knew he'd do it. But if I let him, nothing would change. "No. I want to do this—I *have* to do this."

Blake grinned and jabbed a cucumber with her fork. "You got it. I'll help Nolan with the editing after school. Tomorrow is our only shot, so it will have to be ready."

Alarm flashed through Payton's eyes. "Shit. That's not a lot of time. Are you sure you're okay with this, Regan?"

No. But I also knew this was the kind of thing no one could ever be ready for. "I don't want to pretend anymore. It's time people saw the real me—even if they don't forgive me, I have to at least *try* to undo some of the damage I've done, and the sooner the better, I guess."

Blake raised her water bottle as if preparing to toast. "The sooner the better," she agreed.

Chapter Eighteen

I popped the last bite of my third chicken taco in my mouth, chewing as Mom droned on and on about some new tax bill. As my eyes glazed over and the table around me fell out of focus, I wondered if it were possible to fall into a coma from boredom—or at the very least pass out.

When the doorbell rang, Mom frowned and set her fork on her plate. "Were you expecting anyone, Steven?"

Dad set his napkin aside and stood. "No. Not unless it's Frank returning the edger, but I thought he was going to keep it through the week."

Her frown deepened. As a public figure, unannounced visitors were seldom good things. Despite having an unlisted address, we'd had to call the police more than once to remove lunatics from our porch. Only this time, I had a sinking feeling I knew exactly who the lunatic in question was.

I pushed my chair back so suddenly, it squealed against the hardwood. Both Mom and Dad turned to me with startled expressions. "I'll get it." I jumped to my feet.

"Like hell you will," Mom called after me. "We have no idea who's out there—it could be another crazy person."

Well, she's half right.

"I'll check it out." Dad motioned me back with a wave.

Mom stood and then walked to his side. A noose pulled tight around my chest. If it was Nolan outside, I hoped the inquisition he was about to suffer wouldn't scare him off. I wanted to follow my parents into the foyer, to signal Nolan to run for it, but fear froze me in place.

My parents' footsteps stopped. Mom asked, "Who is it?" in her version of a whisper, which was really a loud hiss, since she only had one volume—loud.

After a pause, Dad answered, "It's Payton and…is that her brother?"

"Let them in, Steven." Mom's voice was a mixture of relief and annoyance. "Regan, your friends are here to see you."

I only hoped that was true. I knew Nolan and Blake were going to work on editing my video after school, but he also mentioned talking to my mom. I couldn't imagine a single scenario where that idea was a good one. "Coming." Dread tightened my muscles as I entered the foyer.

The heavy wooden door gasped when Dad pulled it open. "Payton," he said warmly, "so nice to see you." He nodded at Nolan. "Are you kids working on a school project or something?"

Payton stood between my parents, all smiles. "Not tonight, Mr. Flay." She was practically bouncing on her toes.

Nolan crossed the threshold and joined his sister. He still wore his uniform. And, for the first time ever, his shirttails were tucked in. I couldn't care less what he wore, but the way my mother stared at his unruly hair and scuffed sneakers, I knew he needed every advantage he could get.

Dad, thankfully, wasn't half as rude. His appraisal showed more curiosity than anything. "You're Payton's brother, right?" He snapped his fingers several times in thought. "Nolan?"

He nodded. "Yes, sir."

Dad beamed, clearly pleased his efforts to improve his memory with sudoku were paying off. "So what are you kids up to?"

"Actually, sir," Nolan replied, "I was hoping for a couple minutes of your wife's time." He turned to my mother. "I have a project I would love to discuss with you."

Mom's face smoothed into the unreadable mask she perfected as a politician. I knew that look. She had no idea what was going on, and there was nothing she hated more than to be caught unprepared.

Dad, on the other hand, swept his hand back, inviting Payton and Nolan farther inside the house. "By all means." He glanced at me over his shoulder and gave me a questioning look. I quickly dropped my gaze to the floor. I didn't want any part of the massacre about to take place.

My father led the way into the sitting room. He gestured

Nolan and Payton to the plush sofa in the middle of the room. Dad sat in the love seat angled to the right of it while Mom stood beside him.

I followed them as far as the doorway, but I couldn't bring myself to enter. My heart pounded a frenzied beat against my ribs. My pills were just upstairs. I wondered if I could make it up the steps without passing out and falling to my death—though that might not be such a bad alternative to the current situation.

Nolan, as if sensing my panic, gave me a reassuring smile. Almost immediately, my heartbeat softened.

Mom, who hadn't taken her eyes off of him since he stepped through the door, tilted her head in hawklike observance at the gesture. The corners of her mouth twitched downward, the only sign of her breaking mask.

Payton sniggered under her breath. I shot her the most deadly look I could muster, but she just laughed harder.

Dad, the only person sitting, looked at Mom and patted the cushion beside him. "Why don't you take a seat, dear?"

She folded her arms across her chest and shook her head. "I'd rather stand. That couch isn't good for my back."

I mentally rolled my eyes. There was nothing wrong with her back. Her refusal to sit was part of her power play. Since she had no control of the situation, she was going to snag whatever footing she could. At the moment, all she had to hold on to was the psychological advantage of towering over everyone. It was the same reason she had a footstool placed behind her lectern at all of her public speaking events.

She drummed her fingers along the back of the love seat

and gestured to the couch. "Please everyone, take a seat and then we can begin."

Payton headed for the couch when Nolan caught her arm. "Actually, Mrs. Flay, I was hoping to discuss this with you in private. This project, while your daughter's idea, is kind of a surprise."

Payton stuck out her lip and pouted while Mom arched an eyebrow.

"Fair enough." Dad rose from the love seat. "Come on, girls. I've got a cheesecake in the refrigerator with our names on it."

Payton's pout melted into a smile. "Sweet." She bounded after Dad as he left the room for the kitchen. She paused in the entryway to the dining room and looked back at me over her shoulder. "You coming?"

"Yeah." I glanced back into the sitting room at Mom and Nolan, who both watched me expectantly.

"Well, go on, Regan," Mom said, shooing me away. "Just be careful with the cheesecake. It's an election year, and the camera adds ten pounds."

I frowned before stepping away.

"Wait," she called.

I paused.

Mom motioned to the double French doors. "A little privacy, please?"

With a sigh, I pulled the doors shut. I turned for the kitchen, but not before I heard the muffled voice of my mother asking what this was all about.

From the hallway, Payton motioned me to hurry. The

last thing I heard before I followed her into the kitchen was Nolan's reply.

"It's about the old grade school on Third Street that's about to be torn down," he answered. "I wondered if you could get me access to the bathroom stall doors before it's demolished."

A n hour later, Payton and I sat at the kitchen bar, polishing off our cheesecake while Dad tried to convince us the perfect accompaniment for the dessert was a scoop of ice cream.

Payton giggled. "Sorry, Mr. Flay. I have to be able to fit into my cheerleading skirt."

"Regan?" He arched an eyebrow suggestively.

"No thanks, Dad." While I didn't have a cheerleading skirt to worry about fitting into, after three tacos and cheesecake, I didn't have room in my stomach for another bite.

"Suit yourself." Dad opened the door to the basement where the deep freezer held his stash of ice cream. "I'll be right back."

Once he descended the steps, I turned to Payton and asked the question that had been on my mind for the last hour. "Why does Nolan want a bunch of used bathroom stalls?"

Payton stopped licking her fork and wrinkled her nose. "Gross. Is that really what he wants?"

I shrugged. "I heard him ask my mom about it before we left for the kitchen."

"Ew." She set her fork on her empty plate and pushed it to the far end of the bar. "He is a freak, after all. There's no telling how his mind works."

Nolan was really interested when I told him about the bathroom graffiti. I could only guess he wanted to make a statement somehow—but in what capacity? I chewed on my thumbnail and glanced at the clock. "What do you think is taking so long?"

She smirked. "You know how your mother is. She probably murdered him, and now, she's cleaning up the scene of the crime to make it look like an accident."

"That is *not* funny." Partly because I could almost believe it. "Do you think I should go in there?"

"And become victim number two? I wouldn't."

I drummed my fingers on the counter as I debated what to do. Before I'd made up my mind, I heard the crack of the French doors opening, followed by the sound of my mother's heels.

I jerked upright, every muscle in my body tense and rigid as she walked into the kitchen with Nolan following close behind. Both of them were smiling.

Payton and I exchanged confused glances.

"C'mon, Payton." Nolan waved her toward the door. "We should get going. It's getting late."

"Wait." I jumped off my stool. "You guys were talking forever. Isn't anyone going to fill me in on what's going on?"

"What's going on," Mom said, gliding up to me, "is you

and this young man have an incredible idea that I'm more than happy to assist with. Bullying is such a hot-button issue, and of course I'm eager to help with any program that promotes education and helps prevent it." She patted my shoulder, and my mouth fell open from shock. I couldn't remember the last time she'd given me an encouraging word, let alone touch. "I'm proud of you." She gave me one last pat before looking at Nolan. "I'll call my aide tomorrow and get her working on the details. Of course we'll want the press alerted."

He grinned. "Of course."

"Well then, we'll be in touch." Mom crossed the room to the opposite door. "I'm going to retire early, as I have a lot of work to do tomorrow. You do, too." She nodded at him.

"Talk to you soon," he said.

Mom smiled and left the room.

I leaned against the counter, blinking, trying to make sense of what just happened. Only one explanation came to mind. "You drugged my mother."

Nolan laughed. "I promise you I didn't."

"She was smiling," Payton said. "She never smiles."

"That's proof." I nodded.

Nolan made a face before waving Payton over. "While I hate to interrupt this very important summit meeting of the drama queens, I left Blake at the house editing all by herself. She's probably wondering where the heck I am." He directed his attention to me. "When I left, the video was looking really good. It should be ready for tomorrow. Are you?"

"I…um…" In less than thirteen hours, I'd have no more secrets. The thought wedged a jagged lump inside my throat. The Regan I'd fought to hide from everyone was coming out for good. I sucked in a shaky breath. "I am."

Nolan wrapped his arms around me, pulling me tight against his chest. The smell of citrus and pine enveloped me as the warmth of him seeped into my skin. Slowly, my throat relaxed and the lump disappeared. "You're amazing," he whispered against the top of my head.

Payton made a gagging noise. "Get a room," she groaned.

Nolan's hands released me, and it took all of my strength not to reach for him as he did. He leaned down and rested his forehead against mine. "I'll see you tomorrow before class, okay?"

"Okay."

He slid a hand to the back of my head, and I arched my neck in response. The kiss was quick, thanks to the show Payton made of pretending to vomit, but it warmed my insides nonetheless.

He released me and followed Payton to the kitchen door. He hesitated in the doorway, pointing a finger at me. "Tomorrow," he said and winked.

I forced a smile. "Tomorrow," I echoed, the word swirling inside my head.

Tomorrow.

CHAPTER NINETEEN

The next morning, I pulled into my parking spot several minutes before the warning bell was supposed to sound. Worry zipped through my stomach like a swarm of hornets, keeping me from grabbing my usual morning latte. I pulled the key from the ignition with quivering fingers. I glanced at my purse where I'd stashed my pills. *Maybe I could take just one…*

No. I shook the thought away. Today was too important to hide behind a pill.

There was a rap on my window, and I let out a surprised squeak. Turning, I found Nolan outside my door with his camera open and recording. "How's my star feeling today?"

"I'd feel a lot better if you turned off your camera."

He smiled. "Can't. This footage is necessary for the documentary I'm making on our project."

"The bathroom stall project."

"That's right."

"The one you won't give me any details about."

He adjusted the lens. "And ruin the surprise? I wouldn't dream of it. Now come on. You're going to have to hurry or we're going to be late. You don't want to miss phase one of our plan, do you?"

"Actually…" I pretended to put the keys back in the ignition.

"Very funny." He motioned me to get out. "C'mon."

I rolled my eyes and climbed out of the car. He backed away, filming every move I made.

"How are you feeling?" he asked again. "Nervous? Excited?"

I tightened my hold on the backpack. "All of the above."

"What are you hoping to accomplish with this video?"

I paused and considered the question. "I really want people to know I've changed."

"How so?"

"Well…" I licked my lips. "There's this game you have to play if you want to be popular. The score is tallied in texts, Facebook posts, bathroom graffiti, and tears. The more hurt you inflict, the more you get ahead. It's all about staying one step in front of your opponents. But here's the thing I didn't realize until it was too late: you can play this game for months, years even, and never win because everyone who plays the game is automatically a loser. I don't want to play the game anymore. And I'm sorry I ever did."

Nolan lowered his camera. "That was perfect. I stand by

what I said yesterday—you're amazing."

My cheeks flushed hot. "Before you pile on the compliments too thick, let's see if I can actually walk inside the school building." I glanced at the doors, and my throat went tight just thinking about the video and the students inside who still hated me—who might always hate me.

"Of course you're going to make it inside." He tucked his camera inside his backpack before crouching down in front of me. "I'll be your chauffeur."

I clapped my hands together. "Seriously?"

He jutted his chin over his shoulder. "Hop on."

Giggling, I hopped onto his back and wrapped my arms around his neck. He secured my legs with his arms, stood, and strode toward the entrance. "You're crazy," I told him.

He was quiet a moment. When he finally answered, his voice was devoid of its previous humor. "About you." The warning bell rang. He pulled the door open and stepped inside.

The hornets inside my stomach transformed into hummingbirds that immediately took flight. Who knew that amid the worst moment of my life something so good could happen?

"Where to?" he asked.

After I gave him the room number for my homeroom, I rested my chin on his shoulder as he carried me through the mostly empty halls.

Outside my classroom, he crouched down and I slid off his back. "You're going to be late," I said.

He leaned down and kissed me, a quick brush of lips, but

enough to set my skin on fire. He leaned back and smiled. "Totally worth it."

Stray tendrils of his hair fell across his forehead. I reached up and pushed them behind his ear. "It's so funny, isn't it? I never would have thought you and I would ever be…" I let the words dangle in the air between us, because I wasn't quite sure what we were. So maybe it was best not to put a label on it. I shrugged. "I guess what I'm trying to say is that I'm glad Amber tried to ruin my life. If she hadn't, you and I would never have happened."

The smile left his face and he swallowed. "I'm glad about you and me, too. But—" The late bell rang, cutting him off. He cursed under his breath and took my hands. "Listen, Regan, I really like you, which is why…before I got to know you—the *real* you—I did something really stupid. And I wanted to tell you the night we filmed your apology, but I panicked because I thought you might hate me. I just—"

"Ms. Flay." Mrs. Murphy, my homeroom teacher, suddenly appeared in the doorway. "You're late. Please get inside and take a seat. You can socialize with your boyfriend later." Her words were met with giggles from inside the classroom.

An embarrassed flush burned up my neck, and I gently slipped my hands out of Nolan's. "Sorry, Mrs. Murphy." I looked at Nolan. "We'll talk later?"

He nodded, though he didn't look happy about it. "We will. It's important."

Mrs. Murphy pointed toward the hall. "To class, Nolan." With a nod, he set off in the opposite direction. He paused once to look at me over his shoulder. Something passed through his eyes. Fear? Remorse? I couldn't be sure because it was gone as soon as it arrived.

I wanted to call out to him, but Mrs. Murphy placed a hand on my back and steered me inside the room. I thought about what he'd said as I took my seat. *I did something really stupid.* I slid my backpack between the legs of my chair and sat. What stupid thing could he have done? Obviously we both said some really awful things about each other before—surely he didn't think I'd hold him accountable for that.

Mrs. Murphy took attendance, and I raised my hand when she called my name. When she finished, she switched on the television mounted on the wall.

My heart seized. I'd been so busy thinking about Nolan, I'd completely forgotten about my video confessional, which would be played in a matter of moments. I curled my fingers around my desk and watched seniors Natalie and Dan, the journalism club's morning anchors, rattle off various sports scores and announcements at a card table decorated with poster board to give it the appearance of a news desk.

The wall clock's second hand ticking away drowned out all sound except for the pulse beating inside my head. In mere minutes, everything would change.

Natalie picked up several sheets of papers and stacked them in front of her. "With Ian Riley injured, we have to wonder what chance our wrestling team has this year of making state."

"It doesn't look good," Dan agreed with a frown. He

swiveled in his seat as the camera zoomed in on his face. "That's all for the morning announcements, but please stay tuned. In light of the upcoming Bullying Awareness Week, our producer and president of the broadcasting club, senior Blake Mitchell, has a special presentation."

This is it. Fear squeezed my lungs so each breath was a ragged gasp. But beneath the threads of fear pulling across my chest was something else. A niggle of unease fluttered through me beyond the fact I was about to bear my soul to the entire school. I couldn't help but wonder about the timing of the whole situation. What were the odds all this happened before Bullying Awareness Week?

The camera panned out. Both Dan and Natalie stood and walked off camera. A second later, Blake appeared onscreen and took a seat at the abandoned desk. She licked her lips and fidgeted in her seat before looking at the camera. "Good morning," she said with a quiver in her voice. "For those of you who don't know me, my name is Blake Mitchell and I'm a senior here at Saint Mary's. My best friend, a girl by the name of Jordan Harrison, was supposed to be here with me enjoying the best year of her life. But she's not because of the bullying she suffered here at *this* school."

My gut clenched as wave after wave of nausea washed over me. Something wasn't right. Why was she bringing up Jordan *now* before she was supposed to show my video?

Blake placed her hands on the desk and laced her fingers together. "The video I'm about to play is a documentary I filmed with my friend Nolan Letner. We came up with the idea after Jordan was bullied nearly to death. We wanted to show Jordan's bullies what it was like to spend a day in her shoes. We've titled the project *Life Unaware*."

What the hell was going on? All around me, students stopped doodling in their notebooks and leaned forward in their seats, clearly curious as to what was about to happen. Even Mrs. Murphy had set her iPad aside in order to swivel her desk chair for a better view of the television monitor.

The screen went dark as a piano played a low melody. The words *Life Unaware* flashed on the screen as if being typed by a keyboard, only to disappear one letter at a time.

A two-story brick house appeared on screen. It looked like any house in any middle-class neighborhood. Bushes with pink flowers lined the porch, and the grass was several days past needing to be mowed. A metal mailbox painted to look like a cow stood at an angle at the edge of the yard.

"May, last year," Nolan's voice narrated. At the sound of it, so unexpected, I jerked back in my seat. "Things had been rough before then, but I never knew how bad they had gotten until then. I take some of the blame. I was her boyfriend, so shouldn't I have known? Shouldn't I have done something?"

I held my breath. Had Nolan intended for this video to be shown? A tremor of fear wound down my spine.

The scene switched to a closed door. Whoever held the camera—Nolan, I assumed—tried to twist the knob, but it wouldn't move. "C'mon, Jordan." Nolan's voice was no longer narrating but recorded in the scene. "If we don't leave now we're going to lose our reservation. You've been so down lately I really want to do something special for your birthday. I have the camera recording so you really have no choice but to come out with a smile on your face."

There was a pause, followed by a muffled reply. "I'm not coming out." Sobs punctuated her words.

"Jordan?" The humor vanished from Nolan's voice. "What's the matter?" He tried the handle again, jiggling it several more times. "Are you okay? Let me in."

"Go away," she moaned.

"I'm not going anywhere."

"Doesn't matter." Her voice was barely audible. "Nothing will ever matter again."

"What the hell does that even mean?" Nolan asked.

She didn't answer.

"What the f—k, Jordan?" "Fuck" had been bleeped out, but enough of it remained to come through. Fear laced Nolan's voice. "This isn't funny. I swear to God if you don't open the door, I will break it down."

No reply.

Mrs. Murphy leaned forward in her chair. She reached for the remote, even pointed it at the television, but she never hit the power button. It was apparent she was held captive by the video in the same way I was.

"F—k," Nolan said. "F—k, f—k, f—k." The camera jostled as it was set on something undeterminable due to the angle. Nolan appeared in front of the door a second later. His hair was streaked blue—the color it was all last year. He braced his shoulder against the door, as if testing its strength. His eyes were wide with panic. "This is the last time I'm going to ask you, Jordan. Open up or I'm coming in."

Silence answered him.

He muttered something under his breath, pulled away from the door, and rammed it with his shoulder. The door made an awful crack and bowed in, but it didn't open completely. The frame beside the handle had snapped so the door gaped several inches but still held on.

Nolan rammed it a second time, snapping the frame completely. The door swung wide and struck a boot on the other side with a dull thud. When the shoe didn't budge, it was then I realized it was still being worn.

Nolan ran into the room only to jerk back. "Oh my God, Jordan. What have you done? Is that...bleach?" He fell to his knees beside Jordan's unmoving legs. The rest of her body remained hidden by the door. Nolan reached for her and her legs jerked from the force of being shaken. "Did you drink this, Jordan? Damn it, answer me."

She said something, but it was too low to be heard on camera.

He released her and pulled his phone out of his back pocket.

"I'm calling 911." The screen blurred and faded to black.

My lungs burned, and I realized I'd been holding my breath since the moment Nolan broke down the door. I exhaled loudly and several people around me did the same.

A second later, Nolan appeared onscreen, sitting on the very stool in his room I'd sat on a few days ago. He'd used the green screen to make it look like he was sitting in between a set of railroad tracks in the middle of a field.

"After having her stomach pumped and suffering minor

intestinal damage, Jordan survived her suicide attempt. We'd been dating for more than a year when she broke up with me as soon as she got out of the hospital. She never forgave me for saving her life. Because of her ongoing battle with depression, her parents pulled her out of school so she could get the help she needs." Nolan disappeared, replaced by an image of the city's hospital.

The railroad tracks returned, only this time it was Blake sitting on the stool. "Jordan was my best friend since kindergarten. Up until high school, she was this bubbly, perpetually happy person. She would never have tried to kill herself if she wasn't being tortured on a daily basis." A flush burned up Blake's cheeks and tears welled in her eyes. "I didn't know how bad it was." Her voice cracked. "And I guess that made me a really shitty friend because things must have been pretty bad for her to think the *only* way out was death." Tears rolled down her cheeks, and she quickly wiped them away with her hands. Her gaze shifted beyond the camera. "I need a break." The screen faded to black.

Seconds later, Blake reappeared on the stool, her face no longer red and the tears gone. "Jordan Harrison tried to kill herself because of the torment she endured at school from bullies. She nearly died, may have permanent intestinal damage as well as psychological scarring from what was done to her. Her bullies, however, have suffered no repercussions from their actions. They get to continue to live their lives as they always have, hurting people, making them *suffer*, with no thought to the consequences of the pain they inflict."

Blake shook her head. "I couldn't let that happen. I

couldn't let more people get hurt because of them. And what better way to teach bullies about the consequences of abuse than for them to experience firsthand the very bullying they dished out on others? That's where the idea for *Life Unaware* was born. In order for the experiment to work, we needed the bullies to become targets. We knew that wouldn't be difficult. It's high school after all—everyone has secrets."

I couldn't breathe. I felt as if invisible hands held me by the throat and were slowly strangling me. I had only a moment to wonder what Blake had meant before the setting changed to a green bedroom I knew all too well—Payton's bedroom, only Payton was nowhere to be seen. Nolan sat at her white desk and flipped open her laptop.

"Do you feel bad about what you're about to do?" Blake asked from somewhere behind the camera.

Nolan arched an eyebrow. "I'd feel bad if I didn't do it. If this documentary saves even one life, it's all been totally worth it." He spent several minutes typing and navigating the mouse before he finally smiled. "Bingo," he muttered. He clicked the mouse several more times and the printer came to life with a whirl. Several sheets of paper shot out. Nolan grabbed them and pulled his car keys from his pocket. "Now to get this to a FedEx store. We're going to need *a lot* of copies."

"Copies of what?"

Nolan flipped the pages around. The video had been edited so the names on the pages were blurred, but I could make out enough to know it was a printout of private messages.

My private messages.

Chapter Twenty

Oh my God. Oh my God. Oh my God.

I rubbed my eyes, hoping my mind was playing tricks on me. But no. The papers Nolan held in his hand were the same ones that had been taped to my locker. All this time I thought Amber had been behind the messages, that I'd done something to piss her off and it was her retaliation. Now I realized that wasn't the case. Blake and Nolan had been behind the messages all along.

Nolan—who'd held me in his arms, who'd kissed me, who'd…lied to me this entire time.

The floor slid out from underneath me, and I grasped both sides of my desk as if I could somehow anchor myself. I thought I'd been falling for Nolan, but in reality I was just falling further apart. He told me he cared about me, he'd held me in the bathroom when I couldn't stand, he'd kissed me—had all of it been an act so he could get footage for his documentary?

My stomach clenched painfully tight. My cheeks flushed hot and tears burned in my eyes. I quickly blinked them back before they could fall.

The screen went black as words scrolled across: *We took incriminating messages from one of the offenders and taped them to all the lockers in school. Would the bullies come out of their own social downfall more empathetic?*

A girl appeared onscreen. Her face was blurred out, but the second I saw the purse she carried, I realized with horror I was watching a video of myself. It was the video of my arrival the morning the notes were posted. The girl with the asymmetrical hair whirled around as I tried to pass. Our conversation couldn't be heard over the buzz of students surrounding us. A second later, she smacked the coffee cup out of my hand.

Even now, sitting at my desk, I gasped just like I had that morning. Humiliation washed over me just like it had during the original encounter. The familiar cords of anxiety roped around my body. *Please, God. Let the video be over soon.* I glanced at Mrs. Murphy to find her watching with a strange look of fascination and horror—obviously she wouldn't be turning it off anytime soon.

The students around me sat wide-eyed and rigid in their seats, more awake than I'd ever seen them at eight in the morning.

The scene cut again, and this time I stood in front of Julie Sims's locker as she stared at me with papers clutched in her hands. "Julie, even if you don't believe me, I want you to know I'm very sorry I said those things," Recorded Me said. "I didn't mean them. I was just...being an asshole."

I disappeared from the screen and another girl appeared. Even though her face was blurred out as mine had been, there was no denying who the girl with the hiked-up skirt and stiletto heels was—*Amber*. Words scrolled across the top: *If they learned nothing, would they succumb to the very abuse they dished out?* Amber ripped the pages off a locker and after reading it, tore it into several pieces and threw them across the hall. She marched down a row of lockers and tore the pages off before stuffing them in a trash can.

Would they turn on each other? the scrolling words asked. This time Amber, Payton, and I were onscreen. Amber's shoulders were tight and her fingers curled into fists. "You can drop the innocent act now," she practically spit at me. "I told Payton what you told me—that you thought she was annoying and you were only friends with her because she was good at digging up dirt."

"That's a lie," Onscreen Me shouted.

Another black screen followed by the words: *Would the experience change them? Would they be forced to face their own demons?*

I was back onscreen, my face still blurred—only this time I sat on Nolan's stool in front of the green-screen row of lockers. "I have to be perfect. So *f—king* perfect all the time. Not just at home but at school, at church, at the f—king *grocery store* because everyone's watching. Like the entire world is just waiting for me to screw up. And I've been holding my breath for years because I knew it was only a matter of time before the day came when I slipped up and everything fell apart."

The angle of the camera widened, making me look so small, so frail, among the seemingly never-ending row of lockers. "Some days I think the only thing holding me together are these pills. It's so pathetic. Even more pathetic than the pills, though, are the horrible things I said about other people—the awful things I did. I'm not trying to make excuses because there are none. I just wanted to say I'm sorry for everything—just *everything*. High school is hard enough without other people making it worse, and I'm really sorry I was one of those people."

I disappeared, replaced by the words: *Or would they learn nothing? Would they be so afraid to face the truth about themselves that they would keep on hurting everyone around them?*

These words were replaced with others—blurry, black, and handwritten. Gradually the camera lens focused until the words became readable: DELANEY HICKLER IS A FUCKING WHORE.

It took me a moment to realize where I'd seen those words before—they were written inside the handicap stall in the girls' locker room. The same stall where I recorded— *Oh my God.*

"No." I stood, but no one appeared to notice my outburst. Every eye remained transfixed on the screen. Nolan had taken the footage I'd stupidly left on his camera, and now was about to ruin two lives with it. I whirled around and faced the class behind me. "Please don't listen." I turned to Mrs. Murphy. "Turn it off. Hurry."

She frowned at me and glanced at the remote in her hand, her brow creased in confusion. "Miss Flay, what on earth—?"

Even though I hadn't caught Amber on film, her voice was unmistakable. "I'm sorry," she said.

My heart plummeted to the floor and I realized I was too late. Even if I could stop the video from being shown in my homeroom, I couldn't stop every other class in this school from watching it.

"But not sorry enough to dump that prick Jer—" Christy's voice replied.

Amber sighed. "Jer—'s just for show. You know I couldn't care less about him."

"But that's not what he thinks," Christy countered. "What everyone thinks."

"Fu— what everyone else thinks. We only have to do this for one more year, and then we'll be in college and able to do whatever the fu— we want. One year."

"I guess. The Snowflake Ball is coming up. I just wish—"

"Look," Amber said, "I need to go. We shouldn't risk being caught together like this—especially not at school."

The screen went dark and I waited, with my breath held, for more to come. When it didn't, I turned to discover Mrs. Murphy holding the remote up with a shaking hand, her thumb pressed on the power button. She appeared several shades paler than she had moments ago. "I'm not sure that was appropriate." She said it so softly, I wasn't sure if she was talking to us or herself.

The intercom beeped, making all of us jump.

"I would like Blake Mitchell and Nolan Letner to *immediately* report to my office," Principal McDill announced. Even over the intercom, her anger was unmistakable. "I would also like to personally apologize to all of you for the video just shown. It was in no way authorized by myself or any of the school faculty. The responsible parties will be dealt with. In the meantime, please resume with your classes as scheduled."

Mrs. Murphy dropped the remote onto her desk. "I suppose you should take your textbooks out." Nobody moved. She glanced at me. "Miss Flay, you may take your seat now."

My heart ricocheted off my ribs. Never in my life had I disobeyed a teacher. Still, my legs refused to comply with her request. This video hadn't been an attack on me, but *Amber*. There was no way she hadn't seen it. I knew what it felt like to have your secrets exposed to the entire school.

"Miss Flay. Just where do you think you're going?" Mrs. Murphy demanded. "Return to your desk at once."

Confused, I blinked. Somehow I'd found my way to the classroom door without realizing I was moving. Apparently, on a subconscious level, my body already knew what I had to do. I glanced over my shoulder to find the entire class staring at me in wide-eyed shock. "I'm sorry, Mrs. Murphy. I have to go." I knew I was asking for a detention, but I had to find Amber. Even though she'd played a big part in trying to ruin my life last week, I had to find her—to let her know she wasn't alone in this. After all, how could I expect the school to forgive me my wrongdoings if I wasn't willing to do the same?

I pushed the door open, ignoring Mrs. Murphy's call for me to come back, and dashed out into the empty hallway. *If I were Amber, where would I be?* I couldn't imagine she'd remain in her homeroom, not after her biggest secret was exposed to the entire school.

I raced down the hall, not sure where I was going—all I knew was I *had* to find Amber.

"Regan." Nolan's voice pulled at my body like the strings of a marionette. I slid to a halt but refused to turn around. I couldn't bear to look at the person who'd manipulated and lied to me.

"Regan, *please.*" There was an edge of desperation in his voice. His footsteps drew nearer until they stopped directly behind me. "I had no idea Blake was going to switch the videos. She was supposed to show just your footage—the one we worked on." A hand grabbed my shoulder. "Blake lied to me. She used me."

"Like you used me?" I jerked out of his grasp and whirled around. My hands shook in anger as tears burned the corners of my eyes. My brain couldn't decide if I should scream or cry first. "Like you've been using me this entire time? Setting me up for the big reveal?"

"No." His eyes widened and he took a step backward. "It isn't like that. I mean—yes, maybe it started out like that. After what happened to Jordan, I was so angry. I wanted justice for her. That was before I realized that what Blake and I were doing was no different than what was done to

Jordan. I told her I wanted to abandon the project. I thought she agreed. She must have gotten the footage of you and Amber the night I went to your house and she stayed behind to *edit.*" He rubbed his face with his hands. "God, I'm such an idiot."

That much was true—the rest of it, who knew? It wasn't like I could trust anything he said. "Whatever, Nolan. I don't have time for your bullshit right now, okay?"

Hurt flashed across his eyes, and he jerked back like I'd struck him. "I'm telling you the truth. Blake lied to me. We agreed never to show the original video."

My fingers tightened into fists and I shook my head. "Don't you get it? So what if she lied to you—you lied to *me.* All this time you never said a word when I accused Amber of posting the messages. It doesn't matter that you changed your mind about showing your stupid documentary. The point is you deliberately set out to ruin my life."

He raked his fingers through his hair. "I know. God, Regan, I'm so sorry. When we started filming I was so angry, so hurt...I realize now that's no excuse. I never meant for this to happen. I stopped the documentary when I realized how out of control things were getting. You have to believe me that, in the beginning, I honestly thought I was helping people—helping you, even. I never meant for any of this to happen. I swear. Regan, you're the last person I would ever want to hurt."

I balled my hands into fists. "You're a fucking saint."

"Okay, I deserve that." He held a hand out to me. "You're angry and you have every right to be. We had something really amazing, and I'll never forgive myself if I ruined it. Please, Regan, can we talk about this? Can you just give me a chance?"

"I don't have time to talk." I brushed past him. "I need to find Amber."

His footsteps pounded after me. "I'll help you."

Refusing to look at him, I shook my head. "Don't you have to go to the office?"

"I have to do a lot of things. Right now, you're my number one priority."

I rolled my eyes and continued down the hall. He could say whatever he wanted, but it didn't change the fact I now knew the real Nolan. Whatever act he put on from here on out, I wouldn't be fooled.

I darted around a corner and nearly bumped into Christy. Her face was red and her cheeks wet with tears. She looked between Nolan and me before pointing a shaking finger at us. "*You.* You were working together."

"No. You have it wrong." Nolan raised his hands. "This is all my fault. Regan had nothing to do with this."

Christy grabbed a fistful of his shirt and for several agonizing seconds, I was sure she was going to hit him. "Do you have any idea what you've done?" she spat between clenched teeth. She shoved him, releasing his shirt.

He barely budged. "Please, Christy, none of this was ever my intention."

"Fuck you and your intentions," she answered. "I have to find Amber." She brushed past him, bumping his shoulder.

"Do you know where she went?" I called after her.

Christy stopped and shook her head. Fresh tears spilled down her cheek. "No. We're in the same homeroom together and after the video…" She swallowed hard. "Amber totally lost it. I've—I've never seen her like this. I'm worried."

"Okay." I chewed on my lip, racking my brain for places Amber might have gone. "Why don't you check the parking lot and see if her car is there—if it isn't, she probably went home. I'll keep looking here."

"Okay." Christy nodded before jogging down the hall.

If Amber hadn't left the building, she'd want to go someplace she could be alone where nobody could bother her. Someplace like…the second-floor bathroom. I made a right and started up the staircase with Nolan close at my heels. I prayed I wouldn't find her—that she'd be at Starbucks drowning her sorrows in a mocha latte, or at the MAC counter in Macy's buying away her pain with lipstick and eyeliner.

The intercom crackled as soon as I stepped foot on the second floor. "Nolan Letner *and* Regan Flay, please report to my office at once," Principal McDill ordered.

Apparently Mrs. Murphy had alerted her to my escape. Just what I needed, more trouble. My breath hitched inside my throat, and I reached for my pill bottle hidden inside my purse only to realize I'd left my purse and backpack in homeroom. "Shit," I muttered.

"What is it?" Nolan asked.

"I forgot my pills back in class."

He frowned. "Do you want me to go get them?"

"Yeah, I'm sure you barging into my homeroom would

go over *real* well." I made a face.

"Doesn't matter. I'll do it."

"No." I shook my head. "I don't want you doing anything for me ever again, okay? You've done enough." Before he could respond, I turned around and jogged the rest of the way to the girls' bathroom, hesitating outside the door. My heart pushed up my throat, suffocating me. *Please, Amber. Please don't be here.*

I shoved the door and barged inside. Before the door could swing shut, Nolan skirted in after me.

The bathroom was quiet except for the steady drip from one of the rusted faucets. Amber was nowhere to be seen. My muscles unraveled with relief. "She's not here," I murmured.

"So what do we do now?" he asked.

I whirled on him. "Why don't you get it? There's no *we. You* can go fuck yourself for all I care."

A giggle wafted from under a stall door. "Yeah." Amber's voice echoed off the ceramic tile, only there was something not quite right about it—something I couldn't put my finger on. "Go fuck yourself. Both of you." She erupted in a fit of laughter.

I froze. Fear gripped hold of me with icy fingers. Something was definitely not right. Slowly, I turned in the direction of the stall doors. "Amber?" She didn't answer, so I leaned over and peered beneath the stalls. Amber's long legs were splayed on the floor inside the handicap stall. "Amber, I know you're there. Why don't you come out and talk to me?"

She snorted. "Why the hell would I want to do that? You and your boyfriend didn't get enough footage to completely destroy me?"

Nolan stepped around me and approached the closed stall, pressing a hand against it, testing to see if it was locked. It didn't budge. "Regan had nothing to do with the video. If you want to blame someone, blame me, but at least come out so we can talk."

"F-f-fuck you," she said with a slur in her voice. "We have nothing to talk about. Soon you'll have everything you want."

A tremor shivered down my spine. "*Please,* Amber, come out. You're really freaking me out."

A soft thud answered me. A second later the metal lock of the stall door rattled together. Nolan jerked back as the entire door began to shake.

"What the—" I stepped forward as Nolan crouched down to peer beneath the stall.

"Fuck. Not again." He whipped his head around and looked at me with wide eyes. "She's seizing."

"She's what?" I couldn't make sense of his words. The door continued to rattle. My first thought was we were having an earthquake—but that didn't make sense because nothing else was moving.

Nolan waved me away. "Get back."

Startled, I stumbled backward.

He reached beneath the stall and grabbed Amber's ankles. He slid her out from under the stall; her skirt hiked up around her waist as he did, exposing her black lace underwear. She didn't seem to notice. Her eyes were clenched shut, her teeth bared. Her entire body was rigid and vibrating, like a plucked guitar string.

He let go of her legs and shuffled beside her head. He slapped her cheek lightly. "Amber? Can you hear me? Did you take something? I need to know what you took."

Oh my God. Oh my God. Oh my God. The words looped through my head in a never-ending stream. I wanted to go to her, but fear kept me rooted in place. I could almost convince myself as long as I didn't go to her, didn't *touch* her, this wasn't really happening and somehow I'd fallen inside a nightmare.

Nolan turned to me. "She's not responding. Call 911."

He might as well have spoken Latin. When the pieces of his request finally fell into place, I fumbled through my pockets before remembering I'd left my phone behind. I whimpered, "I don't have a phone."

He pulled an iPhone out of his blazer pocket. After dialing, his hand trembled slightly when he lifted the phone to his face. "I'm in the second-floor bathroom of Saint Mary's high school. I'm with a student I believe overdosed on something. She's having a seizure." He paused, listening. "I have no idea." His eyes flickered to mine. "Regan, see if you can find a pill bottle so we can figure out what she took."

I nodded dumbly and approached Amber's shaking body.

"I don't think she's changing color," Nolan spoke into the phone. "She's still breathing, but her lips look a little blue." He touched Amber's neck and frowned. "Her heart is beating really fast. You guys better get here quick."

I smoothed Amber's skirt down and slipped my fingers inside the pockets to find them empty. Her body twitched beneath my hands. I jerked them away. She made a choking sound and I closed my eyes. Despite going to a Catholic high school and having an ultraconservative mother, I'd never been overly spiritual. Still, I took a moment to mutter a quick prayer for Amber—that she would make it out of this alive.

"Find anything?" Nolan asked.

I opened my eyes and shook my head.

He sighed. "Nothing," he repeated into the phone. He nodded. "Good. Tell them to come to the second floor. We're in the girls' bathroom."

Amber's sweat-soaked hair clung to her forehead. Nolan pushed it back. "Keep looking," he told me.

I nodded and dropped to my knees to peer beneath the stall. Except for the black mold staining the grout around the base of the toilet, nothing stood out. I sat up. "Maybe she didn't take anything," I said hopefully. "Maybe she's epileptic or something?"

"I don't think so." He leaned forward. "Amber, can you hear me? Help is on the way. You're going to be fine, but we really need to know what you took and how much?"

She made a strangled gurgle and swung her trembling arm up to her chest, curling her hand beneath her chin. That was when I saw it—the white cap of a pill bottle protruding from her grasp.

"She has something." I crawled to Amber's side and

grabbed her hand, but it remained locked beneath her chin. With the spasms still coursing through her, I'd never be able to move her arm.

One by one, I pried her fingers from the pill bottle until I wrenched it loose from her grip. It was empty. I only hoped there weren't many to begin with. I read the label. "Bupropion," I told Nolan. "That's what she took."

He repeated the information to the dispatcher.

A chill washed over me. I leaned against the locked stall door as the energy drained from my body. "*Why,* Amber?" I whispered as I closed my fist tight around the bottle. A memory surfaced as if in answer. I remembered lying on my bed a little over a week ago, glancing at my own bottle of pills and thinking how easy it would be to end the pain—to end it all.

I grabbed Amber's hand and squeezed as a sob pushed up my throat. "Please don't die, Amber. *Please.* If you make it through this, things will be different—you'll see. They'll get better."

When I looked up, men in blue uniforms surrounded us. They wrenched my former friend from my grasp and placed her on a stretcher. The moment she was rolled out of the room, time began moving in funny intervals, as if someone kept playing with the fast-forward and play buttons on the remote control of my life.

The principal appeared in front of me, talking, but I couldn't hear a word she said. I closed my eyes, and when I reopened them my mom was there, talking. Everyone was talking—Nolan, a police officer, several teachers, and later a doctor, even though I had no recollection of going to the hospital.

Every so often I picked up a few words from the whispers murmured around me. *Shock. Trauma. Rest.* These words were uttered repeatedly until they swam inside my head and carried me into a sea of unconsciousness.

In my dreams, I saw a body dumped onto a stretcher. A hand fell over the side and a pill bottle slipped from its fingers. Dozens of pink oval pills spilled across the floor. The sound of them hitting the tile echoed off the walls like thunder.

"She's gone," somebody said.

A white sheet was draped across her body. Before her face was covered, I found myself approaching the stretcher for one last look. Even though the eyes were drained of life, there was no mistaking that the color was not the dark brown of Amber's almond eyes, but the pale blue of my own.

A scream gurgled inside my throat but refused to break free.

It could have been me.

CHAPTER TWENTY-ONE

I sat up with a gasp, shattering the dream into fragments. I rubbed my eyes with the heels of my hands until I was sure I was awake and wouldn't succumb to another nightmare. When I finally opened my eyes, I found myself in a hospital bed with a thin, stiff sheet covering my body. I ripped it off to discover I still wore my school uniform. Sunlight filtered through the dusty blinds of a window to my right, creating lines like prison bars on the floor.

"It's okay, honey," Dad said. I whirled around to find him sitting in a chair beside my bed. He wore his oral surgeon scrubs and balanced a coffee cup between his knees. He set it on a nearby counter and stood. "Just sit back. You were in shock, so the doctor gave you something to relax. You've been sleeping for several hours."

Shock.

Hospital.

My heart surged against my ribs. Were they going to commit me? Force me into a bathrobe and lock me in a ward where shoes were stripped of their laces and pencils were replaced with crayons? "I-I don't want to stay. I want to go home."

Dad held up his hands. "You don't have to stay here. We're going to take you home as soon as the doctor sees you're up and gives us the all clear."

I nodded and raked my fingers through my tangled hair, trying to make sense of everything that had happened. There'd been a video…I went looking for Amber…Nolan followed and…*oh God.*

I dropped my hands and snapped my head up. "Amber."

Dad nodded. "So far, so good. It's too early to tell if she's suffered any internal damage, but she's alive, and she wouldn't be if you hadn't found her, honey. You saved her life."

I wasn't so sure. Would she have taken those pills if I hadn't recorded her conversation with Christy? And what about Jordan? Would she have swallowed the bleach if I'd stopped Amber from laughing at her? Hot tears welled in my eyes. I'd wanted to change, but all I'd succeeded in doing was causing more hurt.

"Hey now." Dad pulled several tissues from a nearby box and handed them to me. "Everything is going to be fine. You'll see."

I made a face before dabbing my eyes with the tissue. "You don't get it. *Nothing* will ever be fine again."

Before he could argue, my mother rushed into the room. Her suit was disheveled and several strands of hair had fallen loose from her French twist. "Oh, Regan."

I cringed and pressed my back to the pillows. Knowing my mother, she'd probably heard the entire story by now—everything from my private messages posted on the lockers to the video played at school. I held my breath and waited for the lecture—to be told what a disappointment I was, how she expected more out of me, and how badly I might have hurt her chances for reelection when the media found out.

Mom dropped her purse on the ground. She approached me, her lips pale from being pressed so tightly together. She grabbed me by the shoulders.

I swallowed hard. Here it came.

"Regan, I—" She snapped her jaw shut as if changing her mind and, instead, pulled me against her chest.

The fierceness of her embrace startled me. I tried to pull away, but Mom only tightened her grip. "My baby," she whispered against the top of my head while stroking the ends of my hair. The warmth of her enveloped me, as did her Chanel No. 5—the same jasmine and rose perfume she'd worn since I was a kid. I couldn't remember the last time she'd held me like this. Her arms holding me tight flooded me with memories of life when it had yet to become so *complicated*.

The tears I'd fought so desperately to hold on to finally broke free and spilled down my cheeks. "Mom." A lump wedged inside my throat. "I'm so sorry."

"Shhh," she whispered against the top of my head. "I'm

the one who's sorry, Regan. The school showed me the video. I had no idea what you were going through. I put too much pressure on you. I struggled so hard to get where I am today. I just thought if you succeeded now, life would be so much easier for you than it was for me. I was wrong." She sucked in a ragged breath. "Can you ever forgive me?"

Forgive *her*? Surely the drugs were screwing with my ears. "*I'm* the one who messed everything up. And because I did, everyone at school hates me. And Amber…" I choked back a sob.

"Shhh," she repeated. "We're not going to worry about any of that right now—one day at a time. The important thing is Amber's alive and you're okay."

But I wasn't okay. In a matter of weeks my entire life had slipped out from under me, and I bore the scars from my fall. The things I'd done and the things I'd seen would haunt me forever. I knew this because every time I closed my eyes I saw Jordan's lifeless feet on the television screen in homeroom and Amber's thrashing body on the bathroom floor.

I knew Mom only wanted to make me feel better— to give me a glimmer of hope where there was none. She shouldn't have bothered. At seventeen, I was old enough to know better—to know the truth.

Some things would *never* be okay.

A knock on my bedroom door made me close my book. "Regan?" Mom cracked the door open and smiled. "How's it going?" She looked strange in jeans and a Harvard sweatshirt. Her several-years-old tennis shoes didn't have a speck of dirt on them. I guess she'd never had much use for them before. She hadn't taken a single vacation day since winning her first election a decade ago. When she'd told me in the hospital she'd taken two weeks off to spend with me, I thought she'd go crazy. Surprisingly enough, she appeared more relaxed than I'd ever seen her.

I set my book aside and sat up against my pillows. "I'm good." *Just like I was when you checked a half hour ago,* I mentally added. Still, I didn't mind the frequent check-ins. They were distractions from the dark memories that waited for me when books, internet, and television weren't enough to keep me occupied.

She smiled the same overly enthusiastic grin she usually reserved for campaign fund-raisers. "Great. So I guess that means you're feeling up for a visitor?"

I jerked upright. "It's not—"

"No."

I relaxed. This week, Nolan had shown up at the house twice. Both times I'd hidden in my room and begged my parents to send him away. The second time, Nolan waited for more than an hour before he finally gave up and went home. I knew because I kept checking out the window to see if his car was still in the circular driveway. I had no idea what he could possibly have said to my parents in that amount of time, but I also didn't care. After lying to me like he had—*using* me—I couldn't care less if I never saw him again. "Who is it?" I asked.

"Me," Payton answered, flinging the door open wide. She carried a bulging backpack, which she dropped on the floor with a loud thud. "And I brought a week's worth of homework. Isn't that exciting?" She grinned.

Mom grabbed the backpack and lugged it to my desk. "Thank you, Payton. Regan can't afford to let her grades slip—" She caught herself, biting off the rest of the sentence while shaking her head. "You know what? Why don't we worry about homework tomorrow? We could catch a movie tonight. Hey…maybe Payton would like to join us? It could be a girls' night. What do you think, Payton?"

"Er…" She gave me a sideways glance. "Sure?"

"Excellent." Mom walked to the door. "I'll go check out some showtimes. Be right back."

As soon as she left, Payton turned to me. "Who the hell was that and what has she done with your mother?"

I shrugged. "Don't question it. Alien, demonic possession, or whatever, it's a vast improvement."

"I'll say." Payton jumped onto my bed. "So when are you coming back to school? I have to eat lunch with my brother. It totally sucks."

My throat went tight at the mention of him. I shook my head. "Any word on Amber?"

Payton sighed. "She's alive, that's about all I know. I tried to visit her at the hospital but she was moved to the mental ward once she stabilized. I went to visit her there, too, but she's refusing all visits except for family." She shrugged. "So like I said, at school it's just been me. I really miss you."

I fell back against my pillow. "You're the only one."

"That's not true." She rolled over on her stomach and gave me a meaningful look.

I scowled at her. "I don't want to talk about *him*. Besides, I'm not really sure about the whole school thing. The thought of going back and facing everyone..." I shuddered. "I just don't know when I'll be ready—or if I ever will."

"So you're just going to quit school?"

"Not exactly. Mom and I talked about hiring a tutor for the rest of the year."

"That would be a real shame." Payton plucked a piece of lint from my comforter.

"Why?"

She looked up at me. "Things are different now. Since the whole video-Amber thing. We had this assembly with these speakers who talked about tolerance and stuff." She rolled her eyes. "That part was lame, they were like *forty* or something. What do they really know about what it's like in high school now? Anyway, when they finished, Nolan got up and talked about your project. He said the video of you that didn't get shown was supposed to be phase one, and now he'd like the entire school to help with phase two." She shrugged. "I don't know, it was like he connected with the entire gymnasium or something. Everyone got really excited."

I sat up. "Why the hell would they let Nolan do anything after the whole video incident?"

She looked up at me. "Look, I'm not defending him or anything. I'm still really pissed he broke into my room and took our private messages off my computer. But Blake admitted to the principal that Nolan backed out of the project when you started getting bullied. That pissed Blake off so she went behind his back to continue the project, even going as far as stealing the video you took of Amber and Christy off of Nolan's camera."

The part about Blake didn't surprise me. It didn't take a brain surgeon to figure out she couldn't stand me, and now that I knew why, I couldn't say I blamed her. Hell, I'd done my own fair share of lying and deceiving to get what I wanted. The part that hurt most about Nolan was that because of his lies, I couldn't be sure he'd ever really cared about me. Maybe all of it had been an act to get the information he wanted. I picked up my book and pretended to read the back cover. "Can we talk about something else?"

"The Snowflake Ball is tomorrow. I don't have a date, and if you don't, I thought we could go together," she said hopefully.

I set the book down and made a face. "You're joking, right?"

"Aw. Come on. It could be really fun. We'll get our glam on, dance with a few hotties… *Please, Regan.*"

"I'm sorry." I drew my legs to my chest and wrapped my arms around them. "I don't really feel much like celebrating anything right now. Besides, there's no way I'd be allowed to attend, with me being out of school and all."

"That's not true." Payton scooted closer to me. "I asked Principal McDill and she said she'd love for you to come. If you don't believe me, we'll stay long enough for a song or two, and if you hate it, we'll leave. I promise."

"No." I thought about Amber spending the dance in a psych ward. "I really don't think that would be a good idea."

She flopped against my mattress. "You can't spend the rest of your life hiding out in your room."

"I'm not hiding."

"Yeah?" She arched an eyebrow. "Then prove it. Come to the dance with me."

"Why the hell would I do that? Everyone hates me."

"That's not true." She crawled beside me. "I think a lot of people think you're pretty amazing. After all, not many people would have the strength to make a video apology for the entire school to watch like you did. That took real balls."

"Wait a sec." I jerked back. "How do you know about my video? It never got played."

"Um…" Payton looked at the floor. "That's not entirely true."

"What?"

She twisted her hands inside her sleeves. "I told you about that assembly, right? Nolan played your video—the one you worked on together—before he told the school about your project."

"It's not *our* project," I said, throwing my hands in the air. "I don't know the first thing about it. And who the hell gave him the right to show that video to an assembly anyway?"

Payton shrugged. "He thought you'd be cool with it."

I curled my fingers into my blanket. "I am definitely *not* cool with it. After the last video disaster, I'm done trying to fix anything. Every time the spotlight gets turned on me something goes horribly wrong. I just want to fade away in peace."

Her eyes narrowed. "Fade away?"

"That's not what I meant." Exhaustion crept over me. I leaned forward and raked my fingers through my hair. "I just want to lie low until this whole thing blows over. The less attention I draw to myself, the better."

My mom walked in before Payton could argue. She stared at the iPad in her hands. "That new romantic comedy is showing at seven. Or there's that action flick with Bruce Willis at seven thirty." She sighed happily. "And you *know* how I feel about Bruce." She lowered the iPad when we didn't respond. "Okay, what's the matter?"

Payton folded her arms across her chest. "I was *trying* to convince Regan to go to the dance with me tomorrow."

"That sounds like a wonderful idea." Mom cocked her head. "You never leave the house except to go—" She bit the words off midsentence, not that I needed her to finish. The only time I'd left the house since ending up in the hospital was to visit my therapist. "So what's the problem?"

"The problem," I told her, "is I have no desire to go. I'm just not ready to face the people at school yet."

Mom and Payton exchanged defeated looks. "All right, honey," Mom said. "Nobody is going to force you to do anything. But maybe take the night to think about it before immediately refusing. We could go dress shopping in the morning and get our nails done. Wouldn't that be fun?"

I had to admit, it kinda did sound fun. The most girl time I'd spent with my mom over the last year was when we took a weekend to tour Columbia University. Still, there was no way I was going to the dance. "No, it wouldn't."

She sighed. "Just think about it. In the meantime, I'm going to Fandango these tickets. Payton, why don't you call your mom and make sure it's okay first."

"Sure," she said. "I left my cell phone out in my car. Can I use your phone?"

"Right this way." Mom ushered her out of the room.

Alone, I let out a long sigh. Despite how fun Payton and my mom thought more public humiliation would be, there was no way I was going to that dance. Besides, with the mountain of homework I'd accumulated in my absence, I wasn't going to be doing much of anything if I wanted to get caught up with the rest of my class.

I climbed out of bed and crossed the room to my backpack. It wouldn't hurt to look over my assignments so I had a better idea of what I needed to get done. I unzipped it and dumped the contents onto my desk. Five textbooks and several sheets of paper tumbled out. I was stacking the books and papers by class subject when I noticed the corner of a purple envelope sticking out of the pages of my contemporary lit textbook.

Invisible fingers squeezed my heart. I knew without looking at it the letter was from Nolan. I slid it free from the book. The word "Regan" was scrawled across the front in sloppy handwriting. I stared at the envelope for more than a minute, trying to think of anything Nolan would be able to say to make me want to see or talk to him ever again.

There was nothing.

I tossed the unopened envelope into the trash can beside

my desk. What would be the point of reading it? The letter, just like the school dance, was only another opportunity to cause myself unnecessary pain, and I'd had enough pain to last me a lifetime.

CHAPTER TWENTY-TWO

All across the city, girls were applying one last coat of lipstick, shimmying into sequined dresses, and buckling the straps on their heels. But not me. With zero makeup, I'd slipped on a pair of riding breeches and an extra-soft T-shirt, and now stood in the kitchen looping the elastic bands of my half chaps under the heels of my boots. I had a date with a handsome boy of the equine persuasion.

Mom appeared in the kitchen doorway. Her eyes narrowed. "Why are you dressed like that?"

I grabbed my helmet off the kitchen table. "Because it's been more than a week since I spent time with Rookie. And after all the popcorn and candy we ate at the movies last night, I figured a little exercise couldn't hurt."

Mom nodded. "We did eat an entire year's worth of carbs. Still, we have plenty of time to hit the gym before next November's election."

I made a face. While I appreciated the effort my mom was making with me, it was reassuring in a bizarre sort of way to know my old mom hadn't completely vanished.

Dad entered the room wearing a suit. "There are the two most beautiful women in the world." He handed a blue silk tie to my mother. "Would you please do the honors?"

I watched as her nimble fingers folded and tucked the swatch of silk into a perfect Windsor knot. It never ceased to amaze me how she got it right on the first try without ever having to loosen and adjust the length. When she finished, he kissed her cheek and tucked the tie inside his jacket.

I'd never tied a tie for anyone and wondered if I could duplicate my mom's movements from memory. I closed my eyes and tried to imagine re-creating the movement of my mom's hands. *Wrap. Flip. Tuck.* But in my fantasy, when I stepped back to admire my handiwork, it was Nolan's face smiling down at me.

Ugh.

I opened my eyes and shook my head, hoping to loosen the image from my head. "Where are you guys going?"

Dad sighed. "Another boring political dinner."

Mom elbowed him in the ribs.

"Excuse me." Dad rubbed his side. "I *meant* to say another action-packed political dinner."

"That's better." Mom glanced at the microwave's digital clock. "And we better get going if we don't want to be late." She turned to me. "You know, Regan, you still have time to get ready for the Snowflake Ball if you change your mind."

I fought the urge to snort. Mom had made such an effort to improve our relationship over the last week, I didn't want to fall back into old habits. "I won't change my mind. I called Payton this morning and told her the same thing." I lifted my helmet. "There's only one guy I'm going to dance with tonight, and he weighs fifteen hundred pounds."

"Smart girl." Dad winked. "If you keep choosing horses over boys until you're, say, thirty-five, I'd be a happy man."

"*Dad.*" I smiled and rolled my eyes.

Mom swatted him with her purse. "Come on, Steven. We need to leave."

He walked over and squeezed me against him. His cologne tickled my nose—something spicy and warm. "I'm really proud of you." He pulled away and took Mom's hand. Together, they left through the kitchen door into the garage.

I stared at the closed door for several moments wondering what he meant. *Proud of me? Why?* All I'd done over the last few weeks—actually, more like the last couple of years—was screw things up.

I tucked my helmet under my arm and snatched my keys from the table. Maybe he was just being Dad—saying what he thought would make me feel better. Unfortunately, it hadn't worked—nothing seemed to work, which was exactly why I needed horse therapy. I started for the garage door when the front doorbell rang.

"You've got to be kidding me," I murmured. I set my helmet and keys back down and made my way to the front door. "Payton," I called out, "it better not be you trying to convince me to come to the dance. I already told you I'm not going."

I stopped in front of the door. A shadow shifted on the other side of the frosted glass. "And you better not be a psycho," I added. "My parents are Republicans. We own guns. Lots of them." I cracked open the door and Nolan raised an arm in greeting. He wore jeans, a suit jacket, and a dark shirt underneath. His hair was combed back and gelled into place. He held a suspicious box, the perfect size for a corsage.

"No." I swung the door back in his face. Looked like I was right about the psycho.

Nolan stuck his shoe in the doorjamb before it had a chance to shut. He winced when the door met his foot and it bounced back, opening wide. "Is that what you're wearing to the dance?" He motioned to my riding breeches. "I like it. You get definite points for being original."

He really must be insane if he'd shown up thinking I was going to the dance with him. I folded my arms across my chest. "No. Whatever you're doing here, just *no*."

He cocked his head. "You know what I'm doing here. It's the Snowflake Ball and you agreed to go with me."

"Like hell I did." I practically spit the words at him.

"Uh, *yeah*. You did." He thrust the small cardboard box at me. "For you."

I pushed it away. "I don't want your box. And I never agreed to anything."

He grinned. "Of course you did. It was all in the letter I sent you last night—the one you *obviously* read. In the letter I clearly stated if you didn't want to go to the dance with me, you could either call or text to let me know. Since I didn't hear from you, I knew you accepted my invitation."

Anger burned through my veins and I fought the urge to slam my head against the door. I should have known Nolan would try to use a trick as a dance invitation. Deception was a favorite ploy of his. If only I'd read the damned purple envelope. "That's not—"

"I'm going to assume you're ready to go," he cut me off. "You look beautiful." He gestured to the door. "Shall we?"

To my annoyance, a blush burned up my cheeks. *Get it together, Regan. What do you care what Nolan Letner thinks?* "I'm only going to tell you one more time because you're obviously having trouble understanding. I am not going anywhere with you. End of story."

"What if I told you I had a limo?"

I looked behind him, and sure enough, a black stretch limo waited in the driveway. I shrugged. "I'd tell you you're going to have a lot of room to stretch out inside that limo all by yourself."

"I'm not by myself." He jabbed a thumb over his shoulder. "Payton's with me."

As if on cue, Payton emerged from the sunroof wearing a purple strapless dress. Her hair was piled on top of her head in a mass of curls and rhinestone hair clips. She waved. "Are you ready to go?"

Pressure throbbed beneath my temples. How was it Nolan had been here less than five minutes and I already had a headache brewing? I turned back to him and exhaled loudly. "You could have both Hemsworth brothers inside that limo and I still wouldn't get in. I'm not going. Now please *leave*."

He grabbed my hand before I could reach for the door. I recoiled from his touch as if it'd burned me. His shoulders drooped and the humor left his face. "Regan, I…" He swallowed. "No. This isn't about me. Let me start over."

I folded my arms, waiting.

"I think you're amazing," he said. "What I did to you was unforgivable."

"Yes it was." I grabbed the door and tried to push it closed. "Good-bye."

He stopped the door with his hand. "Please. Let me finish."

I sighed and pinched the bridge of my nose.

"I started *Life Unaware* with Blake because I wanted justice for Jordan. But somehow justice became confused with revenge. By the time I figured that out and decided to scrap the entire project, the damage was done. If I could, I would take back all of the pain I caused you, every ounce of it, even if it meant you and I never got together." He lifted a hand as if he might touch my face. Instead, his fingers hovered in the air so close to my cheek I could feel the heat radiate off his skin.

A lump formed in my throat and I fought the urge to close the distance between us. I hated myself then, the weakness inside me that, despite his betrayal, still longed for his touch.

Luckily, Nolan dropped his hand, and my coiled muscles unwound. "And that's saying something," he said as he curled his fingers into fists. "After Jordan—you know—I thought I'd never be happy again. But you came along and…God." He shook his head. "I knew I should have told you from the beginning, but Regan, I was scared shitless I was going to lose you, and I was desperate not to let that happen. Now that I *have* lost you, it's every bit the hell I imagined it would be."

My chest tightened, making it difficult to breathe. I wanted to believe him, to fall into his arms like I had when Amber was talking shit about me in the bathroom. Only now, he was the one who'd hurt me and there was nowhere to run. "Nolan, please go." I spoke softly to keep my voice from cracking. "And take your bullshit with you."

He nodded as if he'd expected me to say as much. "Okay. I will. But I want you to know our project is being unveiled tonight at the Snowflake Ball."

"*Your* project," I said.

"*Ours*. It was your idea. I just implemented it."

I rolled my eyes. "Doesn't matter."

His head jerked up. "It does. This project is amazing. It's changed the entire school. Once other schools get wind of it, it might change theirs, too. Your mom arranged for the media to be there tonight for the unveiling. I thought you should be there to get the credit you deserve."

I opened my mouth to argue, but he cut me off.

"Even if it means I'm not."

I blinked at him. "*What?*"

He gestured to the limo. "It's yours. Well, yours and Payton's. The driver has already been paid. I can walk home from here, and I promise I won't go to the dance. I want you to be there—to see the amazing thing you created. Stay for five minutes or stay for the whole night—it's up to you. Just go and see what you started." He gave me a sad smile. "You won't be disappointed."

"Are you coming?" Payton called from the limo.

I chewed on my lip. I really had no desire to hang out at the dance, but I couldn't deny the curiosity welling inside me over Nolan's secret project—especially since it was *supposedly* my idea. And if Nolan wasn't going to be there, that only made me want to go more. "I can really leave anytime I want?"

"Anytime." He nodded.

"So I could basically walk in and walk right back out?"

He shrugged. "It's your limo now. You do what you want."

I folded my arms. "I'm not going to put on a dress."

"Fine with me. You look hot no matter what you wear."

I glared at him and he raised his hands in defense. "I'm never going to be anything but honest with you ever again."

I glanced over his shoulder at Payton who waved me over. "Hurry. We're going to be late."

I pushed my shoulders back and sucked in a breath. "Fine. I'll go. But just long enough to see what this secret project has been about, and then I'm out."

"Then you'll need this." He held out the box.

"I told you I'm not getting dressed up. The last thing I want is a corsage."

"You'll need this. Take it." He placed the box in my hand. "Now you better get going. You're not going to want to miss a thing."

Hoping I wasn't making a giant mistake, I locked the front door by punching in a code on the knob. When I approached the limo, the driver was already out and waiting with the door open.

Payton squealed when I ducked inside. "I'm so glad you agreed to come. You won't regret it." The driver shut the door and her smile wavered. She moved to glance out the window. "Wait. What about Nolan?"

I followed her gaze. Nolan stood on the porch and waved. "He said he'd stay home so I could go."

"Oh." Payton sat back against the black leather seat. "That was nice."

I fought the urge to tell her he could make a million *nice* gestures and it still wouldn't cancel out the lying and damage he'd done. Instead, I said, "He gave me this." I lifted the cardboard box.

She quirked an eyebrow. "A corsage? Let's have a look."

"Fine. But I'm not going to wear it." I slid my finger under the lid and popped it open. I'd expected the traditional trio of red roses pinned together with baby's breath. Instead, the box held a single black Sharpie on a bed of tissue paper. "What the—?" I took the Sharpie out of the box and held it to Payton.

Her eyes lit up. She smiled coyly before quickly clasping her hand over her mouth.

"I don't get it." I placed the Sharpie back in the box as the limo pulled onto the street. I resisted the urge to glance through the back window for one last peek at Nolan. "Is this supposed to mean something to me?"

"Not yet." Payton shook her head, still hiding her grin behind her hand. "But it will."

Chapter Twenty-Three

The limo stopped in front of the high school. A moment later the chauffeur pulled our door open and offered his hand. I pointed a finger at him as I climbed out of the car. "Don't go anywhere. I won't be long." I had no intention of lingering inside a gymnasium full of balloons, crepe paper, and formal wear when I still wore my breeches and riding boots. Still, curiosity steeped inside my mind like tea, and I wasn't about to leave until I had the answers I sought.

He gave a curt nod. "Yes ma'am. I'll stay parked out front."

Payton climbed out of the limo after me and grabbed my arm. "Ready?"

Am I? Ribbons of anxiety threaded through my ribs. What waited for me inside?

Payton removed a small square of card stock from her clutch with the words "Saint Mary's Snowflake Ball" printed on the front.

I sucked in a breath when I realized this whole venture was for nothing. "I can't get in. I never bought a ticket."

Payton laughed. "Trust me when I say no one will care."

I frowned. "What does that mean?"

"It means we're late." She tugged my arm. "Come on."

She led me along the sidewalk, past the front school entrance, around the side of the main building to the double glass doors of the gymnasium. A news van was parked on the sidewalk with its antenna extended. Several girls with curled hair and sequined dresses clustered by the front entrance talking and laughing.

A nauseous wave crashed through my stomach. I pulled free from Payton's grip and prayed I wouldn't hurl on the sidewalk.

She stopped, her lips pinched in a frown. "What's up?"

I wrapped an arm around my queasy gut. "Maybe this isn't such a good idea." Inside the building before me were hundreds of students—students who'd seen the video, who knew the things I'd done. Bile burned up my throat. "I can't—I just can't."

"Regan." She held a hand out to me. "I'll be with you. Everything will be fine. You'll see."

"I'm sorry, Pay." I shook my head and took several steps backward. "I just can't."

"Hey, Regan," one of the girls called out to me.

I froze. So much for my getaway. My muscles tensed and

I waited for their insults.

Juliette, a short brunette sophomore wearing a blue satin dress, ran up to me. "Oh my God, I'm so glad you're here. How are you doing? Everyone's been so worried about you."

Two other girls in her group jogged to join us while a third, who obviously wasn't as practiced walking in heels, wobbled precariously. She teetered to the side and caught herself by grasping on to the arm of the girl beside her.

"Yeah," Mindy, a junior I recognized from the pom squad, agreed. "We think your project is amazing. I mean, I know it won't last forever, but the way people have been treating each other is awesome. I actually look forward to coming to school now."

The other girls voiced their agreement.

Confusion rolled through me. I searched Payton's face, to see if this was some kind of joke. She only smiled and shrugged.

"I really love your outfit," the girl who couldn't walk in heels added. "It's so unique—so *you*." The three girls with her nodded their heads, making them look like a cluster of bobbleheads.

"I know." Mindy clapped her hands together. "I'm going to write that down."

"Ooh, great idea," Sarah said. Before I could ask them what they were talking about, they scampered off toward the gymnasium.

I turned to Payton. "What is going on?" I'd expected dirty looks and insults, not...whatever the hell that was.

She laughed as she waved me toward her. "Come on."

Reluctantly, I followed her through the double doors into the wide space outside the gymnasium. The dance committee had a folding table set up next to a Pepsi vending machine. Two bored-looking freshman boys sat behind it wearing white dress shirts and loose-fitting ties. They took tickets from a short line of couples waiting to enter the gymnasium.

"I don't have a ticket," I reminded Payton as the line progressed.

She waved a hand dismissively. The couple in front of us handed their tickets over and we moved to the front of the table. "Here's my ticket." Payton set her ticket on the table. "And this is Regan Flay. She doesn't need a ticket, *obviously.*"

Both boys jerked upright. "Of course not," the one on the left said. "Go right in. Everyone's waiting for her."

I frowned. "Why are people waiting for me?"

Payton snagged my arm and pulled me away from the table before they could answer. "Got that pen ready?"

I touched the Sharpie I'd clipped to my shirt collar — riding breeches didn't exactly have room for pockets. "Why? What's going on?"

A couple who'd been sharing a soda by the door smiled at me. "Good to see you, Regan." The guy tipped the soda can in greeting as I passed by.

I pressed closer to Payton. All this niceness after the weeks of bullying was really starting to freak me out. Had the school been taken over by aliens while I was gone? Or maybe this entire thing was a setup to get me onstage so they could pour blood over my head à la *Carrie*. I shuddered.

"Will you stop freaking out?" Payton whispered in my ear. "Everything is going to be fine. I promise." She stopped in front of the open gymnasium doors. The lights were dim and a dance mix blared from a DJ booth onstage. Throngs of students thrashed together in the middle of the basketball court in a massive sequin-covered mass. "Ready?"

Ice flooded my veins. "No."

"Too bad." She pushed me inside.

I squinted, trying to adjust my eyes to the disco lighting that hung from the ceiling and flashed a rainbow of colored lights and lasers onto the floor.

"It's Regan," came a voice from behind me.

"She's here," another said.

"Stop the music." Several others issued the command until, a minute later, the music was cut off and the gymnasium lights flashed on. The dancers stopped moving, staring confusedly at one another until gradually their gazes turned to me. A low murmuring rumbled through the crowd.

Shit. My heart beat rapidly and a trickle of sweat wove down my spine. What had I just walked into? I took a step back only to collide into Payton.

"Regan. Honey. Over here."

I whipped my head in the direction of the familiar voice. My father stood beside Mrs. Lochte and Principal McDill. All of them smiled warmly and raised their glasses of punch.

"Welcome back," Principal McDill said. "We're all so very proud of you."

I waved my fingers as a nervous flutter spread through my stomach. A million questions surged through my mind. Why was she proud? Why was everyone staring at me? And what on earth was Dad doing here?

I moved to ask him when I realized he wasn't the only one.

Several feet away, a reporter held a microphone to my mother. I edged my way closer. Maybe if I could listen in on her interview I could get some idea of what was going on? Before I reached her, someone stepped in front of me, blocking my path. Christy's hair was pinned to the side of her head, and she wore a long burgundy gown. Unlike everyone else around me, she wasn't smiling.

I took a cautious step back. Of all the people who hated me, Christy had the most right to. After all, if it weren't for the video I took, her girlfriend might not have tried to kill herself. I bit my lip and waited for whatever attack she had planned—it wasn't like I didn't deserve it.

Payton stepped up beside me and gave a reassuring smile. Warmth bubbled through my chest and I smiled back. At least I wouldn't have to face Christy alone.

"I know you weren't responsible for the video being shown," Christy said.

I blinked. That wasn't the reaction I'd expected.

"I also know Blake was the one who sent notes to each of us to get us all in the locker room at the same time," Christy continued. "She used to show up to the same LGBT support group I attend. I guess she somehow figured out who I was seeing and decided to use you to expose Amber."

My throat tightened at the mention on her name. "How is Amber?"

Christy gave a weak smile. "A lot better. Even though being forced out isn't the way for anyone to come out, I think she's relieved that people know. Her parents were actually pretty cool about the whole thing." She bit her lip. "I know a lot of hurt passed between you two, so Amber might never thank you and Nolan for saving her life." She reached for my hand and squeezed it. "But I will. Thank you."

I wanted to say something back, but the words tangled into a knot inside my throat.

Christy released my hand. "I expected this really huge backlash after people found out about me, but I've received nothing but support. I know a large part of that is due to your project. It's had a really huge impact on the school— everyone thinks so."

I glanced over my shoulder to find the motionless dancers still staring at me. They were waiting for something—I just had no idea what. "Um…I wish I could take credit for that but…"

Christy's eyes widened. "Oh my God, that's right. You haven't seen it yet. Come on." She started toward the crowd of dancers and motioned me to follow.

"Go on," Payton urged before giving me a little push.

"Uh, okay." I forced myself to take slow, even steps forward. When I reached the edge of the crowd, the dancers parted, making a path for me to pass through. I swallowed hard and rubbed my damp palms along my pants. Once I stepped forward I'd be surrounded, giving them the perfect opportunity to pelt me with dog food, pig blood, or worse. Still, I wouldn't run. If they wanted revenge for all the pain I'd caused, I'd let them have it. I closed my eyes and stepped forward.

Time to face karma, Regan.

After several steps, when nothing hit me, I opened my eyes. A girl next to me in a floor-length gown started clapping. The guy beside her hooted. He was followed by several more shouts and whistles until the entire gymnasium was filled with thunderous cheers.

My breath caught in my throat. What the hell was going on? My heart raced to match the pace of the growing noise. The sound of it echoed off the ceiling and shook the stacks of bleachers pushed flat against the walls. I continued walking until I emerged from the crowd on the other side of the gymnasium where a row of what appeared to be bathroom stalls stretched across the entire length of the room.

I jerked to a halt. "What the —"

A hand clasped my shoulder. "Pick one," Payton screamed, her voice barely audible over the roar of noise.

"But…that's disgusting." I looked back at the stalls. "You want me to use the bathroom in *public*?"

She laughed. "It's not what you think. Just *go.*"

So was this part of the plan? Lock me inside a bathroom stall and pour shit on me? Would they really do something like that with the media, teachers, and my parents watching? I guessed there was only one way to find out.

I picked the bathroom stall directly in front of me and tested the door to find it unlocked.

"Don't forget your pen," Payton called.

Without turning around, I lifted the Sharpie in the air and pushed inside the stall, letting the door swing shut behind me. The clapping ceased and music started back up.

I took a moment to examine my surroundings. At a glance, it appeared to be a regular bathroom stall, except a folding chair had replaced the toilet. I snapped the lock closed and sat on the edge of the chair. *Okay. Now what?* Just like the school locker room, the inside of this stall was covered in handwritten graffiti. I glanced at the Sharpie in my hand. Was I supposed to add to it?

I leaned forward and read some of the things written.

Jasmine Walker has a beautiful smile.

Peter Doyle is really good at chemistry, and it's awesome how he's willing to tutor people for free.

Olivia Stout is an amazeballs volleyball player. I just know she's going to get a scholarship.

I placed a trembling hand over my mouth as I continued reading the graffiti. Sure, there was still the occasional "I love so-and-so" but unlike most bathroom stalls, there were no notes calling people bitches, sluts, or whores. Each comment written had been meant to uplift instead of tear down. Even more amazing was the fact that there were at least a thousand comments in this stall alone. I couldn't imagine how many more were written on the walls of the surrounding stalls.

The memory of the day Nolan met me at the barn pushed to the front of my mind. We'd been standing so close, me in my dirty breeches, him holding a pink helmet. *Don't you think it's sad some people are only remembered by the graffiti about them on the bathroom stalls?* I'd asked.

But this—there was nothing sad about this. This was how people deserved to be remembered, for the good instead of the bad. Unlike the stalls in the old wing covered in venom, these stalls presented possibility—a chance that we as a school could change not only the way we treat one another, but maybe even the way future classes would treat themselves. These stalls were a promise from every student here that when we graduated, the hope we left behind us would far outweigh the hate.

I placed a hand over my mouth to smother the strangled sob rising inside my throat. I had no idea that when I set out to change myself, I'd started a ripple effect that would change the entire school along with me. And I didn't do it alone. Nolan had somehow tapped into my mind, taken the moment I'd scribbled out "Delaney Hinkler is a fucking whore" and written in "Christy Holder is fucking awesome," and turned it into *this*.

Regardless of my attempt to blink them away, tears spilled down my cheeks. Nolan had done this—lobbied for permission, arranged for pickup and placement of the stalls, and gathered the support and participation of the entire school.

Sure, he'd hurt me. He'd lied to me. But he'd also arranged all *this*. And that had to count for something. With trembling fingers, I pulled the cap off the Sharpie and touched it to a small blank patch on the wall.

Nolan Letner is

I stopped writing, unable to come up with the right word when my heart still bore the scars of his betrayal.

I brought the pen back to the wall.

Nolan Letner is

An asshole. A genius. Conniving. Caring.

"Ugh." I dropped the pen to my side and capped it. So maybe I wasn't ready to finish that sentence. Nolan was a lot of things, too many to sum up in one word. Still, two in particular came to mind.

Nolan Letner is

Not here.

And he should be. Despite my mixed-up feelings over him, this was just as much his project, if not more than mine. And he was missing it all because he wanted me to be happy. It wasn't right.

I stood and unlocked the door.

Payton smiled when she saw me. "What do you think?"

"I think Nolan's not here."

Her brow scrunched in confusion. "What?"

I handed her the Sharpie as I brushed past. I could put my feelings aside long enough to spend a night in a large gymnasium with Nolan. Even if being in the same building with him proved to be too much, I could easily go home. I'd seen what I'd needed to see. It was his turn.

I wove through the throngs of dancers. Some of them smiled and shouted at me as I walked past. I smiled back and quickened my pace.

"Regan," Mom called to me as I reached the doors. "The reporter is looking for you." She frowned when I pushed the door open. "What are you doing?"

"The right thing." I stepped outside and let the door fall shut behind me. True to the driver's word, the limo remained parked out front. Relief fell over me like a warm blanket. I jogged toward it only to stop when I caught sight of *him*.

He no longer wore the suit jacket and his tie had been discarded. He jumped off the tailgate of his truck and strode toward me.

My heart pushed higher inside my throat the closer he came until he stood before me, and I thought I might choke. "What are you doing here? You promised you wouldn't come."

He smiled, tightening things low inside me. "No. I promised I wouldn't come *inside*. I said nothing about the parking lot."

I couldn't help smile. Typical Nolan.

He motioned to the limo. "Leaving already?"

"Actually…" I shifted uncomfortably. "I was on my way to get you."

"Oh?" He arched an eyebrow.

"Yeah. I just…I just didn't think it was fair, you not being here to witness this. You put this together. And it's all so…amazing."

He took a step closer to me, and I was enveloped by the smell of him. My heart thrummed against my ribs. "It was *your* idea."

I licked my suddenly dry lips. "But you did all the legwork. It doesn't seem right I should be inside taking all the credit."

"Credit?" He snorted. "I don't care about that. I only care about you."

My breath hitched inside my throat, and I fought the urge to reach for him and curl against his chest. Instead, I took a step back. "I want to believe you so badly. But you hurt me, Nolan. I wish I could turn the pain off, but I just can't." I looked away.

"I know." He placed a finger under my chin and turned my face to his. "I wouldn't expect you to. That doesn't mean I'm going to stop trying to make things right between us. I wasn't lying when I said I have feelings for you, Regan Flay, and I'm willing to do whatever it takes to win you back."

If only I could put aside the past and believe that. In truth, I ached to wrap my arms around him and bury my head against his shoulder like I had the night in his bedroom when he asked me to pretend that there was no one else in the world but us. And in that moment, we were all that existed. But now a mountain of pain and lies had risen between us, the height of which I wasn't sure I'd ever be able to scale. "I can't promise your efforts will pay off. I can't promise there'll ever be an *us* again." No matter how badly I wanted there to be.

Frowning, he lowered his hand. "What *can* you promise me?"

I wasn't sure I had an answer. But before I could tell Nolan that, a woman's voice called out my name. I turned to find a young black woman wearing a pink pantsuit and heels rushing toward me with a microphone clutched in her hand. Behind her, a skinny man in baggy sweats balanced a large video camera on his shoulder and clambered to keep up.

"Regan Flay?" She arched a perfectly manicured eyebrow.

The cameraman directed the large lens at my face, and I fought not to flinch. "Um, yeah?"

The woman lifted the microphone toward my lips. "Can you please tell me a little about your project?"

With a mother in politics, I was certainly no stranger to a news camera, but having one directed solely at me was an entirely new experience—and an unenjoyable one at that. "Actually, the project was *our* idea." I shot Nolan a pleading look.

With a smirk, he held his hands up and backed away before the reporter could turn the microphone on him. "Not true. The idea was a hundred percent Regan's. I only helped implement."

I tried to shoot him a dirty look, but the reporter shifted between us, blocking my view. "So what was your inspiration behind the project?" She lifted the microphone higher so that only a couple inches separated my lips from its foam cover.

The cameraman inched closer. My throat tightened, and

I found myself unable to look away from the lens. It was like the black, unblinking eye of some terrible monster waiting for me to mess up so it could capture my humiliation and share it with the world.

I closed my eyes and tried to imagine that the person behind the camera was Nolan, the boy I fell for on the night we agreed to have no past. The boy who kissed me until I was dizzy, and who tasted like melting sugar on my tongue. The same boy who'd destroyed me in an instant, breaking my heart into pieces too small, too jagged to ever fit properly together again.

The reporter gave an impatient huff. "What were you hoping to change?" she asked.

"Everything," I murmured, opening my eyes. "I wanted to change everything."

"Like?" she prompted.

I swallowed before answering. "Those bathroom stalls in there? Those are our hearts. Whenever someone says something about us, it gets written inside us, permanently. The good words, the ugly words, it's all right here." I placed a palm against my chest. "Sure, you can scribble out the words or try to paint over them, but beneath the layers of paint and ink, they're still there, branded to our cores like initials carved in a tree.

"So we're walking around with these scars etched inside us, but no one can see them, so no one knows how bad we're hurting. Meanwhile, people keep talking and writing more words, until every inch of our hearts is covered with venom so black even we can no longer see the good in ourselves. So we start to add our own words, and they're darker than the rest, the scars cutting more deeply than the others ever did."

The reporter's eyes were wide. The microphone trembled softly in her hand. "And your project?" Her voice was barely a whisper.

"I did my fair share of talking about other people," I answered. "I realized, too late, all the damage I caused with words I both spoke and typed. Just like bathroom graffiti, those words will be forever written on some people's hearts. They'll walk around for the rest of their lives with scars inflicted by me. Not only did I want to apologize to the people I'd hurt, but I also wanted to stop others from inflicting the same pain I did. While the bathroom stalls in the gym are only a symbol, I have to hope that replacing the poisonous words on our hearts with those of love can heal some of our scars." I shrugged. "At the very least, it's a start."

The reporter stared at me a moment before dropping the microphone to her side. "Thank you, Regan. That's all we need." She nodded to the cameraman, and he lowered the camera. She turned, only to glance at me over her shoulder. "I think you're doing an amazing thing. Who knows how many lives you're going to change. No matter what, you should be proud of that." She gave me a wink before heading off toward the news van parked at the curb.

I couldn't help but smile as I watched them pull away. I could picture the business cards now: *Regan Flay, life changer*. Who knew?

Nolan touched my arm, pulling me from my thoughts. "If I hadn't already thought you were amazing—wow,—that interview would have cinched it."

Still smiling, I rolled my eyes. "Enough with the compliments. Don't think I don't know what you're trying to do."

"Is it working?"

I gave a little laugh. "Tell you what, before the reporter interrupted us, you asked what I could promise you. I think I have an answer."

"Yeah?" His raised his eyebrows, waiting.

"A dance. I totally promise you a dance."

Grinning, he took my hand and led me back to the gymnasium. "For now, that will be enough."

Acknowledgments

First and foremost, thank you to the world's most amazing husband, a man who has not only stood beside me every step of this journey, but also taken my hand in his when my feet grow tired. Thank you for celebrating my quirks, laughing at my stupid jokes, and always being game for last-minute sushi.

Special thanks to my Bub, who's learned to share her mommy with the laptop, but also knows when it's time to pull me away for a *My Little Pony* marathon. No matter how many books I write, you'll always be my most magnificent creation.

This book wouldn't exist if not for my amazing agent, Nicole Resciniti. I have no doubt she secretly dons a cape and fights crime when nobody is looking. She's that kickass.

Another special thanks to Liz Pelletier for giving me

the chance to bring Regan and Nolan to life. This book was not an easy one to write, and I never would have had the strength or courage to attempt it without Liz at my back.

Thank you to Stacy Abrams, Heather Howland, Lydia Sharp, Erin Crum, and the other editorial assistants who made up "Team Edit Until You Bleed." (The T-shirts are on order.) Your brilliant insights are what made this book what it is, and for that I'm truly indebted.

Heather Riccio, thanks for that coffee at RT, and for making me feel like family.

I would be remiss if I didn't mention the amazing publicity efforts of Debbie Suzuki and Jessica Turner. Thank you.

To my therapist, Tonya Kuper, thank you so much for all the late-night phone calls. I love you more than Xanax, girl, and that's saying something.

This book also wouldn't have been possible without my fabulous critique partners, Brad Cook and T.W. Fendley. Thanks for always putting up with my crazy.

And then there are my gin-drinking, Cards Against Humanity playing, we're-supposed-to-be-writing sisters. Sarah Bromley, Shawntelle Coker, Heather Brewer, Emily Hall, LS Murphy, Heather Reid, and Marie Meyer. Words cannot express how much I love you. I'm a Pisces and we're not known for making friends easily, but when we do, we make them for life. Looks like you're stuck with me. Sm**ma 4 Life. (Those T-shirts are also on order.)

Life Unaware **Reading Group Guide**

1. As Regan's story begins, she is presented as manipulative, spiteful, anxiety-ridden, and not very likable. At what point did you begin to feel some empathy for her and her situation? What made her likable to you as a reader?

2. On page 23, Regan states, "There was nowhere in the world I was allowed to be just average." How common is this phenomenon in today's high schools? Are students pushed to achieve too much in order to get into the best colleges and career tracks?

3. Regan's mother's voice guided many of her decisions. How did her mother's advice about life help her? How did it hurt her?

4. On page 72, Regan states that words "were useless sounds passed through lips that faded as soon as they were spoken. Unlike texts, which could be captured, copied, forwarded, and saved." Do you agree with both of these thoughts? Give examples from your own life.

5. Discuss the friendship between Regan and Payton. Is it realistic that Regan would forgive her as she did?

6. It was implied that Amber and Christy could be kicked out of their (Catholic) school for being lesbians. Is this true to life in your experience? How should the girls have handled it? How should the school?

7. Regan relied on pills to relieve her anxiety, but she also used horse therapy as a positive outlet. How do you relieve your stress? What are some positive and negative ways teens can overcome stress in their lives?

8. Could the bullying of Regan, or something similar, happen at your school?

9. Teen suicide is the third leading cause of death for people fifteen to twenty-four years old. Statistics are not always available for suicide attempts. Can friends help someone who is depressed and suicidal? Could anyone have helped Jordan or Amber?

10. What might have happened to Regan if Nolan hadn't been there to save her?

11. What are your thoughts about Regan and Nolan's graffiti project?

12. The title of the book is multilayered. Discuss its meanings.

PAPER OR PLASTIC

by Vivi Barnes

Busted. Lexie Dubois just got caught shoplifting a cheap tube of lipstick at the SmartMart. And her punishment is spending her summer working at the weird cheap-o store, where the only thing stranger than customers are the staff. Coupon cutters, jerk customers, and learning exactly what a "Code B" really is (ew). And for added awkwardness, her new supervisor is the very cute—and least popular guy in school—Noah Grayson. And this summer, she'll learn there's a whole lot more to SmartMart than she ever imagined...

ANOMALY

by Tonya Kuper

What if the world isn't what we think?

What if reality is only an illusion?

What if you were one of the few who could control it?

Yeah, Josie Harper didn't believe it, either, until strange things started happening. And when this hot guy tried to kidnap her... Well, that's when things got real. Now Josie's got it bad for a boy who weakens her every time he's near and a world of enemies want to control her gift. She's going to need more than just her wits if she hopes to survive much longer.

Where You'll Find Me

By Erin Fletcher

When Hanley Helton discovers a boy living in her garage, she knows she should kick him out. But Nate is too charming to be dangerous. He just needs a place to get away, which Hanley understands. Her own escape methods—vodka, black hair dye, and pretending the past didn't happen—are more traditional, but who is she to judge?

Soon, Hanley¹s trading her late night escapades for all-night conversations and stolen kisses. But when Nate¹s recognized as the missing teen from the news, Hanley isn't sure which is worse: that she's harboring a fugitive, or that she's in love with one.

Lola Carlyle's 12-Step Romance

By Danielle Younge-Ullman

While the idea of a summer in rehab is a terrible idea (especially when her biggest addiction is organic chocolate), Lola Carlyle finds herself tempted by the promise of spa-like accommodations and her major hottie crush. Unfortunately, Sunrise Rehabilitation Center isn't quite what she expected. Her best friend has gone AWOL, the facility is definitely more jail than spa, and boys are completely off-limits...except for Lola's infuriating(and irritatingly hot) mentor, Adam. Worse still, she might have found the one messy, invasive place where life actually makes sense.